A

~~MATTER~~

~~OF~~

~~LIFE~~

~~AND~~

~~DEATH~~

~~OR~~

~~SOMETHING~~

BEN
STEPHENSON

*

A Matter OF LIFE and DEATH OR Something

A NOVEL

Douglas & McIntyre
D&M PUBLISHERS INC.
Vancouver/Toronto

Douglas & McIntyre
An imprint of D&M Publishers Inc.
2323 Quebec Street, Suite 201
Vancouver BC Canada V5T 4S7
www.douglas-mcintyre.com

Cataloguing data available from Library and Archives Canada

ISBN 978-1-926812-71-7 (pbk.)
ISBN 978-1-926812-72-4 (ebook)

Editing by Barbara Berson
Copy editing by Pam Robertson
Cover and text design by Jessica Sullivan
Cover illustration by Jessica Sullivan
Interior illustrations by Ben Stephenson
Printed and bound in Canada by Friesens
Text printed on acid-free paper

We gratefully acknowledge the financial support of the Canada Council for the Arts, the British Columbia Arts Council, the Province of British Columbia through the Book Publishing Tax Credit and the Government of Canada through the Canada Book Fund for our publishing activities.

FOR MY PARENTS:
as real as they come

ACKNOWLEDGEMENTS

THE BYLINE on the front of this book is lying. It should not just say "Ben Stephenson" like that. The truth is that this pesky little book *could not* have existed without the encouragement, patience, hand-holding, and, if you really think about it, the *birth* of a huge number of entities, and so even the most condensed version of its byline should read:

Ben Stephenson and everyone I'm made out of, in chronological and alphabetical disorder: my parents, my sisters, my grandparents; Jenner-Brooke Berger (for more than is mentionable in a full other novel or trilogy); Andrew Mazerolle and Allison Higgins (for everything all the while); every one of my teachers, but especially Dan O'Neill (the first to tell me it might be possible, whether he remembers or not), Donna Morrissey, and Michael Fernandes; Carol Bruneau (for the early edit, and even more so for all the follow-up smiles); Leah Ellingwood (for telling me about Rosie); Fraser Lockerbie; Richard Light (expert librarian/editor/friend); Jennifer McGraw (another great editor); Peter Richard (for all the thoughts, theories, rants, rice puddings, and pigeons); the Greek Village Restaurant; the Good Food Emporium; Normand Carrey, Gwen Davies, and the Tatamagouche Centre (for the time alone); each of the millions of people involved in growing, harvesting, roasting, transporting, and sometimes brewing all the coffee; the manufacturers of proton pump inhibitors; Rosie Swale-Pope (a real live person); Barbara Berson (for faith, and for making me make damn hard choices); John Pearce (for taking a chance); Jesus Christ, Saint Francis de Sales, His Holiness the Dalai Lama, J.D. Salinger, and all other patrons; Charlotte (for being such a prophetic, immediate, and tiny friend); Katherine, Linda, and J.P.; Spencer Clayton and his wonderful family; Simon Richards and Steve MacLeod (for times infinitely more valuable than they may have seemed); anyone I've forgotten so far and still won't manage to remember by the end of this list; Chris Labonté; Jessica Sullivan; Seymour, Buddy, Franny, Zooey, Bessie, Les, De Daumier-Smith, and Holden and Phoebe Caulfield; Brynn McNab; Matthew Stackhouse; Laurë Nolte; Hannah Guinan; Danika Vandersteen; the beautiful Banff Centre; Jacqueline Baker; Richard Francis Ivan Charlie Burlock Eva Clark-Bailey; Lily Mead Martin; and Arthur

except of course that this would be a book designer's most vivid nightmare. And even *this* byline merely skims the surface. So for anyone to read the drastically severed one on the cover and actually come to believe that "Ben Stephenson" wrote this book *all by himself* should require a very dicey leap of faith indeed, and one I really can't recommend under any circumstance.

(I'm eternally indebted to and deeply grateful for all those whose names are written on this book's cover in invisible ink.)

A

MATTER

OF

LIFE

AND

DEATH

OR

SOMETHING

WE WATCH

WE HEAR everything. In the wind we whisper secrets—it is true. We speak it all softly and simply, as human mothers send promises through the tiny ears of their little ones. Translate our language and hear it flow ambient and foreign, a banquet hall murmur, the airy breath of ten million hushed opinions in a crowd. Hear the constant rush of wind through our branches.

Feel the sounds brush our leaves—the boy's small steps rustling, his boots pressing brittle twigs and shuffling soil; the man's breathing, steady, ragged. The signals quivering in tiniest branches then passed inward through thicker limbs, deep into our trunks.

And see everything. See the sunlight spark through the quick spots between leaves. See the light reflecting off it all, even reaching us from such distances. See it bounce off so many surfaces—the bright rim of fuzz along the man's cotton shoulder, his feet drawing twin arcs in white; a gleam from the notebook's cover tilting in the boy's hand. The light's history leaves its imprint; its colour and texture and intensity are not lost on our skin. We see it all. See houses ascending, falling, mountains sinking into seas, cities blooming and deserted. The images, not only the light, feed us. It is the images, the sounds, the moments and the stories that sustain us. We thrive on all life projects to us in its subtle signals, and we understand.

See us as one, strung together at the roots. Joined by all we bear witness to, we know only one moment: this full and eternal *now* which is everything. But it's the humans who fascinate us most. Their desires, flaws, their will, their hopes race between us at impossible speeds, never stopping nor starting, never frozen; constant. Beneath our branches their movements blaze a hyper-blur of every colour, a woven web of speeding light. Something about it never tires.

So we slow and focus on certain threads; we bend to a point of view and a pace synchronized with its person. Some strands we revisit often, some we never leave. In this way we've learned much, have collected so much, but still we wonder. And so we watch.

A DELIGHTFULLY HAPPY CHILD

MEANWHILE my *real* dad was hot air ballooning off the coast of California all by himself, trying to make the long flight over the Pacific alone without dying. He had, obviously, packed suitcases full of enough food for ten weeks, and enough leisure suits for one. My real dad was not the kind of man to wear the same outfit twice in a row, even if he was alone a kilometre above the sea, so when laundry day came around he'd send his parrots down to the surface with their talons gripping custom-tailored slacks and their beaks full of detergent. It hadn't failed him yet.

He Made a List of Things the Ocean Was:
- A wrinkly blanket
- Pale blue
- Scarier than anything
- Covered in cold mist
- Infinitely huge

He spent most of his days writing in his log book and listening to his favourite records on his mini Victrola. Occasionally he'd smoke a pipe of tobacco and write a letter home to my real mother, and promise to be back soon. Every Sunday he'd crank

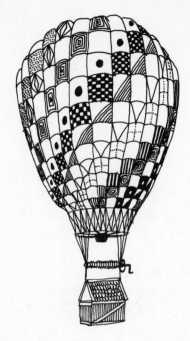

a lever to extend all the ropes of his airship way down until the basket floated gently on the waves, five hundred feet below the balloon, and he would cast his rod and fish for his weekly feast. Most of the time, he'd hook a great white shark and wrestle it to the floor of the basket until it practically *begged* to be cooked, but if he was tired, a giant squid would have to do instead. My real dad won every squid-wrestling contest he ever entered.

When he had a break from being amazing, my real dad would just sit and think. He'd stare at the horizon. He'd try to count the days since he'd last seen land. He would lose count. He'd think about his father, and wonder what ever happened to his own son. He'd catch a glimpse of his six-foot beard reflecting in his gold pocket watch and think, "How stupid must a man be to remember everything but his razor?"

THEN SIMON—the guy who pretends to be my dad—tapped my shoulder to get my attention back. "Arthur?" The balloon flew out through my skull and away from my brain.

"Hmm?"

I was supposed to be doing algebra.

"You daydreaming again?"

"No, I was calculating. I was *trying* to work it out in my head."

"Try to pay attention, chief. We're almost done."

The math book flipped to a new page and I looked past Simon's shoulder and out the window to the tall trees, moving back and forth from the wind. There's a pretty nice bit of woods by our house, and I like it a lot in there. We live in this fat dark grey house that has white windows and a wood porch attached to the front, and it isn't really in the city, but it's also not in the country or anything crazy like that, it's just on this long street by the river, and there's lots of amazing trees all around. What I mean is, the city and the skyscrapers and the noise and all that stuff isn't that far away really, if you take a car for about fifteen minutes, but where we live it's just houses and a river and trees. Simon says I spend too much time in the woods. I *don't* though. He pretty much lets me do what I want, I guess, but one time he said it might not be healthy for me to be alone in the woods all the time. And he knew how I felt about Finch and Victoria, but he still said I should ask them to play sometimes. "Even if they *are* so annoying."

It was in those exact woods where I was about to find the most excruciating thing I'll probably ever find, and half an hour later my life was about to never be the same again, but I didn't even know that yet. These past couple weeks have felt like a thousand weeks, and they've definitely been the craziest days of my life so far—well but maybe I should just give you the basic scoop first of all, so I can make sense. I promise it won't take forever or anything.

First off, I know it's confusing, but Simon Arthur Williams is not actually my real dad. Even though it probably looks like he is. But he adopted me when I was still a tiny foetus or something, I guess because he wanted a kid pretty bad, and he named me, and everything. And I had been living there forever pretending like he was my dad even though he wasn't. Because someone else was my real dad and mom but they decided not to be. I know it's confusing. The most confusing part was how last Christmas break I asked if we could go see them one day but it turned out I wasn't allowed to.

Simon has big square glasses and wispy soft hair and he's really tall and boring. Compared to Uncle Max or even Aunt Maxine, he's boring. And compared to most of the other grown-ups I know, too. His job has always been something on the computer that he does at home, in the room with the wooden sliding door beside the kitchen, and he'd never had a girlfriend or frenched any babes or anything. But that was OK with me, because if he had a girlfriend she might think she could just start being my mom if she wanted, which obviously would be so annoying. Simon always thought that he could teach me better than schools could, so the room beside our kitchen is also where I go to school. I guess he must be an alright teacher, because I'm supposed to be in grade five Math, but I'm really in grade eight. And I'm in grade six English, and grade seven Social Studies, and grade *nine* Science.

Simon's got a younger sister named Maxine and, unbelievably, she married this guy named Max. Since he is her husband, and she is Simon's sister, that makes Max and Maxine almost my aunt and uncle. They've always acted like they really were my aunt and uncle, but mostly I don't mind that, because mostly, I like them. Simon likes them a lot too, especially Max, so they come over to our house a lot and it's usually pretty fun when they do. They both like talking to me, but in different ways.

Uncle Max is hilarious, because of when he tries to be, but also because of when he doesn't try to be. I mean, he's pretty good at telling jokes and giving me funny presents and things, but he's also afraid of lots of things. *Lots* of things. Uncle Max is afraid of spiders, and tall places, and rats. He's afraid of swimming, and boats, and driving—Aunt Maxine drives most of the time—and paper cuts, and spilling hot drinks, and mermaids. Some of his fears are a lot more serious than others. Some of them are mostly jokes.

Whenever some tiny little thing scares him when I'm around, he'll usually yelp or jump at first, and then go right into doing an impression of whatever the thing is. I think if he makes fun of the thing, he gets revenge.

He'll see a spider and get the shakes and I'll laugh at him.

"Oooh-hooo, *spider*," he'll say.

Then he'll bend his arms and stick them out funny and crawl around on the floor, and try to climb up my pantleg. It's only happened a few times, but I usually try to gently stomp him, to help him get over the fear. Then he twitches upside-down on the ground and I put him out of his misery. Or,

"How are you today, Uncle Max?"

"Not bad, Arthur, not bad, except your aunt's busy so *I* had to drive. You know how much I hate driving."

He'll open his eyes as wide as they go and grab the invisible steering wheel and start crashing into things in my bedroom and puffing out his chest like an airbag. What I'll do is, I'll grab hold of the wheel and I'll throw the emergency brake on and steer us to safety. Then I'll ask him to step out of the vehicle and suspend his licence.

My Uncle Max is not afraid of talking about what he is afraid of though, and that's what I like most about him. He's an obvious guy. And he has good skills with the ladies even though he's got a hairy moustache. He's always making up funny love songs about Maxine and the sun and cheesecake and stuff, and singing them to me and playing his electric organ. Also, he is not afraid of the dark. He says that when it's dark, he can't possibly see any of the things he's afraid of anymore, so it's OK. Plus I doubt my Uncle Max can do a very good impression of "the dark."

Aunt Maxine is different. I don't think she's afraid of anything at all. She gives great hugs and she always writes me letters and usually sends them in the mail, even though she could easily send them to my Gmail account, and even though they only live about twenty minutes away. Her letters are always written on pale blue paper and neatly folded into white envelopes. She said that she wanted to be pen pals so that I could practise my writing skills and my politeness and things, and so she could send me amazing true facts and interesting words. But really, there were usually hidden important things that were the *real* reason she wrote.

April 8th

Dearest Arthur,

How are you, sweetheart? I'm terribly sorry that I haven't written in a while. Your silly uncle has been in bed stiff as a two-by-four for six days, he's got very mild pneumonia [new-moan-yuh] and is delighted to make me serve him like a prince whenever I'm home. Speaking of two-by-fours, how is your old treehouse holding up? Do you still spend much time in it? I hope so.

OK, the vocabulary word this time is: "transmigration." It can mean one of two things: the departure from one's native

land to settle in another, or the passage of a soul after death
into another body.

Love as always,
Aunt Maxine

P.S.—I really do hope you still play in that old treehouse. I
remember when you and Si built it. You were such a delightfully happy child in that era. Are you still?

P.P.S.—I know it must be hard, this business about wanting to
know. I just hope you know how special you are to us.

See what I mean? Aunt Maxine really likes movies, and she
knows what all the really *good* ones are. Her favourite part about
movies, I think, is when the guy (or girl) has this thing happen,
some big gigantic thing or sometimes a really small but important thing, which sort of changes the guy's life. Something that
makes the guy snap out of it, or makes him *stronger,* or something. It's like she'd always try to do that to *me* sometimes, in
her letters, even though I was absolutely fine and could take care
of my own snapping out of things. I would write back, usually,
but I'd just hand her my letter next time she came over, because
what kind of ten-year-old could afford a stamp every week?

Dear Maxine.
I'm absolutely fine. I still play and pretend stuff in the treehouse from time to times. It's weird that Max would let himself
get pneumonia because I would think that he's probably affraid
of pneumonia. Come over to visit soon so I can transmigrate
this letter to you. I think that I am still a delightfully happy
child. Bring some of your cinnimin buns.

by Arthur.

P.S.—Obviously I'm special. I'm Arthur.

I'd usually try to write the vocabulary word somewhere to show her how much smarter I was getting. I'd hand her my letter and she'd say thanks and put it right in her purse and probably not read it until she got home.

When I was still a little baby me and Simon built a big treehouse in the woods, on a cliff near the water, and I used to play in it every day. That's what Aunt Maxine was talking about. But then I didn't really go in the treehouse too much anymore, after a while. Not because I didn't like it anymore, but because I just got a *little* too old for it, and I liked exploring other parts of the woods instead. It wasn't a big deal or anything, but maybe I just sort of grew out of it.

Anyway, you never know what you might find in the woods. Every day there's a new universe in there. Some things I've found in the woods are a rock shaped exactly like a human brain, a half of a steering wheel, and a couple shotgun shells that Simon said must have been from hunters, way before we moved in. There are animals, too. One time I chased a squirrel around for an eternity (for fun, not because I'm a hunter or anything) until he scampered up into a pine tree and straight past this *huge* black porcupine. That big guy gave me quite the staring contest. There was a bare patch on the trunk next to him where he must have been eating the bark, like how Victoria told me her dad once murdered a porcupine with a rifle because it was killing their trees. The porcupine *I* saw just kept staring at me, which was a little scary because he looked sharp of course, but we both minded our own business. I was being pretty brave. Everyone thinks porcupines shoot their quills at you. That's ridiculous. As if they have gunpowder blood or something.

Whenever I find something good in the woods, I'll draw it. I'm a really good drawer. I drew the Leaning Tower of Pisa before, and

I was pretty proud of it. I hung it on my wall with all my other drawings and lists and things. A couple nights after I drew it, I had a dream where I went to Spain to hunt down the *real* leaning tower, and I drew a giant picture of it in full-scale size. I drew it with a gigantic yellow pencil, and made it really wide and flat, on sheets of white paper the size of apartment buildings. Months later, when I was finally finished the drawing, my team of engineers and architects helped me lift the paper with cranes and wrap it around the whole tower. The biggest roll of masking tape ever was needed to hold it in place. The thing was, I made it so that when you looked at it with my drawing on top, it wasn't leaning anymore. It was just the Regular Tower of Pisa, like it was always supposed to be. The tourists stopped staring at it, because it was like any other building around. It was perfectly normal. I know it doesn't make sense, but that's what my dream was.

When I woke up I thought, "You idiot. It's in *Italy*."

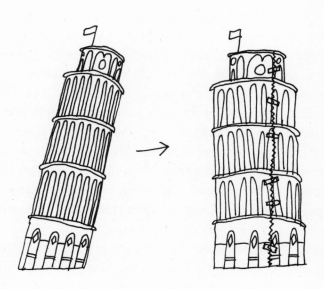

Part of the reason I drew everything I found was so I could remember it. Because, whenever I discovered anything in the woods, I always put it back exactly where I found it. Instead of keeping all the things I found, I would just make really exquisite drawings of them, and then put them back where they came from.

Other Things I Found in The Woods:
- A rusted silver tag from a dog who was named Crusader, which is about the most moronic name for a dog ever
- The pit from a peach
- A squishy thing that I had to do a ton of internet researching about to figure out that it was a used condom.

It's just that the woods are so gigantic. The trees are a thousand times taller than me, and hundreds of years older, and the rocks and leaves and plants and animals never do anything silly like kill each other or fall in love or grow up. So I always felt like the woods was very nice for letting me walk around in it in the first place, and I should at least be careful to leave things where they were. It's like, the woods doesn't go around moving everything everywhere, so I didn't think I should either. Even when I found things that were obviously garbage from sloppy people, like the peach pit and stuff, I still left it where it was because the woods was used to having it there, and maybe it wasn't garbage to the woods. I mean, who knows? There's lots of garbage in my desk at home that if anyone threw it out I would want to punch them, except I wouldn't actually punch them, because punching is something I'm not very good at.

When I go walking around in the woods it always feels like time stops. The problem is, it doesn't *really*. Time is the one thing I'll never understand. One minute I'm leaving the house and my watch says 4:00 and one minute later Simon is calling me for supper and it's 6:30. Probably everyone wishes they had a time machine, and I probably do, too.

Some Obvious Places I Would Go in My Time Machine:
- The time when Adam and Eve were around and didn't eat the apples yet, and were still naked (to tell them to be careful)
- The time when Finch fell in the mud *so* hard and it was really funny
- The time when the first pizza ever was invented and I could have the very first slice
- The time when I crawled out of my real mom's vagina, and I would make myself memorize who was in the room
- The time when Jesus is supposed to come back again (to see if he will still wear a beard or not)
- The time when the history book writers had to start rewriting all the history books because of how much I was changing with my time machine
- The instant right before Phil was about to make himself die.

WE WAIT

WE SEE HIM. See the man walking under our branches, between our trunks, toward the river, carrying only a notebook. See him wearing white. He is bright and clear to us in white jeans, a clean white t-shirt and white sneakers. It's a warm morning though it's late fall, nearly winter—the soil is damp but holds no snow, and beneath us the sunlight sometimes reaches the man, and he glows.

He walks with slow confidence, stepping carefully down the hill, his arms held at forty-five-degree angles to his body. He places one foot in front of the other and walks along a thick root until it nearly meets another. He stretches out his leg and switches to the next root, his arms still suspended, notebook in right hand; he balances and keeps his head down and walks almost musically, as if watching intently while treading along a piano, and picking out all the right notes in a melody he makes with his footsteps: bright, slow, rhythmic and lingering. He walks on our roots like this for some time, crossing a series of linked dark tightropes over the green-brown earth.

He hops down and his thin black hair bounces and lands in his eyes. He brushes it aside and finds a nearby rock to sit on. He looks toward the river, watches the surface of the water in the small cove: an expanse of warm glass. He crosses his right leg over his left and continues to stare. He shuts his eyes so hard his face fills with creases, and he holds them shut. We see his teeth clenched. He opens the notebook and drapes it over his leg, takes a pen from his pants pocket and writes something quickly. He studies the top of the page with dark eyebrows drawn together, daring the word to stand up and swim away. He crosses it out and writes another. Immediately he crosses the second out as well. We watch him make seven more attempts before deciding.

The next words come quickly, and he puts them down meticulously, precisely on the page. He seems as if he's recalling a long phrase he's never quite heard, but is transcribing it flawlessly. When he stops writing we watch him take a small translucent bottle from his pocket, and the sun plays in the bottle's orangeness, silhouetting the tiny contents at the bottom against the colour of iodine. He twists the cap off and pours a small pile of fine white crystals into his left hand. With one finger he pushes the grains around, making patterns on his palm. Abruptly, as if of its own will, his hand raises and tips them into his mouth, and he tries to swallow.

We watch him stare. He waits.

Immediately he is writing again, almost illegibly, the words striking the page and landing where they must. More and more words charge at him and he writes.

Then he is eliminating. He draws long lines, slashing through the abundance, shedding words and banishing them.

Few are left when his body begins to ask itself what is happening. We hear his breathing grow heavy. We watch him shut the notebook and jump up, turning in all directions, wild and urgent. We see the book fall to the forest floor. We watch his muscles tense as he pulls his white clothes off. Carrying them with him, he heads for the beach, the book forgotten. It remains.

We hear his feet crushing the gravel so roughly, so loud. His steps echo over the calm water, and across the river more of us are listening. More are watching. We watch his chest contract, as if strapped with belts quickly tightening. We listen as he coughs deeply, relentlessly. He stumbles along the gravel and then the grey sand, past thick tangles of driftwood collected on the shore. We hear his sloshing steps cutting into the shallow water and his splash into the deep.

We wait in the silence. We listen for the next shimmering splash, the returning splash. We listen for the next rough breath breaking surface, and it does not come. And it still does not come.

AN UGLY DUCKLING

AFTER ALGEBRA I came home from school—which is what I like to call it when I'm done my lessons and I can run from the kitchen into the woods, because obviously there isn't much difference between home and school for me—and I was in an amazingly bad mood. Simon was getting on top of my nerves, because during Math my brain wouldn't stop thinking about the real dads and he wouldn't stop telling me to pay attention.

But God was in a good mood I think, 'cause it was just barely spring but he was shining all the light he could on our neighbourhood *all day*. He decided that the day needed no wind, or rain, or even clouds, and he painted the sky the prettiest of blues, as if he was a huge fan of postcards.

So there God was making this amazing day, and there I was solving the hardest algebra ever. I couldn't pay attention, and all I could focus on was how it was extraordinarily beautiful outside and how much I wanted to get out of the stupid house. I kept asking God to please make Simon get sick or get hurt (just a little) or even just fall asleep, but I think he was too busy painting the day, so I came home from school at 3:00 as usual. Does that guy *ever* do anything you ask him to?

So Simon was on top of my nerves, or I was on top of his, and either way when school was finally done I walked across the yard and into the woods thinking angry things.

(Meanwhile my real dad was pulling his solid gold car into his huge driveway, after a long day of work at the Mint. He was exhausted from a long hard day of printing money. My real dad was very important and respected at the Mint, so they let him choose his own salary and print off as much money for himself as he wanted. So he made money for twenty-two hours a day, and the Mint didn't keep track anymore.

He turned the ruby doorknob and burst through the door of his mansion and all seven of my real sisters and brothers jumped on him like leeches who only wanted hugs, not blood. He called them all by name and kissed them all on their foreheads, one by one, and then they all said together, "What did you bring us today, Daddy?"

With a cunning smile he distributioned to them all of their favourite chocolate bars and slipped misprinted twenty dollar bills into their tuxedo pockets so that they could play stock market later. He went into one of his ten bathrooms and clapped for the tap to turn on, then washed the green and blue ink stains from his shining hands.

My real mom came and leaned against the door frame in her tangerine-orange summer dress and took off her sunglasses, then leaned in and frenched my real dad for about five minutes. Then she said "Honey, a boy named Arthur is calling for you on line three ... he says he's your son?"

"Nonsense," my real dad swiftly replied, "Put him on hold. Can't you see I'm ever so tired from such a long day of printing money?"

My real mom strutted back over to the phone and pushed the HOLD button, hung up, and put a kettle on to make coffee.)

Jazz piano hold-music was stuck in my head as I walked underneath the huge skinny trees. I took out my almost-great-grandfather's binoculars and peeped around, except when Simon gave them to me he said that my almost-great-grandfather actually would have called them "field glasses" instead of binoculars. Looking through the field glasses, I only spied all the ordinary things: a sticky-looking bird's nest, my favourite boulder shaped like a sea turtle, a couple squirrels squirrelling around in the roof of shadowy branches, and the treehouse sitting way over there on the cliff. For a millisecond I thought maybe I'd go in the treehouse and work on some stuff but then I thought I should just stick to the woods.

The Woods By My House:
- The trees are all cedar and birch, with a couple pines and spruces and fat oaks popping up every once in a while.
- A bunch of little hills covered in brown pine needles, crushed up old leaves, dirt, a little bit of old snow.
- Some jagged cliffs by the water, a tiny gully, a clearing, and, farther down, a not-very-sandy beach.
- Rocks with creeping green moss like soft emeralds, bright orange lichens that look like when cars rust apart and get flaky, and white stringy stuff like cauliflower spaghetti.
- Spiderwebs that always get wrapped around your face but then you can't find the spider.
- Trees so tall and skinny that it feels like wandering through an NBA team's potluck dinner party on your knees.
- A rotten smell that is kind of sweet and isn't gross.
- In the summer you look up and there's a smudge of different greens against the blinding sky light so bright, and dark thin trunks stretching up and kind of jumping towards it.

– Ants.
– Paths that aren't *real* paths, they're only kind-of-paths, because I walk on them so much.

I reached one of my favourite spots in the woods. It's this small clearing with no trees except on the sides, which are very nice to sit under. It was so beautiful out that day, and spring was coming up quick. That was amazing, because kind of soon after that it would be summer vacation. The snow had been disappearing: the street was extraordinarily clear, but it still stuck around the ground in the woods. The snow was 50% still there. I wandered through the trees, thanking God for not making winter last forever.

I didn't know why Simon worried about me playing in the woods so much. One time he called me a "little escapist" when I was going out the door, and I didn't know what that meant, so I decided to have fun in the woods and forget about it instead of figuring it out. I found out later that it means someone who chains themself up and dunks themself underwater but gets out without drowning. Which is weird, and I *still* didn't know why Simon called me that; it's not like I ever pretended to be an escapist or anything.

I sat down on the sea turtle rock and photosynthesized. I let the sun hit me in the face and make me feel glowy. In the shade it was chilly, so I was wearing my green jacket over my t-shirt, but in the sunlight it was so warm. I thought about the trees and how they were basically doing the same thing: letting the sun warm them up and keep them alive. I thought about some other things.

Like how my street was so long, and all the houses stood far apart like they hated each other. And a bunch of people lived inside the houses, but I didn't know any of them yet. As far as kids my age, there's only Finch and Victoria. Simon Alexander

Finch is an annoying boy one year younger than me, who lives three houses away, which is way farther than it sounds, because of how separate the houses are. I already have enough Simons in my life as it is, obviously, so I just call him Finch. Finch and I only saw each other once in a blue mood, and that was fine by me.

I mean I didn't *hate* Finch. Sometimes I wanted to call him my nemesis, but that was only because I liked the word "nemesis," and not because it was the 100% truth. The truth is that I just didn't care much about him at all, really, and that's why we weren't friends. The thing is that his mom and my Simon thought that Finch and me were superb friends, so sometimes they *made* us play. It also didn't help that Finch was confused for some reason into thinking we were friends.

Finch just thinks he's the best at everything. If you're playing soccer with him, he's going to tell you what a rainbow kick is, for the billionth time, and show you how he's *so* good at doing them. And the thing is, he's just not even good at doing them. I'm not either, to be honest, but it's not like I go around *telling* everybody I am or something.

Like one day a couple months before, Finch was in my woods with me, and we were over by the treehouse because Finch loves the treehouse because he doesn't have his own one, so he always wants to go look at it. So one second he's telling me about how awesome my treehouse is, and then one second later he's showing me some mistake that me and Simon made building it, and telling me that if *he'd* made it, it would've been ten times stronger and ten times bigger and ten times cooler. But I couldn't think of anything ten times less true. I doubt he even owns a hammer. Then like always he asked why can't we just play in the treehouse, and I told him because it was so boring in there, but he climbed up anyway.

Then, to top it all off, he starts bragging to me.

"Victoria said she wants to be my girlfriend."

He was *always* trying to make Victoria be his girlfriend.

"Finch, quit being so moronic. And she's *way* too much of a babe for you."

Victoria Brown *is* too much of a babe for Finch. Victoria's a girl that me and Finch know, who lives way up our street. She's a year older than Finch and the same age as me, and I am a *way* better match for her. But I don't like her, if you're wondering. I mean she's beautiful and she's a babe and she's not a moron and all that, but I don't care if she's my girlfriend or not. Because I don't think I'm old enough yet that I like girls much, and also because I have too much self-esteem.

"You'll see," Finch said, climbing up the ladder to the top floor. "And I already said stop calling me 'Finch.'"

Victoria Brown had brown eyes and brown hair and her skin was just slightly browner than say, mine or Finch's, more like Uncle Max's. Anyway, her last name was perfect for her, and one time I told her that and she said "I know!" The only part that wasn't brown was that she always wore these white dresses. She lived so far up the street, she even lived three or four houses farther away than the *hermit,* for God's saints.

That's a weird thing: people always said there was a hermit living in the small grey house close to Victoria's. The house was kind of dirty and scary looking, like some Halloween cottage or something stupid like that. It really *was* pretty scary though. Everyone said all this stuff about the hermit doing all these evil things. Like all he ever did was really *bad* things. No one ever told a nice story about him petting a dog or anything like that. He'd probably be sawing the dog in half. I didn't know anything about hermits, other than the hermit crabs we'd sometimes find if Maxine drove us way out to the ocean. I liked to imagine the hermit on our street poking his claws out from under the bottom of his old grey shack and kind of scuttling all over the neighbourhood, eating up the deer and stuff. But I didn't think he ever *really* did that; I figured he was the kind of hermit who didn't move around. Simon never talked about him though, even when I asked. He always said if there was a hermit on our street, he'd never met him. To which obviously I said "That's because you don't *meet* hermits." Simon didn't say anything else. That's just what he's like—sometimes he acts all quiet and mysterious. It's *so* annoying. I usually wouldn't even bother asking him about stuff. Anyway I won't tell you every single thing I heard the hermit did right now, but it was all really evil.

I was sitting on the sea turtle rock forever, because I was thinking about infinities and infinities of things. I do that a lot. I know it's weird. I think because of how much I think about stuff, grown-ups sometimes call me things like "smart" or "special" or "delightful," and Finch always calls me a "weirdo." I guess I know what they're all talking about. The good thing about being so weird is that I can kind of be friends with all types of people, because I have so many thoughts that I usually have one in common with everyone. I mean like I can sort of be friends with most grown-ups if I want, and kids, and also kids who act like grown-ups and also grown-ups who act like kids. The bad thing is that I'm usually too weird to have more than one thing in common with anyone, so really I guess I'm nobody's friend except myself.

Then *BLAM!* A huge sharp sound ripped through the air, and the river echoed it over and over. I jumped to the ground behind the rock and waited with my heart shaking. Nothing else happened. I waited more. The loudest part of a big noise is the quiet afterwards. I could hear nothing but a few branches rustling, and one of my crazy neighbours dropping a pin somewhere. I coughed, to break the ice a little, and realized that I was lying on my side, with my legs scrunched up like a baby still inside a vagina.

Finally I remembered that it was probably just someone hunting ducks. I'd heard the same sound lots of times before, but it still scared the heck out of me and it was still good to use my excellent reflexes just in case. I slowly got back up and sat on the rock. I felt a little bit sick when I thought about how something had probably just died, so close to where I was. I mean, *something* probably dies every millisecond, I know, but still. I thought that a duck would have a family, and if it wasn't an idiot it might have friends, and maybe even a girlfriend if it wasn't an ugly duckling or anything, and if it was rich. Anyway, there were other ducks out there, somewhere, and when that one duck didn't show up at home that night, they would wonder where he might have gone and probably be excruciatingly depressed. I shivered but I wasn't cold.

I took a swig of milk from my thermos. It was very relaxing, sitting on the sea turtle rock drinking milk and ice cubes and forgetting about death and things. I tipped my thermos up and took another sip of milk with the bright sun closing my eyes, and when I tipped my head back down I saw something strange on the ground. Down the hill a ways, there was a corner of something sticking out from some leaves. I figured I probably had a milk moustache as usual, so I shaved it. Then I slid off the rock and climbed down to check out the whatever-it-was.

It was a book. A splotchy black and white notebook, beat up and damp, half covered in leaves. I knelt down and pulled it out from the mucky leaves and brushed it off like a palaeontologist. I looked around for a second to check if there was anyone else on the hill, or up in the clearing, anyone who might have lost it. But

I realized that the thing looked like it had been there for ice ages. Obviously, whoever owned it must have lost it a while ago and had no idea where it went.

The cover was black and white like I said, this small speckly pattern of strange black shapes and strange white shapes crashing into each other and covering each other up. Someone had written their name on the cover, but their last name was all smudged.

I hiked back up to the rock again and sat and opened it up. I examined the first page. Faded and sketchy handwriting filled the paper, written in black ink all attacked by the rain and wind and bugs and racoons and whatever else it had dealt with. I flipped through the rest of the book and found a bunch of pages pretty similar to the first. Most of them were filled with black handwriting, and each page was numbered in the top corner, because the book must have came with numbers already printed in it. Big parts of the writing were really hard to read because of how wet they'd gotten, and the ink was so runny. There were a couple diagrams, and there was a lot of stuff that was crossed out. Some pages looked like they were written carefully and slowly, with nice loopy letters and perfect spaces, like an intelligent sloth might write, but then some pages were more mashed together and had writing at weird angles, kind of angry looking. It must have been someone's journal.

"Aaaarrrr-thurrrr!"

I was almost all the way to the beach but I could still hear Simon's voice. It was time to eat.

I went over and put the book back on the ground where it was, but then I picked it up again. I was having a mid-life crisis. For some reason, I skimmed through the pages over and over, like I was having a case of Alzheimer's right there in the woods. Like I said, I'd found lots of things in the woods, all the time, but I always put them back where they came from. I'd just never found anything that was so *obviously* someone else's before.

"Aaaaaarrrrrr-thurrrrrr!"

"Ohhhhh-kayyyyy!"

I put the notebook into my little white backpack with my thermos and my sketchbook and my field glasses. Before I zipped it up, I looked at it again, and I looked at the spot where I found it. I measured it in steps, and memorized that it was five steps from the bent tree, heading away from the river, and one step sideways towards the house. I was breaking my own rules. I was breaking the rules that I thought the woods had. I looked up to the trees for advice, kind of, but they obviously said nothing. They just whooshed in the breeze. I decided that I would put it back where it had really come from, which was in the hands of whoever wrote it. Still. I was breaking the rules. I put my backpack on over my shoulders and it felt like it weighed a ton.

"Aaaaaaaarrrrrrrr-thurrrrrrrr!"

"OOOOOOOHHHHHHH-KAAAYYY!"

I went home and slid the book under my pillow and ate supper.

OTHER GALAXIES

I REALLY did have Alzheimer's. It wasn't until the next day that I even thought about the notebook again. Simon and I had finished my school, and I was using the computer. I had just solved the hardest equation known to man, and I was proud of myself, so I celebrated with a cold glass of milk and a visit to www.rosiearoundtheworld.co.uk to see how Rosie was doing. Rosie is a woman whose husband died of cancer, and she's running around the world because she knows that you only get one life and you have to grab it by its horns, and also because orphan kids need lots of money which she will raise for them. I'd found out about her about a year before when I was searching the internet for extraordinary people. She was about 80% finished her run around the world. I knew this because there was a picture on the site that showed the whole world and the line she was making around it, and I made a big drawing of it myself to keep track of her, with a star for where she started in Wales. Something about her really expired me. A lot of things about her did. I mean, she even ran through *Siberia,* for crying outside.

Anyway, her website was updated every three days, on average, and I visited it just as often. It had lots of pictures of her all over the world—on the side of snowy highways, in the hot sun

with sweat pouring off of her, smiling in front of famous statues, just her and Icebird. Icebird was the trailer that she pulled behind her everywhere she went because it kept everything she needed to survive inside of it, and sometimes I think she even slept in it.

It was really crazy because on the website that day there was an update saying that she would actually be running through our town on April 19th, if everything went according to schedule. This was amazing news. I had been expecting that she might come somewhere nearby, but I mean I wasn't expecting her to go through my exact *town* in a week. I went over to the *National Geographic* photo calendar on our fridge and wrote her name on the 19th. Even if she didn't come exactly on that day, it was good to be prepared.

It was right then, when I was staring at all the numbers on the calendar, that I finally remembered. The book! Simon was taking over the computer to do work stuff as I left the kitchen and walked through the living room and down the short hallway to my room. I couldn't believe I'd forgotten about that book.

I'd hid it under my pillow to keep it safe but then it was so well hidden that it had just fallen right out of my brain. My pillow felt kinda hard and flat with that thing under there. No wonder I had so many dreams. I took it out.

It was exactly the same as I remembered it being, except I hadn't remembered it. The black and white speckled cover, bulging and warped from the rain. The black ink running in places, all shaky. Hundreds of pages all stiff and brittle, crackly in the margins. The wire coil made of rust. The page numbers, the crossed out words.

I spent a long time reading it. Basically, it seemed like a long story about a man named Phil, and also written by him. Only it was confusing because he didn't always tell the story like a normal person, like saying "I did this and then I did this." He did talk like that sometimes, but then sometimes it was like he was talking about someone else doing everything but he was saying the name Phil so I think he was still talking about himself. I mean, half the time he would talk like "*Phil* did this, *Phil* did that." He was sometimes really mean, or sad. He was sometimes kind of nice and funny too, but mostly he seemed kind of angry. It was sorta weird. Some of the things I read I didn't understand, but most things I did.

I looked at the cover again:

Of course his last name was all smudged out. That's the way it always was in crazy detective shows. I got out my magnifying glass and examined the half-signature really close up, just in case, but I still couldn't read it. I did find something weird though. I realized that the long ink blob had a pattern to it: it ended in sort of a fingerprint. It seemed like whoever this "Phil" guy was, he had tried to get rid of the last name on purpose, like he licked his finger and blurred out his own name.

"A curious specimen," I said out loud for some reason. Sometimes I say things out loud by accident. I don't know why it happens. Then I drew an amazing picture of the fingerprint, which took me forever, and I put it away in a drawer in my desk. But I was still curious. I opened to the inside back cover, and saw that he had made a list of quotes like on the backs of grown-up books:

"Without a fraction of a scrap of a doubt our best living journal-writer... [his] prose glistens with such slippery dripping intellect... [the journal] will leave you entirely speechless."
—*The New York Times*

"One of the worst things they've ever sent us to review, and that's saying a lot."
—*Rolling Stone*

"The only thing that's come along in the past bundle of decades just shimmery enough to lead me—nearly against my will, and with no stingy amount of hand-holding—out of the house, let alone to the bookstore."
—*J.D. Salinger*

I kept reading. I just sat at my desk for a long time, reading parts of the book and getting more confused. Was he making the stuff up or was it all real? It seemed like one second he would be talking about one thing and the next he was way off somewhere else. Or I couldn't figure out the order he was putting it in. It made sense but at the same time it didn't. It was weird because I kind of liked it that way, how strange it was, but I felt other things about it too and I didn't know what those things were. I could never tell if he was actually upset about something or if he was just pretending or what. It was confusing, and I kept reading it.

Then I flipped way ahead in the book and I found the part I wish I never had to find and that I don't really like talking about. I found Page 43. The handwriting at first was way more steady than the other pages, like it was written a lot slower. He was more organized. It was also kind of like a list, and I liked that. There was some stuff about a beach, and other stuff. He had a lot of things crossed out too, almost all of it, but I could still read it all. Then as the page went on his writing got more crazy again and everything was crossed out except a couple of words that didn't make whole sentences, and then the empty sentences started to make me feel weird. I read it and read it again. I kind of stared at it, that one page, until my throat got tingly, and like it was poking my stomach in the elbow, trying to get its attention. My stomach was just feeling huge and empty. Finally I turned to the next page but there was no next page. Page 44 didn't exist. The whole rest of the notebook was all blank.

I shoved the book back under my pillow and me and my throat and my stomach all sat on my bed for a long while, trying to think about nothing and getting nowhere.

Then Simon called me to eat supper, so I went and ate supper. We had macaroni and cheese, which was barely even cheesy at all because Simon only puts half the cheese package in. After supper Simon said he had to go meet someone for coffee, which was weird, because it was almost nighttime, but I didn't ask him who he was meeting or why, mostly because I had a huge amount of things to think about and I was just excited to be the man of the house.

Hours later I was working on a list at my desk and Simon opened my door.

"Storytime yet?" he asked.

I didn't hear our squeaky car come back and I hadn't even noticed my window get dark. I must have been listing for years.

"Five minutes?" I said.

"Sure thing, boss. Get ready for bed."

I was getting a little old for storytime, but I could tell that Simon was not. He always wanted to read to me. Mostly it was pretty annoying, him always wanting to read to me, but that night I thought maybe it would be OK. I don't know why.

I went to the bathroom mirror and watched the Arthur behind it. I practised a few faces for a second: an angry one, a surprise party one, a fat fish one, a heartbroken one, a squinty but focused one, a cyclopsed one. I thought about trying a Phil one, but didn't know how and I was too nervous, so I didn't. Then I took my green toothbrush out of the medicine cabinet on the wall next to the mirror. I rinsed the toothbrush with scalding water for fifteen seconds and all the germs living in it burned up. I took my toothpaste and squeezed a blob of it out of the tube and onto my toothbrush. Right as I started to brush, a reflection of Simon appeared in the mirror over Reflection Arthur's right shoulder and at the same time the actual Simon was behind my actual left shoulder.

"Anything good in there today?" Simon and his reflection asked at the same time, leaning on door frames.

"Im ma teef?" I said, looking at Simon's reflection's eyes, and almost spitting out green foam everywhere.

The Simons laughed.

"No, in the woods. Anything good?"

"Na," I said, still brushing, "nuffing ard all."

"Same old?"

I spit into the sink and turned the tap on.

"No. I mean, yes."

As I was rinsing off my toothbrush Simon started doing this extremely annoying thing he does where he takes his thumb and finger and flicks the top of my head, not to hurt my head, but to move pieces of my hair around. I filled up a glass of water for rinsing my mouth, and he just kept flicking tufts of my hair around while I did it. I looked at his reflection's eyes.

"Stop it," I said.

He messed up my entire hairdo for a second with his hand, like he brushed it all around and then stopped. I drank my little glass of water quickly, then took the black plastic comb from inside the medicine cabinet and slowly and carefully started combing my hair, practising frowns.

"If you *want* to know about it," I said, "I heard a *gun*shot because someone was probably shooting ducks like they always do."

"Oh, wow," Simon said. "They're really getting an early start. I don't even think that's legal."

I dragged the comb down the right side of my head and the left side of my reflection's head, to part my hair where I always do.

"Maybe there's just a lot of people wanting duck hats this year. Maybe the mayor ordered this one special guy to shoot just one for him, so he could have the very first hat of—"

"What?" Simon said.

"The very first hat of the year?"

"Ducks don't get made into *hats*, chief."

"What?"

"Ducks get eaten. And sometimes made into pillows and jackets."

I thought about how a duck might taste, with all that grease soaked into it from its raincoat, and I figured it would be disgusting. Then I thought about how uncomfortable it would be, really, to sleep with your head on a duck, or to try to fit your arms into one.

"Why don't they just make them into hats?" I said.

The Simons laughed at me.

"The whole duck? Or just the feathers?"

I put the comb back in the cabinet, and walked down the hall to my room. Simon followed me. I sat at my desk and got a piece of blank paper from my drawer. I made him a quick picture of what I always figured duck hats looked like, with the guy's head, and then a duck. Simon watched over my shoulder.

"So it's just a whole duck sitting on your head."

"I guess."

He laughed at me.

"Well, they make racoon hats don't they?" I walked slowly around my room and acted like I was pointing at something, because it's easier to explain things when you do that. "Plus, if a duck hunter was smart, he'd make one into a hat for himself first, and then use scuba gear and maybe an underwater gun, like a harpoon gun or something, and then he would stay under the water but with the duck hat sticking out above like it was swimming, and sneak up to a normal duck like 'Hey, how's it going?' and then *BLAM!*"

Simon laughed and then didn't say anything. He was standing around staring at the papers on my wall like a tourist in a museum.

"Who lives in there?" he asked while pointing at my drawing of the hot-air balloon.

"How should I know?" I went and sat on my bed.

He shrugged and slowly walked over to me.

"Arthur, will you please change your bedsheets tomorrow? It's been a while. Unless you want me to have to do it for you."

"No! I'll do it myself. Tomorrow."

Then he suddenly tackled me onto my bed and tickled the heck out of me. So annoying. I am so ticklish and I'm way too old to be getting tickled. I eventually yelled and bit his arm enough to break free and he started reading to me. I can't even remember what book he was reading, because he reads so many different books, and because I wasn't really paying attention. I couldn't concentrate.

(Meanwhile my *real* dad was busy accepting his Nobel Prize and giving a speech to the press and the fans. He had created an all-new perforated bread loaf, and it was easily the best thing since sliced. Other than the obvious cool looks, perforated bread also let you choose the thickness of your slice, so thick and thin sandwich fans could both live off the same loaf. Also, you could create the all-new "half sandwich," "ring sandwich" and even "zig-zag sandwich" types amazingly easy:

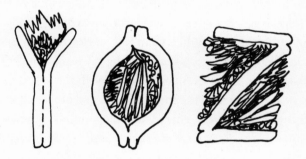

On a lucky side note, a chemical my real dad's research team invented to inject into the yeast and make the bread stretchy also turned out to be excruciatingly anti-cancerous, and it was the greatest scientific surprise in decades.

"But I'm not just here to brag about curing cancer," he said. "I'd like to thank my heroes: Neil Armstrong, Albert Einstein, Aunt Jemima, of course my extremely beautiful wife Marsha, and my son James, a perfect example of excellence in bloom."

He looked around the gigantic auditorium and squinted.

"...I feel like I'm forgetting someone," he said.

I stared out over the rest of the crowd from my back row seat, and tried to make eye contact with him. He kept glancing over me and beside me and really close to me, but no luck.

"... Oh yes!" he exclaimed, "how could I forget my wonderful German shepherd, Tilly!?"

A drooling dog ran onto the stage and the crowd thundered in applause. As the standing ovation started I ran straight out the front doors of that stupid theatre and fell into a bottomless dark abyss and a bunch of dreams.)

WHEN I WOKE up the next morning I was back in my room again. I woke up too early and I stayed there for a while before going to eat breakfast. Maybe I should give you a tour.

My room is reddish purplish navyish, a dark kind of colour that it has been ever since I existed, and that I didn't choose, but I kind of like anyway. When you come in the door you see my desk in the back corner on the right and my bed on the left. My bedsheets are usually the ones with space all over them, they're all navy and black with the constellations and other galaxies. In another galaxy, I think, there would be another room exactly like mine, right down to every little detail, except everything was mirrored backwards, and an extraterrestrial boy named Ruhtra lived in it instead. The universe is so infinitely big that that galaxy's gotta be *some*where.

In the corner next to where my closet sticks out is my igloo. That's one good thing Simon did. For Christmas he'd got me this igloo building kit that I really wanted. It's from the science store downtown, and it's just basically this *huge* box, full of all these styrofoam bricks, white bricks like snowblocks that don't melt. And they all have a little number on the bottom and you put it all together using this big diagram page. The thing is that the bricks never really fit perfectly even though the kit costs about a million dollars so that it's your main Christmas present and it doesn't even work that well. I'd been trying to build the crazy thing for like four months, but I just couldn't do it all at once. So instead, almost every day, when I remembered, I'd work on another brick. I'd break them a bit and cut them with a ruler and a knife from the kitchen to make them fit, and then carefully add them in. But then every once in a while, or all the time, it would just fall in on itself completely, 'cause maybe by accident I forgot not to breathe on it or something, and then I couldn't try it again for weeks because it was so annoying. I'd stomp down to the basement for the vacuum and settle down my emotions about the stupid igloo by sucking up all the foam particles off my floor. Once I asked Simon if we could get some crazy glue to help it stick together but he said glue wouldn't work on foam, and besides did I have any idea how toxic that stuff was? I thought if the igloo ever actually *did* work, it would be amazing: all the whiteness inside surrounding me. The light coming in through the cracks. I could curl up into a ball and sleep forever.

My desk is another pretty important thing. That's where I do a lot of the things I do when I'm not in the woods or at school beside the kitchen. I've got this nice white desk with red drawers on the right side and it's pushed up against the wall. In the top drawer I have:

- pens and pencils and paper for drawing
- paperclips
- pushpins
- duct tape, masking tape, and electrical tape
- a can of golden spray paint that's mostly empty
- a bunch of elastics

- blank cassette tapes
- a pad of tracing paper (even though I never trace because I don't have to)
- some fingernails I should throw out
- a magnifying glass
- the chunky black tape recorder Simon once bought me at a yard sale that actually works.

In the bottom drawer I just keep piles of drawings, old lists I don't need hung up anymore, letters from Aunt Maxine and other stuff. Anyway, that's enough about my room, I think. It's kind of boring stuff.

Before I went for breakfast that morning I tried to start my routine. I checked a few things off some of my lists, and then I added another brick to the igloo, brick #17, which took eternities because I had to saw it a ton first. I swept all the styrofoam shavings from my desk into my hand and threw them out. I was about to open my door and go check Rosie's website again but that was as long as I lasted making myself not think about Phil. I got the book out from my pillow and opened it up. I read it for a long while, not skipping around so much, until I had read the whole thing, right up to Page 43. It was easy to read it for a couple of hours. I mean, I could barely stop. Then I read Page 43 again.

"Maybe it's not so bad," my brain said, "maybe we could just put it back in the woods where we found it and live happily ever after."

"It *is* pretty bad," Page 43 said, "it's *really* bad."

Inside me, my heart felt stuffed up. It felt all swollen and stuffed, like it had the worst cold ever and just wanted to lie in bed all day. I shut the book again. I sat there waiting to see if my heart would tell me a message about what the heck I was supposed to do now. I waited and waited forever but it said nothing. I waited so long I could tell the next ice age would come at any second, and my room got excruciatingly cold and my heart got icicles hanging off it and I had no clue what to do, and I opened my door but my life was buried under a kilometre of snow and there was no way out.

SEPTEMBER 27TH

~~She's gone. I went to her house and she was just~~

OCTOBER 21ST
SNOW

I need this. This is what I need. I'm coming at this at breakneck speed because I need to just I need to get this down. Because it will help.

I need to get this down, how the snow was there for me. I'm going so fucking crazy.

Start with *tonight*. I went to the store. I was in a good mood. (This is how crazy I am.) I was in a good mood, and it's only just barely officially fall but already the air smelled of tree bark and ice. I hurried to the 24-hour on the other side of the park, jogging in the dark on the frozen-stiff grass fields with my hands in my pockets. It's hands-in-pockets time again.

Keep going, I entered the store, and the lady at the counter who talks too much said Hello and I returned it, making sure not to give her enough eye contact as to appear to be searching for conversation. I scanned the aisles and picked out the things I needed. Oatmeal. Eggs. Milk. Had I wanted to I could have also very easily purchased: sports drinks, birthday cards, white bread, brown sugar, gambling scams, an entire chicken carcass, an orange toque, motor oil, baby wipes, lung cancer, fresh breath, *The Best of AC/DC,* overpriced cereal, the leftover bits of every part of various animals ground together into a paste, pencils, UV protection, several books of pictures of men putting their penises inside of multiple women, and many other items.

Then I saw this notebook. I mean I saw the two stacks of notebooks that look exactly like this notebook, the one I am writing in, which I bought from that exact specific unchanged shelf like three months ago. This notebook, which I haven't used like I told myself I would.

Dear Journal I'm sorry I neglected you and couldn't guess your real worth. If I could have written, I would have. I need you now—do you forgive me? I can't explain but I just feel every single muscle of me tilting towards you now and this is fun, Journal, this is good, to talk to you.

Nice to meet you. I'm Phil. At least for now. Other times I look at me and I'm really not certain. I wonder how I would know. Let's not get into it—I'm getting sidetracked.

Tonight I got sidetracked. I stared at the notebooks. I've always loved the cover on these—it's so beautifully disorienting. And so iconic. Anyway I suddenly knew keeping a journal would be a good idea. Like it would be *necessary.* It felt like a solution—something about the stack of all those composition notebooks, and just how many there were. I've tried this before, as you probably recall—or I'm just going to go ahead and assume you recall, because I don't think I can go on living in a world where a person's past journals don't telepathically communicate with their current ones. I tried a while ago and gave up. Now you remember me.

So. I brought the stuff to the counter. The talkative lady said Is that everything? Yes. Eleven dollars, eleven cents. Make a wish. I gave her the money and with all my will I wished she wouldn't get into it, as she does. She started to hand me my change, but then she was staring at it instead, and then smelling her hands and smiling, as if she hoped their scent might transfer to my money?

I've got this new cocoa butter, she said.

Ohh, awesome.

It might be too strong, but I just love the smell.

Yeah, it smells great. (And I wasn't lying. It smelled exactly like both cocoa *and* butter.) I can smell it from here. (I was in a good mood.)

I used to have mint stuff, but this is much better. So rich.

Mmm-hmm.

She laughed.

O...K.......

I opened the door and started to move outside.

It's cold out there tonight.

I turned around in the doorway.

Yeah, so cold.

They're calling it a *cold snap*. Yesterday was pretty bad, but I think today's even worse.

Whoa, probably.

I took a step through the doorway.

It's so strange. Radio said it might get to minus ten!

Wow. No way. OK, see ya!

Have a good night!

You too, I said, but made the fatal mistake of turning around as I spoke. I have to just stop answering. I have to find a less convenient store.

Oh look, it's snowing! she said, looking past me. I turned my head, nodded, and finally made it out.

It was the first snowfall of the season. It shouldn't be snowing yet. "Cold snap." It shouldn't snow again for months. Of course I didn't expect it, so I had my little white shoes on, and I was sliding all over the slanted parking lot. There was only the thinnest layer of fluffy snow forming on the ground, and my feet melted through and exposed the dark pavement below. I left a trail of fresh black tracks behind me.

Walking home, I began to look back at my trail every once in a while, almost with some strange form of very recent nostalgia. My footprints were the only ones around, and I found them so endearing. They meant I was actually going somewhere: that I had started in one place and could show concretely and precisely how I'd proceeded to my destination. Or that I had finally started moving. No, it was that I'd travelled in such a *straight forward* way—not how I would have pictured them. My footprints didn't falter or wonder at anything, they had purpose and kept straight and true—simple. I appreciated them how they were, but then I wanted to push them a little. I started to play with them.

I leapt forward and my slippery landing drew two black lines, the right twice as long as the left. I headed back through the park on the pavement pathway, and there was no one around: it was Wednesday at 3:00 AM. I started walking a symmetric zig-zag evenly across the path, turning around now and then to check its aesthetic value. Perfect. I walked rigidly straight for a while, determined, but then pulled a loop-de-loop and spiralled insanely before continuing in the same direction. I zigged more and zagged more and made longer loops. I got so into it that I wasn't even thinking. I watched myself draw the most futile line possible through the park. The Phil I watched was having a great time. He hopped on one foot for a while. He backtracked and carefully added a third leg in one section. At one point he noted the only other prints of the trip, some animal's, maybe canine, and he veered off to follow its route before returning to his own. Each step and each gesture—tangential, calculated, improvised—was recorded. He looked back occasionally and took joy in his madman's map. The end couldn't have possibly accounted for the means.

It was childish, but soon he wished he might have had an audience. Not necessarily right then, but soon after. At least somebody. Someone to laugh at the process. Would she have liked it? I could never predict her. I shouldn't even try.

As the snowflakes got bigger and more frequent, it became clear that my dark trail would be filled in and bleached white before long. ~~Nothing stays. (The hardest and blandest truth.)~~

I walked in a heart shape, and once I'd made the whole outline I considered it a while, then trod through the middle and broke it in two. That one was so cheesy it made me feel dirty, so I kept walking and trying for greater things. In a large area where two paths met, I set my grocery bag down—I set my whole self down, and I walked out a masterpiece.

It was way out of character, how much time I spent on it. It felt right at the time, but now it doesn't seem like something I would ever do. It was simple enough; it was footprints after all. But I made her huge, fifteen times the size of the original. I outlined her and then sort of framed her in a rectangle. I couldn't remember the background, so I improvised and filled in what seemed right: a rudimentary tree, a mountain.

It was unmistakably the Mona Lisa, although highly simplified. But my Mona didn't seem as happy. Everyone knows about how long he supposedly spent on the lips. I didn't have the patience or the eye for detail, so mine looked more... concerned?

Of course I hoped someone might see it. I checked around the giant park again but still there was no one. I was alone in the falling snow. The park looked brilliant then, some kind of big aquarium filled only with a wide darkness, its floor sprinkled with lamp posts turning the water near them pale yellow in the midst of all the dark dark purple. The yellow-white flakes sinking down lazily, drifting back and forth and settling to the bottom.

I admired my masterpiece for a final moment, as every second it vanished more and more.

Then I picked up my bag and walked home, mostly in straight lines from then on: my feet were numb. And now I'm writing this.

Whatever this is.

Because I realized on the walk home that I actually felt fine? If I was honest with myself, it was fine that no one might notice what I made, and probably that was the fun of it—it existed either way, in its own right, because *I* know it did, and *that's* what I was trying to say. And I'm making it sound like it was some out-of-body thing, like I was once again just watching myself do some distant thing—but this was different. This was, it was like I was watching not someone doing something way out of character, no, it was actually the opposite of that. For at least half an hour, I was almost completely free of thought. It was like something pure. It sounds insane but that was Phil. I knew for sure that whoever I saw making that thing was real. I was *really* there—I swear.

UNIVERSE

The way it all came to exist can be very clearly explained, these days, in our infinite wisdom. (It's simple, really):

Everything in the universe just exploded from some cold and random point, at some random time before "time," for a random reason before reasons. Before this, there was nothing. An inconceivable black nothingness filled every corner of nothing, except that there were no corners, and there was no "black." Then suddenly, out of this non-situation, this absolute nothing, before a "thing" was even imaginable in any terms, suddenly everything burst forth. A non-existing pin pricked through the enormous tension of the nothing, and all the matter banged through the massive void, tearing the nothing wide open, erupting into existence. In a fraction of a tiny fraction of time, nothing became everything. This was not a miracle.

Massive planets and balls of burning gas were hurled from this exploding point. They bumped into one another, socialized, flirted, split up, ran away, kept moving; they were thrown far far far into an emptiness out of which they carved space for themselves, and to this day they continue along these same paths. No force propels them, other than the initial bang, which was of course not a miracle.

The waitress just called me "honey." When I came in she acted like she knew me, like we were pals. It's kind of nice, actually, they're starting to know me here. In the kitchen they're laughing about how I'm wearing the same clothes as yesterday. The crazy guy in white clothes who gets nine hundred coffees and sits scrawling in his little book until close. That's funny—I just noticed everyone in here is eating alone. It's so quiet. Where else would we all go on a day like today? Off topic.

The matter fell into groups along the way. Some of the planets found other planets and stuck together for a time, since they were headed the same way anyway. Some of the luckier groups found great glowing suns. They were pulled from their drifting, and were slowly reeled in. They were spun around and warmed, drawn close to new caretakers.

On one of these lucky rocks, an even luckier thing was about to take place. The planet happened to be held a certain distance from its sun, and happened to contain all the necessary ingredients so that, when held there, and with enough time, the perfect energy from the planet's sun allowed something to emerge—something which would later call itself "Life." And so it did emerge. First, in a tiny but enormously consequential way—similar to the initial bang, and most things—in little groupings of molecules that did something when they merged, something foreign and cyclical and self-perpetuating. This something they did continued and continued, and Life spread its way around the planet timidly but unquestionably. It was wiped out and it began again. It kept on. The details were a bit fuzzy (unlike all the details previous to this point) but this something became dinosaurs, became nothing, became amoebas again, became fish, became crawling fish, became billions of other animals, became almost-monkeys, then monkeys, then a-bit-more-than-monkeys, then humans.

It stopped at humans, because the humans told it to.

(The humans wrote a book about this whole process a while after it happened, and they wrote it in the proper order, and they had fun writing it, and they called it Genesis. But the book was a bad book, and eventually everyone hated it, because although it had the order basically right, it forgot about the dinosaurs, and it played around too much, and it used silly characters and metaphors that weren't necessary to the central plot, so it lacked sense.)

Oh I think they're closing in like fifteen minutes. Shit.

The humans were now conscious of what had happened. They put their penises inside their vaginas and created more and more Life. They talked about Life, often. For a while it was all they talked about, because it was all that was worth talking about, even though it was truly so bland. It was merely the luck of the cosmic draw. After all, any other planet in the universe which was positioned the proper distance from its sun, and which housed a similar system of proper elements, could also create Life. The odds had nothing to do with it, even though they were incredibly rare (some humans calculated less than a 0.01% chance over a span of four billion years) because Life was simply the exception to the universal rule—special, but not *that* special. And it wasn't a *miracle,* because a miracle had to both happen, and not make sense. And although all of this happened, it, of course, made perfect sense.

AS THEY SAY

FINALLY I had it. What I would do was I would do an investigation. I would just go around and ask the neighbours a few questions. Our neighbourhood was pretty big, but there weren't actually that many people in it, and I'd just check out all the neighbours' houses and see if anyone knew anything about someone named Phil. If something like that really happened, people would know about it. Unless they were complete idiots. I would make sure to check every single house in the neighbourhood and try to figure out where it came from and whose it was and if I could give it back. And if no one on the whole street knew anything well then I'd have to figure out a bigger investigation, or if I absolutely had to I might get a grown-up to do something, but only if I tried *everything* and it was still impossible.

I opened my closet door and dragged out this cork bulletin board I had but had never used yet. Then I took some scrap sheets of paper and tore them very carefully into a couple different-sized pieces. I wrote a fact on each piece, and a title for the list on the biggest one. It wasn't *really* helpful, but it was just a start:

CLUES:
- It was in the woods.
- It must have been there a while.

- Because of the mud and water and rust.
- From the bent tree you take five steps away from the river
  and one sideways towards the house.
- Someone named Phil.

And I would keep adding more and more pieces every time I found a clue, and keep the clues organized in alphabetical order, or in order of hardest to discover to easiest, or in order of how true I thought they were, or a better system I would figure out later, and I would think hard about all the clues and rearrange them and come up with theories and illustrations and explanations et cetera and eventually get to the bottom of it.

And my investigation would start that very afternoon, right after algebra.

SO THEN LATER I was sitting in the woods on that mossy sea turtle rock, right before I went to check out the first house. I was thinking about Phil's UNIVERSE. It was the middle of a grey Thursday afternoon, and I was sitting there thinking about it and adding my own parts in my head:

(Only, a few of the humans weren't sure exactly which penis had been placed into exactly which vagina, and exactly which vagina they crawled out of. The universe, or whatever, had tossed them to somebody else, just to mix things up. The universe *loved* to mix things up.)

I kept drawing all the nothing in my sketchbook by pencilling the whole page black, and then I flipped my pencil around to the eraser side and erased the everything into it. I erased one tiny little explosion for the big bang, then the suns, the stars, the planets, including Saturn which is my favourite, Earth, the UFOs, the faraway galaxies, the penises and the vaginas, and everything else.

It didn't make sense though.

I mean, how can a universe of nothing just turn into everything all the sudden? And if there is everything now, how could there have ever been *nothing?* This was a thing that I thought about quite often, to be honest with you, and sometimes I talked to people about it, like Finch, and smarter people, and it seemed like no one really knew what to say about it. Obviously no one knew what to say. But I mean I never even heard anyone with any really good ideas about it. No one even cared.

So I drew it in my sketchbook like I said, and I tried to imagine it that way, but no matter how I imagined it, I couldn't imagine it. Between the nothing and the everything must be something else. Like, what was around before the big bang? There had to be *something,* or else how could the big bang have even happened? If there was nothing, that meant there was no sketchbook first of all, and no eraser, and no me. If there was no eraser and no page and no me, then how did the erasing happen?

If all that existed was a big, like, *void* or something, like a big black page, then that means there's nothing different outside the page that could turn into the everything. Because *everything* is nothing. But if there was a something extra separate from the void, a little atom or something, it was still just as confusing because you can't ask where *it* came from, or else you're just asking the same question all over again.

So: there was either nothing and then suddenly everything—which just doesn't make sense—or there was nothing, plus another something that must have just been around *forever,* before the everything, before the nothing, and it was just always around. That didn't make a lot of sense either, but maybe a *little* more sense.

I decided that it was the guy with the eraser who was the thing that was around since forever. Most people just called the erasing guy "God," I think, because what the heck else are you supposed to call something like that, and so I guessed I usually did too. But I also realized that no one could know for sure about anything before the big bang, and it was really too scary to look back farther than that, which made me kind of angry and sad at the same time, especially because what if it was a question that made me angry and sad for the rest of my entire life?

After I erased the universe I made the page black again a few times and I kept thinking about the questions without answers, and eventually my page started to get all messy. It started to look kind of like the cover of Phil's notebook, just white and black splotches all over.

Then I swept the eraser shavings off of the edge of the messy universe and they fell and bounced off of the crinkly leaves on the forest floor. Where did the shavings fit into the puzzle? They were the rubber that was used to create everything from nothing. I thought hard. Maybe they were dreams? I didn't want to even start to wonder where they went after slipping through the cracks between the dead leaves and into the soil.

So I slapped myself in the face pretty hard. I looked at my watch, and was shocked. It was almost 5:00 PM already, and it was time to stop thinking. I had a house to check out.

I snapped my sketchbook shut and headed out of the woods and had supper with Simon. It was nothing special, it was the usual: meat, potatoes, carrots, green beans and white milk. I finished my milk, shaved my moustache, and asked to be excused.

"Where are you rushing off to?"

"Frankly," I said, "I've still got a lot of work to do in the woods," but obviously I was lying because where I was rushing off to was actually the beginning of my investigation.

"Alright, I guess. Be home before dark though, Arthur?"

"Yup!" I slid off my chair.

"Oh, Arthur, will you change those sheets, please?" Simon said for the nine-thousandth time.

"Dooon't wooorrryyy," I crooned while heading for the door.

I picked up my backpack from the floor near the hallway and shoved my arms through the straps. Phil was in there.

I shut the front door behind me, dropped off the porch and headed up the street. It was still grey outside, and kinda damp from the rain the day before. There were shrivelling worms on the side of the road every once in a while, who had evacuated their burrows when the flood had started, but then didn't make it back home afterwards. Aha! They had transmigrated, in the first meaning of the word. And maybe in the second meaning too. Two or three of them were still moist and slimy though, so those ones I picked up and put in the grass on the side, where they had probably come from. Then I kept walking.

My stomach felt a little funny, I don't know why. I pictured the potatoes in there with all the carrots and the steak and the milk. The mashed potatoes trying to calm everyone else down. One thing I like about potatoes, now that I think about it, is I like how when potatoes sit on your counter and get old they just grow more eyes. I like how they're called "eyes," and not warts or lumps or chicken pox or anything stupid. It would be nice if by the time I was twenty I would have another eye grow somewhere, like on the back of my hand, or right above my belly button. I would cut holes in the belly of all my shirts so I could look around with that eye too, and check out things without anyone noticing, like secretly check the soles of their shoes to draw their footprints if I was investigating them or something. Then I'd keep growing more eyes every couple of years, and the older I got the more directions I could see in, and by the time I was eighty I'd be *covered*. All over my arms and legs and everywhere. I would have so many eyes that if I rolled them backwards far enough I could see everything inside all of me. And when I blinked them all it would make a sound like someone jumping up and clacking their shoes together at the heels, and sometimes, obviously, I would actually do that at the same time as I blinked. And my clothes would look like moths had eaten holes through every inch of them, but really it was because I was getting so old that I could see in all directions at once and never miss anything.

I'd decided to use the most obvious system, which was beginning at the houses closest to my own house, and working my way farther and farther up the street. So, going by this plan, the first house I'd check out would be the house of these people called the Beckhams. There was actually a house before them, but no one lived there 'cause it was for sale, then Finch's was next, but I wasn't going to put Finch's or Victoria's houses on the list of houses I had to check, obviously, because if Finch's parents or Victoria's dad actually read any of Phil they might think I was being a weirdo, and they might call Simon on the phone or something. Then next I would check the house that said "PETERSON" on the mailbox, and then, if I absolutely *had* to, the hermit's.

When I got to the Beckhams' driveway, I stood on the seam between the old dusty grey pavement of our street and their fresh black tar. I think that they had the only driveway on our street that wasn't gravel. Maybe it would be less noisy to walk on. I stood there for a while and observed the scene. There were no cars in the yard, the garage was closed, and the lawn was a bit tall.

"Maybe no one is home," I said out loud by accident.

I tried to think of the last time I'd actually *seen* the Beckhams. All I could come up with was a time where I walked along the side of the road and they drove past me and smiled and waved. I felt like that happened often. I tried to think of a time other than those times when I had seen the Beckhams, and I couldn't. I could barely even picture them, except that I thought Mrs. Beckham had blond hair.

I started to wobble back and forth on my feet and kick rocks.

"Ahh, who cares about Phil," one of the voices inside my brain said.

I turned around to leave.

"Wait, I do," the other voice said.

I turned around again.

In the cartoon of myself standing almost in the driveway, there was an angel on one of my shoulders and a devil on the other. In the cartoon, I looked at the devil, he smiled and winked, or something, and then I looked at the angel. He raised his eyebrows and nodded his head slowly. I knew that what I should do was I should pick the angel, and walk up to the Beckhams' and ring the doorbell and try to find out clues about Phil. Because in the cartoon of my life, if I picked the devil, I might have an easier day, but I might also get flattened by a steamroller, or exploded by dynamite, or accordioned by a giant anvil.

"Excuse me?" said someone. Mrs. Beckham was on her doorstep, with the door open behind her.

I stared at her, trying to think of what to say.

"Yes," I said.

She did have blond hair. It was straight, a bit longer than most moms', and looked dry. I couldn't tell if it was real blond or fake blond. She was wearing a yellow apron that looked like it was too small, tied right overtop of a navy blue business-man suit.

"Sorry?" she said.

"Yes!" I said again but I didn't know why.

"Yes, what?"

I tried to do some unboggling of my mind for a moment but it was hard work.

"What's that?" she said, pointing at me.

"Huh?" I thought, it's *me*, obviously. I walked slowly up the quiet new pavement.

"What's that on your shoulder?" she said as I got to the door-way. I wondered if it was the angel or the devil. But it was just a leaf.

"Oh, it's a leaf there," she said.

I said nothing.

"A leaf there, just there on your shoulder," she said in a jumpy way. She was almost singing. "Did you need something, honey?"

I took the leaf off my shoulder.

"Uhhhm, I'm kind of investigating," I said, giving myself away right at the start.

"Oooh, investigating me?"

"No. No. I was just wanting to talk to you, though."

After a second, she said "Sure!" and invited me inside.

It was really weird to go into someone-I-didn't-know's house by myself, and I felt like I was a house intruder even though I was invited. I took off my red rubber boots and left my backpack on. She walked through a doorway on the left and into the white kitchen, and she offered me a chocolate chip cookie. I accepted, obviously. I sat at the kitchen table, even though I might as well have been sitting on a chair alone in the corner, or behind a big brick wall or inside a jail cell or something, because the table was *covered* in stuff. It piled up over my head. Laundry baskets, a couple dishes, a stapler, a ball of yarn, plastic bags of things, other things on top of more things, a roll of masking tape, a vase of flowers, and everything else, covered the table. The wall of stuff was so tall that I couldn't even really see Mrs. Beckham on the other side of the kitchen. I felt like I was a prisoner in sanitary confinement. On one side the mess spilled onto the floor. I looked around. The whole house was like that: walls of stuff.

I took the little black tape recorder that Simon gave me for my birthday out of my backpack and put it on top of a book called *Basic Gardening*.

"How professional!" said Mrs. Beckham when she saw my tape recorder.

I pushed RECORD.

"So, Mrs. Beckham—"

"Brenda."

"So Brenda. What are you doing this evening?"

"Arthur, right?"

"Arthur Williams."

"Well Arthur, I took the day off of work. I called in sick. I told them I was up to my neck in mucus and I might be back tomorrow. Really, I wanted to dig up my garden."

"Spring fever," I said cleverly.

She laughed. "Certainly!"

"Isn't it too early for that still?"

"Well maybe," she said. "Who knows."

I knew. The ground was probably still frozen solid. But that wasn't the point so I kept interviewing.

"Where is everybody else?"

"Sam's at work still. He works late. The kids are all moved out of course, well you know that. Yup, too many cowboys and not enough Indians, as they say."

"Native Americans," I said.

"Hmm?"

"It's 'too many cowboys and not enough Native Americans.'"

"Oh yes, yes of course."

"Also First Nations."

My brain started to boggle itself. It was a good thing she was a good talker, because I was not a good interviewer. It was really hard to figure out what we were talking about, so I didn't even know which questions to ask. But she was kind of interviewing herself anyway.

"So, I've just had my fingers in all the pies this afternoon—cleaning the house, reading, doing this and that, well you can probably tell."

I couldn't tell.

"—And I haven't even *got* to the garden yet! But you know, a stitch in time saves nine."

I nodded.

"Umm, so what do you need all this stuff for?" I asked.

"Which stuff?"

"I mean, well, nevermind."

I wanted to get the heck out of there. Mrs. Beckham had sat down on a chair across the table and across the fort made of stuff, and I peeped over the top, between a checkery shirt and the edge of a DVD case. She was giving me a funny look, like kind of serious. I didn't want to waste any more time.

"What I really wanted to talk about was this," I said.

"Brass tacks."

"What? No," I said. I took the notebook from my backpack.

"What've you got there?"

"I found this book in the woods, and someone named Phil wrote it."

"You think it's Phil's?"

"Well, I know it's Phil's," I said. "It's got his name on it. And also everywhere inside it." I held the book out way up high for her to have a look, but she didn't move her hand to take it from me, and she didn't even really look at it. She looked like she was thinking, like she was staring at something, and her eyes were moving backward and forward. My arm got a little sore of holding Phil in the air so I stopped reaching and slowly put Phil down in my lap. Mrs. Beckham's shiny lips were mumbling things under her breath.

"Five, four... well, it's probably only four or five there, right now," she said. "I'll try him!"

She got up and rushed over to the phone, and then I realized what I hadn't been realizing yet. There was a person I'd entirely forgotten about, and he was Mrs. Beckham's son, and his name was Phil Beckham. Once, a long time ago, he babysat me. Just once.

"No, that's okay," I said pretty loudly, "it's probably not—"

"Oh don't worry about it," she said, "I was going to call him today anyway."

She dialled the numbers.

"You'll never *guess* where he lives now," she said to me, as if she had something amazingly interesting to say. I didn't guess.

"*Phil*adelphia!"

She yelped out a bunch of laughs at herself, not seeming to care whether I found it very funny or not. I didn't, by the way. Then her laughter was cut off by a muffled sound in the top part of the phone.

"—Phil! Hello dear. How's *Phil*adelphia today?" She started laughing again, and miles and miles away, I bet Phil Beckham probably laughed too. I'd seen him laugh a couple times.

I put my head inside of my hands and bent down under the stack of laundry under a small piece of plywood under a round clock under a stack of books under my tape recorder, so that the wall came up really tall between me and Brenda. I laid my forehead down on the cover of Phil's book, rubbed my eyes and took a bunch of deep breaths.

On the tape, you can hear Brenda and the impostor Phil's conversation going on and on behind the wall of stuff for an entire twelve and a half minutes before you hear the loud roar sounds of the tape recorder being stuffed into my backpack. I decided to leave. I sat up in stealth mode and slipped Phil back into my backpack too, zipped the zipper and put it on my back. I sneaked my way out of the kitchen and into the living room while Brenda's back was turned to me. I stood in there and considered my next move. I could just barely see into the kitchen from where I was, and I could see the curly white phone cord wiggling around in the air, and tap tapping against the fridge.

A pile of jeans on the living room couch bulged up out of nowhere, and a poofy white cat silently hopped to the floor. It looked at me with its yellow eyes, and then strolled its way over to my feet. He or she seemed friendly enough, and actually started to wrap itself around my legs and go around and around between them, kind of in the shape of the symbol for infinity, which is called a "lemniscate." While the cat was lemniscating I leaned down and got small, and I touched its smooth back and it shot up like a gigantic inchworm. I didn't really know that many cats. It sniffed my bare feet, and I felt a bit smelly, but I don't think it cared, because it started to sort of lick my toes. It licked my big toe, then the next, then the next, then all of them at once. It felt *exactly* like wet sandpaper.

I kind of giggled even though I wasn't in the mood to laugh, because it was really tickling. Brenda peeked out from the kitchen door, and looked at me, smiling, with the phone cord yanked out straight behind her.

"Oh Phil, I almost forgot! Little Arthur—you remember Arthur Williams? No, yes. Yes exactly. He was wondering if you lost a book."

The cat finished my toe bath and softly hurried up a few of the grey carpeted stairs to the second floor, and sat there watching me.

"No, a black and white notebook. What? Yes, black and white—speckled. Yes. No? Okay, I would've figured as much. Yes. Would've figured as much."

She put her hand over the bottom part of the phone and whispered, "He says it's not his," and went back into the kitchen to keep phoning.

"Obviously," I whispered to the cat.

I tiptoed down the hall and shoved my boots on and opened the door to outside. It was almost dark.

"Well, Phil, nice to talk to you. Just wanted to separate sheep from goats, you know, as—"

I shut the door as softly as I could, tiptoed half of the driveway and then ran the rest. When I finally got to the street I slumped all the way back home, picking up twigs every once in a while and snapping them in half.

I got home and went past the kitchen and the room beside, where Simon was doing work on the computer, and I went to my room and opened my closet and stared at the bulletin board. I thought about Brenda, and the piles of stuff. I thought about the chocolate chip cookie, and the frozen garden. I thought about the whole stupid evening, and tried to think of something I might have learned. Years later, I wrote on another scrap of paper and tacked it up with the rest.

CLUES:
- From the bent tree you take five steps away from the river and one sideways towards the house.
- It must have been there a while.
- Because of the mud and water and rust.
- How you can't possibly think of anything else.
- It was in the woods.
- Someone named Phil.
- How the cat's tongue felt *exactly* like wet sandpaper.

THEY BUILD it together. We see another man, a man with glasses and slim limbs, a man carrying on his square shoulder a young boy, kicking squirming laughing. He always carries the boy this way, at least every time we see them come to build: he holds the boy's waist and flings him up onto his shoulder and they walk among us. The man places his steps with visible caution: he is walking for two. With his other hand, on the non-boy side, he carries a red toolbox. When they get to the spot, the man bows and the boy's small feet touch the ground as the toolbox's scuffed bottom does the same.

Though the man does the bulk of the work, he makes sure the boy always has some task, some skill to contribute: see him pass the box of nails to the man when he asks. See the boy holding the level, the man asking if the bubble is centred, the boy checking and screaming yes. The boy sitting with his back to the man, stacking small towers of dusty scraps of wood, humming structureless wandering songs that he invents as he goes.

The man places the boards of the ragged frame and the plywood to clothe it. The wood they use is from a pile of leftovers from the building of their house, years ago. The man starts the nails with his hammer, leaving an inch for the boy to finish with his own boy-sized hammer. Often the boy bends a nail in half, and the man starts another one just beside. Sometimes the boy demands to use the big hammer, making the man use the small one instead.

Between three of us, a small triangular floor soon sits. A moment later, a top floor as well. Then two ladders, one for each level, and a roof: a wavy bit of mint-green fibreglass blazing translucent in sunlight. The man watches the boy climb the ladder to the top floor for the first time.

The whole treehouse is a "house" in fashion only. This is no shelter, no residence. It provides for no physical need. But in the moments to come, it transforms from fort to castle to clinic to airship to hotel to laboratory to lifeboat. To the boy running climbing stomping and yelling, to the boy growing, it is anything.

We don't mind this, this use. As much as they confuse us, we trust the humans. What reason would they have to let us go to waste? They can sense our value, in some way they must feel it. However, one thing we do find confusing. Sometimes after we are cut, they will count the rings exposed on our cross-sections. They count our layers, and this counting seems somehow important. Is it a game? "This one is fifty years old," they say. "This one is almost a hundred." Is it a joke? Surely they know that we, who have seen nearly every age, who have been here for so long, passing our vision through time in all directions, we who live in all time as in a single moment—surely we are not *years old*. Why do they want the rings' number? Do they even notice their shape?

Now the man and boy return; again they are building. The boy is taller and needs a bigger palace.

The two builders drive a circuit of the neighbourhood, searching for supplies in roadside junk piles. It is "spring cleaning." They collect as many building blocks as will fit into their car and they return home.

They are adding and climbing and reimagining. This addition will be several times larger than the first; in a sense it will make the original an annex. Like its tinier parent, it also gets two floors, built of varied length two-by-four and other scrap beams. Inside, a ladder leads from top floor to bottom, then a set of stairs connects the bottom to the soft leafy earth.

See them stitch its walls together like wooden quilts, like pages of a wooden scrapbook, tightly sewing in all their neighbours' discarded window frames, their rusted screens with holes punched through, a gunrack that will never again hold a gun, sturdy railings draped with stiff wire mesh, a small family of shingles, a burgundy paint-peeled door. See them top it with a half tin, half mint-fibreglass roof.

The man places a four-foot piece of ply between each of the first floors connecting old to new, the boy nails the bridge down and the treehouse becomes a whole. They sit in the top floor eating ham and cheese sandwiches, swatting mosquitoes and watching the river.

The boy darts around in the treehouse's crow's nest. It pours. His ship has taken in too much water. He bails it over the railing with an orange bucket.

He stands on the bottom floor's stage; it's a hot afternoon. He's narrating his first one-man play, about a boulder who wishes it were an acorn. It's opening night and a chipmunk watches, apparently captivated.

He balances on the outside of the wall, with his stomach and spread arms pressed against it. His feet perch on whatever jutting beam or convenient branch might support his weight, exactly as the man had made him promise never to do. But he is inching along one final rock face and he is so close to the summit.

Then he is not here. When the book falls and the man walks to the water, the boy is not in the treehouse. It sits empty. We still see the boy, and he is often near us, but the boards of the treehouse hover virtually untouched. Now they've weathered so much rain and snow and wind that they match the colour of our skin. The shrine's mossy wood blends seamlessly into our bark and we embrace it. The boy still leaves it alone. Should someone come and pull out every one of its nails, we know the treehouse will still float here, fused to us.

~~NOW~~
~~ALONE~~
~~ONLY~~
~~HEART~~
<u>HER</u>

I haven't written in days. I was feeling quite a bit better for a
while there but now today it's hopeless. I've literally been pac-
ing down the hall for like an hour. Lost. Can't sort out the
tasks involved in making anything more than cereal, and so I
eat cereal for breakfast lunch supper, this whole week so far. I
thought about making a sandwich today and just stared into the
fridge. Can't even begin to expect anything of today. It's making me so fucking antsy to write! Not calming at all! I feel pulled
in so many directions and like there's all this stuff I should be
doing—can't do any of it—give it up.

 And half the time I wake up and almost call her. My mind
accepts no order. Chronological least of all. Things don't happen chronologically to me—they never did. Things never "did,"
and then "do," and then "will." They would and then they do and
then they will and did. They mix themselves around even while
happening, and once they become memory it's even more help-
less. As far as I can see, everything in my life happened at once.

 AND → THERE'S → NOTHING → LIKE → THIS,

                    MORE
IT'S   ALWAYS   MUCH
        THIS.   ~~USUALLY~~
     LIKE

When someone tells me a story in which some events happen to them in some kind of time-based order, I assume they're either lying or insane. If someone wrote my biography (not that they would or should) I'd make them play fifty-two pick-up with the final draft.

FIRSTLY, (as if anything else ever happened to me) let's begin with E. Yes, we'll just leave it at "E," upper-case E, like an eye-test chart. Which was one of the many things she was, to put it horribly. To put it horribly, there were some parts of her that I always had to squint at and still couldn't read.

E
WAS
THE FIRST —
AND ONLY—PERSON I
COULD SAY THAT I HONESTLY, WITHOUT
A SPECK OF DOUBT, LOVED, SOMETIMES DESPITE
MY BEST REASONING, AND DESPITE ALL EVIDENCE
THAT I HAD NO IDEA HOW TO DO IT, WAS NEVER CUT
OUT FOR IT, DESPITE ALL FEARS THAT I THEREFORE
WASN'T MEANT TO BE OF ANY USE TO ANYONE, DESPITE
THE TERRIFYING NOTION THAT MY INSECURITY AND MY NEED TO
FEEL CONTAINED AND CERTAIN MUST MEAN THAT I WAS ROTTEN, GREEDY,
LUSTFUL AND UNCARING, MUST MEAN THAT I WAS A MONSTER, DESPITE HOW
MUCH I ONLY WANTED WHAT SHE WANTED FOR HERSELF, AND ALL OF ME BELIEVED ALL
OF HER WAS SO PERFECT, BUT HOW THE HIDDEN PARTS OF ME I COULDN'T PREDICT OR ACCOUNT FOR
TRIED SO HARD TO CHANGE HER, TO CONTAIN HER, TO JUST CONVINCE HER THAT WHAT SHE WAS SUPPOSED TO BE WAS *MINE*.

And if I can just get it all down—big and small—then it's mine. And it's *over*, and I can stop. I can't bring any of it back. I can't summon you, but at least I'll have tried.

We met in our last year of school. We were both trying to finish. There was no dramatic story about our meeting, we were just in the same class. You just walked around the studios like you were lost but wouldn't have had it any other way. You would later say that I walked around like a puppy whose leash was "too slow." Eventually I talked to you, and after a few days of the first talks I was shocked because we actually *were* talking: we were talking about actual things. We were agreeing and disagreeing, we were arguing and laughing, we were spending eight hours together, we were plotting.

I fell for you so hard that all I could do was worry about falling for you—about turning you into something you weren't, some muse or divine icon, so I vowed not to, but then I couldn't imagine how I might dream up anything better than the full, actual you. You made me think thoughts that dangerous.

You were someone so dangerously close to the person I'd always (subconsciously) dreamed of meeting that you caused me to (consciously) adjust the idea of that person, to completely discard it, because you'd trumped it. You could tell, couldn't you?

You were beautiful, and not in a way where I noticed things about you that were beautiful and could point them out—I could do this, and I did, but it never seemed to have much to do with the true you—you were beautiful in a way that was its whole own thing, you seemed a complete—something—and whatever you were I knew I didn't want to change one thing about it. I wasn't exaggerating.

Sometimes you were peppy and confused and honest and shrugged your shoulders and laughed and said Oh Well to the world. Other times the world weighed down on you tremendously for weeks at a time, and I did all I could to make it easier, but all I could do was not much.

When you spoke, you said things without the slang you were supposed to use, and in tones of voices I'd never heard, only imagined. Your sentences were unpredictable. Sometimes you would actually sing them, and I didn't know what to do except laugh. You were funny. You didn't think anyone got your jokes. I'm not convinced anyone did—no one could have been ready for you. Sometimes you would pause in the middle of a sentence and then switch to something extraneous that at first glance didn't seem to complete the initial thought, but to someone who knew you, you made sense in some hilarious and abstract way that went beyond language. You made something better than "sense."

I thought I understood that I would never understand you, but then maybe I secretly thought I understood you.

You understood me. You put me back inside myself. You made me think I was OK, like I was normal. (Like I was nowhere near normal and that was fine.) Like I was *good*. Remember? I couldn't explain myself to you, but then I didn't have to explain. I wanted to be like one of your thoughts, like one of those unexpectedly and vaguely completed things. You finished my sentences in ways I myself never could have. You came from some other reality with such detail and integrity that it terrified me. You terrified me. I loved you. (Remember?) You loved me too, somehow, and of course I didn't know why at first, but gradually I did. Maybe I didn't believe it at first, but does anyone? Maybe you helped me see things that had always been there. Things like me. When we were together, I reminded me of myself. And you were yourself, and who else was there? Maybe there were no secrets anymore. Why would there be? Maybe we lived in a world totally without secrets, and perhaps we couldn't imagine living in any other. Maybe I only wanted what I already had.

(And maybe you didn't need me.)

MORE

There's no way to tell it. No way that would serve my real purpose, of course. And so now, as many classic failures have before me, I'll probably write all frantic and calculated about my mental block, about my inability to write (to *express!*) and this, yes *this,* of course, what a surprise, won't lead anywhere either, other than straight down a spiralling stairwell of self-consciousness and wasted wit, ending in some dingy gallery of bad, bad writing and shameless narcissism and meta-nothing. And so here I am, standing in this awkward position, and wondering with clenched fists, while browsing around the space, wondering if wait, maybe, yes,

maybe I *can* get there from here if only I could just lower my expectations (Hooray!), and sincerely admit that no, I cannot write these things yet, and even if I could, I could never do what I really want and must do: Live Them Again. Even though every stitch of me, every tiny ruthless cell of me is convinced it needs to. But of course my life lives itself chronologically only when it's least appropriate. Of course there's no way to get back even the worst, even the fights, and that should be almost a comfort, but no, it's a weight in my gut, a well-known weight: the ache of wondering, and also of knowing, having known I was pushing and losing her then and knowing that I continue to lose her more and more now as I keep going, and knowing how I should have changed it all, should have just *tried harder.* But how back then every word spoken was its own battlefield, every exchange something to be won or lost, and how I *was* trying then, and making a great tour of it, winning them all, and her retreating, vanishing in defeat. If I could've just seen her *once* more, or sent *one* more email to cap off the series—I could've made it a real live masterpiece. Five epic paragraphs dripping with all the rationality of love, the horror but the inevitability of it, and littered with cross-references to evidence against its decline. I know I tried, but not HARD ENOUGH and now here I am, layers upon layers later, months later, still reminiscing all the fights and all the self-hating and the time when I could no longer speak a word of kindness. When every good intention had its own twisted moral code. When my heart declared civil war, with my mind allied against it. Against me. ~~When my mind boiled over and sizzled on the stove element, wreaking havoc and slicing~~ When my mind in fact just turned off, but not before willing my heart to surrender to numbness. When the fighting became automatic, and there wasn't even *that* for fun anymore. When we had said everything. When there was nothing more to say. And how, looking back on it, the agony was probably caused in the first place by some desire born out of this scrambled omelette brain, a sick desire for MORE emotion, for MORE drama, not an end to it, and how I was truly in my glory days then, oh man, staying at her apartment until all hours of the morning, refusing to leave, sitting hunched on the edge of her bed letting the words just continue and continue until I finally made my point and made her cry, and then finally I could. And how of course it's not the job of a relationship to provide such prizefights, night after night. And of course we didn't *have* a "relationship" anymore. And what about how EVERYTHING always worked in these complementary ways whereby I, at the end, seemed so emotional—hateful irritable hopeless—yet how inside—as already stated—I was almost entirely numb.

And how, *complementarily,* she put up a barrier of faux-numbness to protect herself from how hurt she was by my every move. What about how it was all my fault? And how my numbness escalated in secret, only peaking and revealing itself to me far past all turning points when on that one night, in front of her house, after a full two-hour walk of stubbornness and looking for things and pushing her further and always further, when in an honest attempt to right all wrongs, I pulled her in and said I love you. What about how she couldn't answer—What about how you just didn't answer?—and immediately started trembling because of how much you were straining to see it in me— to believe it—but WHERE HAD IT GONE OR WHAT HAD IT TURNED INTO? What about how you said nothing and went inside as if you would lock the door? THERE'S NO WAY TO TELL how we both knew how far my version of the word "love" had shifted towards the past tense—how much it sounded like WANTED—

THERE'S NO WAY TO TELL THIS
there's no way.

CAT

Last night I was actually out, at a bar, dancing with people. It was this Thursday night thing, and it was fun, for a while. I like dancing with people. With people who don't care. People whose dances don't care. I went with June, or I mean, she had called me and told me I should go. I actually did. She was with people I didn't know. It was alright, I just got into this zone where it didn't seem to matter whether I was there or not? I was pretty drunk. I think that was it—I was probably drunk, but it was fun to just dance silly under the coloured lights, and then eventually everyone moved outside for a cigarette and I followed. It was the exact type of situation that makes me wish I was a smoker, and I asked for a cigarette and someone gave me one, I lit it, immediately coughing like an amateur and standing with the rest of the small crowd, everyone talking about nothing. I wasn't talking, though. I wasn't hearing. I was somewhere else—nowhere exactly. Then I was around the corner of the brick building in the dark, looking for a spot hidden behind anything to pee and smoking the stupid cigarette which was so fun to let slowly kill me, and there was a cat. There was a cat in the alley by itself, no collar, no people. It didn't really look dangerous, it wasn't a mangy stray wrought with rabies. It looked pretty, and scared.

I tossed my cigarette and got down on my knees on the pavement and made myself very small and unthreatening—one thing that comes naturally to me—and I slowly held my hand out, rubbed my thumb and finger together and said come here you, cat, come here please now and the cat twitched its grey head to one side, flashing its white whiskers in the dim light, moving an inch closer, with one paw, then another, then strolling over, keeping focused orange eyes on this shrunken man kneeling in the alley, but still moving its soft angular head to the man's hand, then sliding its feathery grey cheek along it, marking the man. I scratched behind the little cat's ears for a while, its eyes narrowed to tiny black wisps, sound holes in miniature violins.

Then I picked it up and it didn't care. I held the cat and stood up in the alley and walked back around the corner to the people. They all lit up when they saw me with the little guy, and some of them petted it and whispered things to it in human languages it didn't speak. When they spoke to it they didn't expect replies. The cat didn't need to carry on a conversation or be in on the jokes. Everyone just enjoyed the cat for what it was: a cat. They hung around touching it, scratching it, gently tugging its whiskers, giving it kisses.

But then the cat was struggling. It'd had enough holding and prodding and love and confusion for one night, for seemingly a lifetime, and it was squirming and shifting its weight, swimming in the man's arms, with me determined, telling it no with my mind, No, stay, you have no idea how good I will be for you. Stop squirming. Aren't you a stray? You can be mine instead. Look, it will be better for you: I will feed you and give you shelter and all the things essential to being a cat. I will give you so much, everything—until it brought out the claws and teeth and I had to release my grip. The quick thing fell to the sidewalk, absorbing the impact with front paws, and rear, and shot across the street and into another part of the night.

That was weird: I was just staring out the window—I'm eating pizza downtown—and I was looking right at these two people and not noticing, I was zoned out and just blurry and the seeing and recognizing parts of me weren't connected on any level, but then they connected and after a while I noticed these people were staring at me too, like they'd stopped in the middle of the sidewalk across the street, and they were waving at me? I waved back, and they laughed and waved more and then kept going on their way. It was that red-haired girl from that film history class, and her friend I always see around. Why would they wave? People are friendly. Maybe they thought I was someone else. Maybe they were there last night, I can't remember.

Inside the bar they were all dancing again. I danced too but it wasn't the same. I was suddenly so aware of everyone there and so convinced of something, it's hard now to remember exactly what its shape was, I was just like bombarded with self-consciousness, my body was foreign, I tried, but it just wasn't going to be one of those nights—those moments of uncautiousness and epic foolishness, shamelessness... it wasn't one of them. I was moving my arms and legs, hips even, instead of them moving me. I was swaying and trying to just be funny, like everyone with all their glad smiles; I was there in the same moment with all of them, making the same motions, being turned the same reds and yellows and greens and oranges under the same lights, but I wasn't really there anymore and then I couldn't decide if I'd ever arrived. And there was something else there now, larger, and hitting me more with every stab at movement, with every beat. Had the cat caused it? Had anything? I was listening to the music and *then* dancing, and in that separation was this tremendous effort that was leaving a large part of me—my heart?—so blatantly out of it all, so I went outside and started my walk home. I had to go.

On a parallel street two blocks down, the cat was finally slowing down its run. It was thinking of the man who had snatched it up. The way he had held on. It was so forceful, wrong. The cat had enjoyed being petted by the man and his friends and had felt safe for a time. ~~But when the man continued to hold on, when the man wouldn't let go~~

But when the man clutched and refused
when he couldn't accept

when he couldn't give up
~~when he didn't understand~~
when he just *wouldn't let go,* the cat had to get away.

It remembered the scent of the man.
It would be more careful around this kind of man in the future.

PART OF THE REASON WHY IT RAINS

TWO DAYS after my interview with Mrs. Beckham it was a Saturday, and Max and Maxine and Simon and me all went on a trip. We woke up early and took Max and Maxine's little green car and sped down the highway. Simon sat up front beside Maxine, who was driving. Uncle Max sat in the back seat with me, and me and him played a game where one person draws a scribble on a page, without thinking about it, and then the other person has to make a drawing out of it. The game was Max's idea, and it was really fun. Uncle Max handed me back my sketchbook with the next scribble he'd just made.

"Good luck with that one."

The scribble was one lonely line (that was the rules), but it zig-zagged and curved around and made all these pockets in between. It was a real mess of a scribble. I turned the page around to look at it from all angles. On one side, the top was pointy so I thought about making it into a NASA rocket, but it was too fat on the bottom. Then when I turned it another way, two of the points kind of made legs, or I could have made them into legs, I mean, except they were spread out legs at stupid angles. The point of the game wasn't really to make famous masterpieces or anything, but I couldn't see how to make anything at all out of the scribble. Then, I drew a tiny dot at the end of the line, and put wings on it. I passed it to Uncle Max.

"What's this?" he asked.

"It's a fly. The scribbly part is just the way the fly decided to fly."

"Looks like we're going to have to make a new rule, smart-guy."

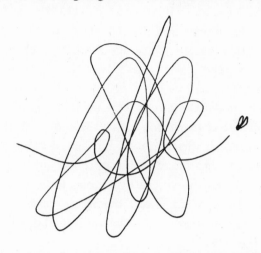

After that, I drew a really hard scribble for Max and he made a bendy telescope out of it, then I made a pair of shoes that had three shoes instead of two, where the middle one wasn't left or right, just middle, and then Max made a jaguar with five legs. We kept making drawings like that for probably an hour. It was hard because we were driving on the highway and the car bumped our pencil around. Max was actually pretty good at drawing. Not as good as me, but I wasn't surprised. It's hard to be as good at drawing as me. But his drawings all had this thing about them where you could tell they were all drawn by Uncle Max. They *looked* like they were drawn by him. I liked that.

"So how exactly do they make the syrup at this place?" I asked, after we had stopped scribbling.

Aunt Maxine's eyes looked at mine in the rear-view mirror.

"They use taps—well, I don't want to tell you everything and take the magic out. It's breathtaking there. You'll see." When she talked her eyes went from looking at me in the mirror to looking at the road and then back again.

"How would you like it if I stuck a tap in *you*," Uncle Max said, and pushed his thumb into the side of my shoulder. He pretended to turn a faucet sticking out of me. "Would you let us make Arthur syrup?"

I laughed. "No."

Uncle Max pulled the tap out of my arm.

"That sounds like something the hermit would do," I said.

Simon turned his head around and looked at me because I knew I wasn't supposed to say mean things about the crazy hermit even though everyone else did constantly. And I said it because Finch once said he heard the hermit made smoothies out of people's bone marrow. And he was so evil he even had a shadow in the dark.

I rolled my eyes at Simon so much that I could see my brain upside down like a fishbowl with my annoyed thoughts floating in it upside down and I said "Sorry" in a voice that meant I wasn't actually that sorry.

Out the window it was sunny. It was one of those weird days where it's really sunny but also really wintery. Back at our house, winter was pretty much over, but the farther we drove the more wintery it seemed to get. Along the side of the road there were still some little snow piles with pebbles on top, like clean salt that had put pepper on itself for some reason. Farther off the road in the forest there was still a couple inches of snow, like a blanket around the bottoms of the trees so that only their roots were hidden under the white. It looked like the trees were just stabbed into the ground like birthday candles into that shiny kind of cake icing that's the good kind you have to boil. The car bumped along and I watched it all whiz by. The sun made my forehead sweaty.

"I hope this place is more civilized than that pigeon farm you dragged me to," Max said, moving his head to find Maxine's eyes in the mirror.

Aunt Maxine smiled. "Oh lord," she said.

"What pigeon farm?" I asked.

Aunt Maxine's green eyes spied mine in the mirror. Her yellow hair was blowing on the left side because her window was just barely open at the top.

"Oh, I took your uncle on a beautiful trip a few years back, but he apparently won't let me live it down."

"Beautiful?" Uncle Max laughed, "If your idea of beautiful is me getting chased out of a barn by a lunatic with an axe, then yes, it was—"

"Maybe that *is* my idea of beautiful," Maxine laughed. "Maybe it's my *definition* of beautiful."

"What are you talking about?" I asked.

"Your aunt used to date this insane—"

"I have an old friend who breeds pigeons on a farm, as a hobby. His name's Peter, and he has all these really extravagant—"

"He belongs to the National Pigeon Fanciers Association," Max said, and he looked at me and rolled his eyes into his brain.

"Pigeon breeding is a serious pastime," Maxine said.

Simon was squinting and looking at Maxine too, listening.

"... You have to be very dedicated and patient. If you do it right, Arthur, you can make all these incredible types of pigeons, ones like you never see in nature. They have very curious genetics, with all these different traits they can get. Strange coloured ones, oranges and yellows, spotted ones, some with puffy feathers covering their feet, some with little hoods on their necks. Some of them are really skinny, or have big bubbled-out chests, and long white wings, almost anything you can imagine. The neatest pigeons you've ever seen, and almost as many types as there are types of people, really. Except, they don't so much look like pigeons anymore, more like little roosters or cockatiels, or—"

"*Some* of them are born blind, and only live a few short months," Uncle Max said. "Some of them can barely stand up they're so horribly deformed. They're doomed, but man they look pretty."

Aunt Maxine made a big sigh.

"Well it's the truth!" Max said.

"Max got into a fight with Peter about it," Maxine said.

"I asked him some perfectly legitimate questions."

"You *asked* him what gave him the right to play God."

"I don't think that's a quote."

"Anyway Max got chased out—"

"With an *axe*."

"He happened to be holding the axe at the time. You don't harass someone who's holding an—"

"Either way."

Maxine took a loud breath and everyone was quiet for a second. I usually get confused when I try to figure out if Max and Maxine are fighting for real or for fake, so I didn't try too hard.

"Anyway," Maxine said, "I haven't heard a word from Peter since."

Simon laughed. "So how exactly do they get these different types?"

"Of pigeons? Well, that's the thing." Maxine steered us out into the other lane for a second to miss a pothole. "You have to be very careful and do a *lot* of research, because if you breed the wrong ones, I'm not sure, but say if you breed two rare ones, they can just default back to the plain old grey pigeon. The rock dove. So there's a whole math and science to it."

"But what, they isolate them in couples and mate different combinations?" Simon asked.

"Yeah, they have all these little cubbyholes, oh it's so fascinating, I wish you could see it Arthur. Maybe someday, if *someone* hasn't completely burnt our bridge."

"Arthur doesn't want to see that freak show anyway," Uncle Max said, lightly elbowing me in my side and smiling.

"I don't know," I said. "Maybe it would be fun?" I didn't know what to say 'cause Max was putting me on a hot seat.

Max held his hands over his heart and pretended to faint a little. "You're killing me, Arthur!"

"Sorry, Uncle Max."

I watched the window and I was confused about why Max was so upset about the pigeons. I mean, it did sound pretty messed up and weird, but also it sounded exactly like what humans did. Well grown-up humans anyway. They did lots of research about each other and were very careful and then got sexy in cubbyholes in different combinations. Then lots of normal grey ones came out, and sometimes really pretty ones, but they were all doomed in their own ways. Like, they were blind, or could barely stand up, so they fell over all the time. Some of them looked exactly like the two pigeons they came from and some of them didn't so much, and others of them got moved to a different cubbyhole somewhere else, because the pigeons they came from didn't actually want them around. And those ones were so small they couldn't even remember whether the pigeons they came from were grey pigeons or blind pigeons that fell on their faces, or why they had to get moved. I didn't know why Max seemed to think it was so out of the ordinary, and it made me feel confused because usually grown-ups never cared about things that were messed up. Maybe he was just pretending to care about it to make the drive go by.

"It's okay Arthur, I'm joking." Uncle Max reached his arm forward and gently tickled the back of Aunt Maxine's neck through the hole in the headrest. "You know I'm joking, right?"

Aunt Maxine sighed one more time but in the mirror I saw her smile, and kind of roll her eyes a bit, but not far enough to see her brain or Uncle Max upside down. She said "Of course."

Then she started searching around the car with one hand while she was still driving. She swept along the dashboard, felt around in some drawers in the front of the car, then reached over and opened the glove compartment. I kept my eyes on the road through the windshield and held on tight to my door handle. The car swerved towards the ditch a bit and Uncle Max made a kind of girly scream.

"Be careful!"

"What are you looking for?" Simon asked, so that he could find it for her and she could go back to driving and making sure that we didn't all get killed. He found a tape for her and put it into the tape player. It was a woman with a beautiful voice like a soft bird and she played a funny banjo. I liked it.

(Max and Maxine's car listened to tapes instead of CDs. Aunt Maxine was a teacher; she taught grade one, but she had also taught grade three before. She liked grade one better. She was in charge of twenty-three kids that were all six years old. She showed them how to read words and print words and add up numbers and all that easy stuff, and when they got things right she bought them all ice creams and when they got things wrong she put them in the corner, because that is what it's like in public school. If I was in public school, I would have been in grade five, but Maxine had never taught a grade that high. That didn't mean I was smarter than her though; Maxine was actually really smart.

Simon said Uncle Max was "between jobs." He used to be a miner. He worked at some place kind of far away, mining coal. I think that he liked doing it, too. He told me that before I was born he had mined diamonds out and polished them up for the Queen of England, but I didn't believe him. I think he was just pretending. I pictured Max in some dark tunnel thousands of kilometres under the earth, all covered in black dust with a flashlight-hat on, swinging at walls with a metal pick. I sometimes couldn't believe that that's what his job used to be, with all his fears, and with how silly he was. I had heard stories about canaries dying in mines, and people too, but Max never talked about being afraid of his job. He didn't talk about his job at all, actually. I always had to ask Simon about it. Simon said Max's job was like another life to him, buried underneath his main life. But that was weird too 'cause I always thought when you grew up it was the other way around, and you had to dig really hard to mine out your real life. Max was looking for a new job, but I don't think he was looking very hard.

Public school teachers didn't exactly have money-vault rooms filled with hundred-dollar bills they went skinny-dipping in, and Uncle Max didn't make any cash at all, so anyway the point is that Max and Maxine's car listened to tapes instead of CDs.)

We were still driving, and Max was doing impressions of Maxine's driving, and that lady on the tape was still chirping away and plucking her wobbly banjo. I thought it would be neat, maybe, to pop in the tape I had recorded of the Brenda Beckham interview, not that I had brought it with me or anything. I just liked picturing us driving around in a car on the speeding highway, and everyone listening to me talk and interview people. It would be like I had my very own radio show called *Why Did I Have to Find a Book About a Guy Who Died in the Woods by My House?* Anyone who listened to the radio would have to listen to *me.* Then I remembered how many interesting and useful things I'd actually learned from the Brenda interview—zero—and I knew that no one would tune in to my radio show except me and I would lose my job. Maybe I could ask Uncle Max to help me out with the investigation, since he had so much free time and since I was in way over my brain. I wouldn't tell him about Page 43, because I wouldn't want to scare him or anything—plus what if he did an impression—but maybe he could still help without knowing that part.

The banjoing lady's saddish song faded out and then she started playing a quick happy one. It was a good song. It was getting even sunnier outside the window. The car zoomed along this skinny highway along this big hill, and I just watched everything out the window and hoped the long drive would end soon. Out the right side of the car—my side—was a big steep drop-off of forest and after that, way far down, was this kind of meadowy area with light brown and gold diamond-shaped fields dotted with snow leftovers and some farmhouses with pointy roofs, and barns. On the left side of the car—Uncle Max's side—was a wall of orange rock that had been exploded with dynamite because the road had to be there instead. The rock had all these lines in it, diagonal slanting layers of white and orange, like the kind of rock called "shale" that grenades apart when you throw it, except orangey instead of grey. There were probably so many fossils in there.

A fossil is a thing, like an animal or something, that gets killed and then trapped in rock, or it *becomes* rock, I guess, and leaves a statue of itself inside the rock forever, so that later on someone can find it, like a palaeontologist, which is one of the things I will someday be. The palaeontologist will know so much about the rock and the history of the place where it was, and about everything in general, that he or she will know exactly when and where the fossilized animal came from, and maybe even why it became a fossil. Someday when I was older I figured I'd have a car, or probably a bike because bikes don't use "fossil fuels," which are bad, and are different than what I am talking about, and I would ride my bike way back out there to the orange rock and collect fossils. Plus, by that time I would have actually invented a type of engine that goes on the back of my bike and runs on another kind of fossil fuels, which would be an engine with a glass box in it that you put a fossil into and lasers scan it and learn everything about it, and the bike wheels are turned by all the wisdom that the bike learns. I would fill my bike up with the fossil fuel and do wheelies back to the laboratory.

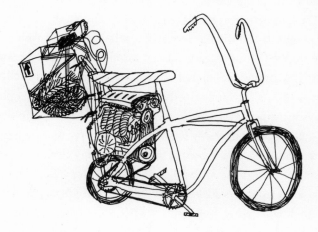

"Are we there yet?" Uncle Max said.

"We're about ten minutes away," said Aunt Maxine, and about ten minutes later, we were there. We saw a sign that was wood-coloured with old-fashioned white writing on the front; I couldn't read it 'cause Maxine speeded by, but it was The Something Family Maple Sugar Farm. We turned off the highway and onto a long curvy driveway.

Aunt Maxine slammed on the brakes and we stopped at the end of the snowy driveway in front of a log-cabin type house up on a tiny hill, and another barn type thing not much bigger than the house. The two buildings were close together, like the two parts of my old treehouse, except they didn't have a bridge in between them. There was kind of a circle of nothing around the small buildings, and then after that was trees. Different ones than at our house: skinnier and straighter and darker and taller ones. Through the space between the two buildings I could see a faraway group of people, maybe six or seven of them wearing bright-coloured winter and spring coats, wandering into the woods. Most of them turned their heads around to look at us speeding up in our car.

The four of us got out of the car at pretty much the same time. The people in the woods were still staring at us but eventually they stopped. Aunt Maxine looked through her purse for something, leaning with her back against the car. Simon took his glasses off his face and wiped them on the bottom of his black coat, squinting. Max stretched his mouth wide open and made the loudest yawn ever. My legs were just waking up, so I jiggled them, and I reached my arms way up over my head to stretch myself out. Then we all walked to the smaller building, Aunt Maxine in front, because she was kind of being the teacher on our field trip.

I shut the red door behind us. The house was weird inside: it had a tiny front room first with a desk and lots of windows, and then in behind it down a hall were other rooms, like bedrooms and kitchens and bathrooms and things. It was like a family house with an office just nailed onto the front. At the desk there was a girl with shiny brown hair probably in grade nine, leaning over a magazine and chewing. She looked up at us and blew a bubble gum bubble and it popped. She didn't say anything, as if that bubble was supposed to talk for her.

So Maxine said, "We're here for—"

"—The tour. What's your name?" The girl moved her magazine over to look at a notebook underneath, with things scribbled in it. I thought that she had no idea how lucky she was because her notebook probably didn't have any excruciatingly scary or weird or sad things to find inside.

"I think I put it under 'Arthur,'" Maxine said.

"Aren't *you* special," Max whispered to me.

The girl looked in her book and wrote something down. "You're late," she said.

I checked my watch and it said 11:39 AM.

"Okay Mrs. Arthur," the girl said, "just sign here, and then you can go catch up I guess. Hurry up though."

Aunt Maxine scribbled on the paper and we went back out the front door.

"You didn't sign as that, I hope," Max said when we were back outside.

Maxine laughed. "I didn't want to correct her."

"*Mrs. Arthur,*" Max said, "can you believe that?" He punched my shoulder amazingly gentle. "You trying to steal my woman?" he yelled. He picked me up off the ground and swung me around like we were the weirdest helicopter. "YOU TRYING TO STEAL MY WOMAN?"

The people on the tour were little lines of bright colours between the trees, and from where we were they looked kind of like those yellow and orange barcodes that the postal service prints on your envelopes when you mail them. We headed towards them, trying to walk up quietly because a man was speaking, but little twigs and bits of snow snapped and crunched under our boots as we got close to the crowd. The talking man was kind of old, older than Simon, but not as old as an old man. He had curly reddish hair poking out the bottom of his hat with earflaps, and a black and white plaid shirt on underneath an orange vest. He looked like a picnic blanket going hunting. His outfit was kind of funny to me because it somehow showed that he looked funny, but was obviously in charge.

The man-in-charge pulled a metal bucket off a tap in a tree and showed it to the people standing nearby. I squeezed my head through a couple of jackets so I could get a closer look. He held the bucket out in front of him and walked along for each person to get a peek. When he got to me I stuck my head almost inside the bucket. It was filled with clear liquid with some dirt floating in it. Maple sap. It smelled like soaking wet wood. I lifted my head up and the man-in-charge smiled and moved along to the next people. Another boy about my age was there with his little sister. They didn't even look at the sap; they were too busy pushing each other around and stepping on each other's boots.

The man-in-charge walked over and poured the sap bucket into a way huger bucket thing on top of this wagon with really tall wheels.

"How often do you collect it?" asked a short woman with a round belly and short black hair.

"Every day till the buds come out," the man-in-charge said. "Some places, they use a tube system these days, just run plastic hoses straight to the cabin, just collects itself and then you put it through the evaporator. We like doing it with the buckets. It's how we've always done it."

I looked around the forest. The trees were spread out farther than the trees at home, and they were basically all maple trees. And every one of the trees had a tap stabbed into it, and a shiny grey bucket dangling. Every single tree was getting drained.

"Listen everybody," the man-in-charge said, and he put his pointer finger to his lips to mean "Shhh." Everybody shut up after a second, even the fighting kids.

I listened.

When everything was quiet and the wind died down, I could hear the dripping. I could hear these plinking sounds, drips hitting bottoms of buckets or puddles of other sap drips. I could pick out the sounds one by one, but at the same time there were so many of them that they made music.

plink plink plonk, plink plonk.
plink plink plonk, plink plonk.

It was one of the saddest songs I'd ever heard.

"How long have you been doing it for?" the questioning lady asked.

"Three generations now, roughly a hundred years."

My eyebrows frowned. A hundred years? They'd been sucking those poor trees dry for ten times as long as I had even been *alive?* I decided to ask a question.

"Does it hurt the trees, you stabbing them with taps?"

The man-in-charge smiled and I didn't.

"Nope," he said. "It's just like a blood test from a healthy person. Like going to the hospital and getting your blood work done. The trees'll make more sap soon, and they'll be fine. I'll bet your dad'll tell you what it's like to get a blood test." He looked at Uncle Max, for some reason.

"Actually, my *uncle* said blood tests hurt like crazy. One time he had to get a blood test, and it hurt so bad he got confused and fainted and had a nightmare about falling off a cliff."

I looked at Max and he had shocked eyes and a serious face but he gave me a very small nod.

"Well anyway," the man-in-charge said, "it doesn't hurt the trees."

I wasn't convinced. Maybe it didn't *hurt* the trees, like how scraping your knee hurts, but it definitely couldn't do them any good. It wasn't the right thing to do, to just be pouring the trees' blood out like that. It didn't matter that they were just trees, I mean, they didn't even ask them. You can't ask a tree if it wants to give a blood donation or not, so you can't just go around *taking* it from them. This guy was a tree vampire, sucking the blood and then drinking it later on, and he pretended like he really loved the trees but he didn't. He just wanted the sap. What about how big and how old the trees were? What about everything that had happened to them? And what about all the maple syrup I had eaten for my whole life because I didn't know?

Everyone turned around to walk back towards the buildings, but I stayed behind, looking at all the buckets hanging, trying to hear the song again. I stood there listening forever and making a sad list in my head.

I Realized:
- that the hundreds of silver buckets reflecting the sunlight looked really pretty, hanging there in rows, polka-dotting the woods.
- that it was even worse that the buckets had to look so pretty, because of the thing that they were doing.
- that what I should do was run through the place ripping all the taps out and then come back another day with band-aids and maybe an invention I'd have to invent that could inject the sap back into the trees so that they would all be OK.
- that what I should do was ten times bigger than what I could do.

Simon put his hands on my shoulders and said, "You alright, chief?"

How could I expect him to understand? And plus had he been standing there the whole time?

"Yeah," I said, looking at my boots. "I'm fine."

"Let's get going," he said, and we walked out of the woods and into the second cabin and he tried to wrap his arm around my shoulders but I didn't let him because I had to make him believe I was fine.

Inside, the murderer-in-charge was showing everyone this big square metal machine called the evaporator that he used to boil the tree blood and get the water out so he could sell it to people to put on their pancakes. All the people, even Simon and Maxine and Max, were listening very closely.

What if trees had souls just like animals and humans? I mean, I didn't know if they did or not, but what if they did? If they drained the trees long enough, would their souls seep out too, and would their bark get lighter and lighter every day until one day they were transparent so you couldn't even see them anymore, and there would be no forest, just a big space filled with nothing? Where did all the broken parts of their souls go once the sap got evaporated into syrup? Did they stay in the syrup, or did they maybe float in the steam up into the clouds, way up, and then did God have to look at them, and did he pull the water molecules into himself and piece them back together in the right order and then cry for the trees, and was that part of the reason why it rains?

I almost wanted to punch the man-in-charge but punching is something I am not very good at, so I just made myself ignore everything, which is something I'm better at, and something I do all the time when there are big stacks of thoughts piling up

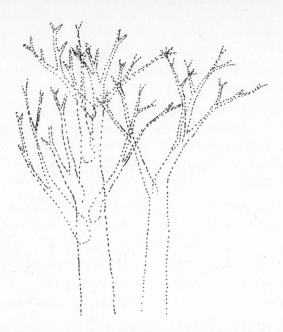

in my brain and they are making walls and there is nowhere for me to go.

(Meanwhile my real dad was relaxing in a rocking chair in his house on his pigeon farm. He was a pigeon breeder, but he didn't do it to come up with mutated cool-looking ones. My real dad knew a way to breed pigeons that were normal looking, except they were almost as big as Great Danes, and they had strong biceps underneath all the feathers. They were farming pigeons.

My real mom had helped develop the formula for it. Also, she was in charge of teaching the pigeons to speak English, so that they could understand the commands well. She had written a textbook on Englishing animals, especially pigeons, and it was a bestseller. The most interesting thing that her research found was that pigeons were extraordinarily good at learning English except that, for some reason, they had a huge amount of trouble with verbs and the order that stuff happened in. Her book was one of those really expiring books that people liked to read together in clubs, and this television lady liked to talk about.

While my real mom was out of town to be on the television lady's show, my real dad was rocking in his chair, thinking about how easy life was for him. He was thinking about how all he had to do was make the pigeons do everything, and sit around and wait for the money to pour in. He was not thinking about me. He was also not lonely and wondering if I turned into an amazing drawer or not. Then one of the strongest and greyest pigeons flew in through the open window and landed in front of him.

"We are sickening of the way you treated us," the pigeon said. "We haven't going to be taken it anymore."

Hundreds of other huge pigeons flew in through the window and made a crowd behind the first one.

"We tire of watching you sitting in your about to be rocked chair while we slaved in the fields in the sun," said another bird from the back row, and he swooped in with ropes and tied my real dad to the rocking chair.

"Let's see you having been relaxed *now*," they all said, and pushed the chair way back and let it swing way forward. They rocked him back and forth, back and forth.

"But I don't understand," said my dizzy dad, "I gave you everything you have! I put a roof over your heads, food on your tables, I give you plenty of vacation time!"

"We have been *pigeons*," the first pigeon said. "We are not needing roofs over our heads, we have needed to be flying. We will be able to have found our own food, with no tables, and our vacations will have lasted forever! We will have been—")

Then there was a loud popping sound and I was sitting at a big table with everyone in a dining room, getting served pancake breakfast. The bubble gum girl from the desk was coming towards the table with two plates stacked with pancakes that were almost as big as the plates. She dropped one off in front of me, and one in front of Simon, who was cleaning his glasses across the table from me. "Thank you very much," Simon said, and the girl said nothing at all and walked back to the kitchen and came back with pancakes for Max and Maxine too. "Thank you," said Aunt Maxine, and Uncle Max said, "Wow." Simon pulled his black coat off his shoulders and hung it on the back of his seat. I watched him reach for the little jug of maple syrup and carefully pour it on top of his pancakes. He started with a big dot in the centre and then spiralled it outwards in a snail-shell pattern, almost as fast as a snail, too. "Please pass it after you're done with it, Arthur," Maxine said. Simon handed me the little jug and I didn't use it, I just passed it sideways to Maxine. "You don't want any?" she asked.

"I'm not hungry."

Simon frowned at me.

"But you love pancakes."

"Sometimes," I said.

I examined the pancakes. They were possibly the nicest pancakes I had ever seen, really, and I know what makes a good pancake good. These ones were perfectly yellow with hints of golden brown painted on top. They were big, almost perfect circles, and when you poked them they felt like a delicious pillow, not like a rubbery tire. Simon had his hands folded and his eyes closed, because he was saying a little prayer before eating. I usually did that too, not because I wanted to be like Simon or anything, but because I thought it was good to say thank you for getting to eat. But this time I had to say a prayer about *not* eating.

"Hello God," I said in my brain, "thanks for the pancakes. If you care about the syrup and the trees and everything, please tell me somehow and I won't eat it. Okay goodbye."

I opened my eyes and looked around at all the people, stuffing the food into their mouths. I cut off a piece of my pancake and chewed on it. It was only about 60% good-tasting. I know what makes a good pancake good, and pancakes without syrup are pretty terrible.

"Mmm," Uncle Max mumbled with his mouth full. Aunt Maxine smiled.

I reached for the syrup and somehow—I have no idea how, because I am *not* a clumsy person—I knocked over the little jug and syrup spilled out all over the table. That was kind of a disaster, because the tablecloth was bright white and very clean.

"Uh oh," Simon said, and he turned the jug back over. There was a gigantic puddle of brown on the tablecloth and it was soaking in. At least it was syrup, so it didn't shoot everywhere and get people wet, but it was just sitting there soaking in and laughing at me for being so clumsy.

Simon and Maxine were dabbing the table with napkins to clean up the huge sticky mess I made, and then I felt something on my shoulder. I turned my head around and it was the man-in-charge. He said "Is everything alright?" and Simon said "We had a bit of a spill but it's fine," and the man-in-charge still had his big hairy hand on my shoulder, like grown-ups always do—they think they can just put their stupid hands on your shoulders, and mess your hair up and touch you on the cheek—and the man-in-charge asked me if I was enjoying my pancakes and I said "Don't touch me." And he lifted his hand away and held it floating in the air like I was a hot burner on a stove, and he said "Easy, little guy" and he gave me a look like I was doing something wrong. He said "What's the matter?" and I thought about the trees losing all their sap and turning into transparent nothing and him not even caring, and I thought about ripping all the taps out and I said "I'm going to punch you," and I transformed my hand into a fist and turned my teeth into shark teeth. The man-in-charge shook his head and looked angry but *I* was the one who was angry, and I didn't punch him but finally he walked away and Simon was staring at me like I was something gross he'd never seen before. And I didn't feel happy like you're supposed to feel when you win against someone in a fight; I didn't feel happy at all and I was even less happy because I realized I'd made my fist wrong, and not the way Max showed me one time, because I tucked my thumb inside my fingers so even if I was an expert puncher and punched the man-in-charge as hard as I ever could, I still wouldn't have actually won because I would have broken my own stupid thumb in half.

"I have to go to the bathroom," I said, and I left Simon and everyone else and the sticky mess and went outside. I ran over to the other house and went in and that weird girl was at the desk again. She was everywhere at the same time; she was an octuplet or something. I asked about the bathroom and she said it was down the hall, so I ran down the hall and into this tiny white bathroom with red towels and my breaths were really fast. I didn't have to pee, I just needed to go away and to run somewhere. And I needed to have a sit-down. So I sat on the edge of the bathtub for about as long as it takes to pretend you're going pee. Then I stood back up and flushed the toilet and washed my hands, but I was still scared to leave the bathroom and I was still breathing excruciatingly fast so I sat back down for a couple more ice ages and thought about my deep breaths and thought about how punching doesn't make anything easier.

When I finally came out, the girl at the desk smiled at me and said, "How old are you?"

"Why?"

"Just wondering." Her bubble gum exploded again.

"I'm ten," I said. "How old are you?"

"I'm fifteen. My birthday was three days ago."

"Happy birthday," I said. "My birthday is December 5th."

"You're pretty cute for ten," she said.

"No I'm not," I lied, and I walked out the door.

I carefully looked through the door of the dining room building but I didn't see the man-in-charge anywhere so I walked towards the table. Maxine was still eating, and Max and Simon seemed like they had been having a long important conversation and it was just about to end. I knew that because Simon was doing this thing he does where he leans back in his chair with his hands folded behind his head sort of like he's sunbathing, and he was shaking his head like "No," staring straight ahead, and smiling really big. If he was doing all that, it usually meant that he had made up his mind on something, and if the next thing he did was take his glasses off his face and hold them out and stare through them like field glasses, that meant that no matter what, he would *never* change his mind.

"No, it would be fine," I heard Max say as I was getting close to them. "It wouldn't be a big deal, and she—well, it wouldn't be a big deal."

"I don't know," Simon said in his tanning position. "We'll see."

"We'll see" with Simon usually meant "No way," but he didn't do the glasses-binoculars thing, so it was a little curious. I had no idea what they were talking about. Grown-up stuff probably. Banks and retiring and buying cars. Maybe we were finally getting a new car.

"What are you guys talking about?" I asked Simon as I sat down again.

"Adult stuff," Uncle Max said. "Boring."

"Let's get the *hell* out of here," I said. I didn't really care what they were talking about. Simon said "Arthur," 'cause I said "hell," so I said "Sorry" and we got my pancakes boxed up for later and we left.

IN THE CAR on the drive home Max and me played the scribble game in my sketchbook again, but soon it got boring and I couldn't stop thinking about the most important and serious thing I had to do in my life at that moment, which was obviously to figure out where the Phil notebook came from, and what I was supposed to do with it, and if anyone could help me out. I was almost thinking maybe I should just phone 9-1-1, and also in the two days since my interview with Mrs. Beckham I must have almost-searched the internet for him a hundred times. But every time I was about to click the button I got the biggest throat lump. And once I clicked it and then closed the window right away 'cause Simon came into the kitchen, so I didn't see anything and I was glad. Both searching him and calling the police scared the heck out of me, and also for some reason it felt like I wouldn't find the right clues that way.

So when we drove past the orange fossil rock again, which was on my side this time, Max passed me a scribble and I looked at it for a bit, acting like I was scheming about what to draw, but I really wasn't. Max had his head against the window, checking out the scenery and the sun that was falling down in the sky but wasn't quite setting yet. I flipped the page and wrote him a little note instead of a drawing.

UNCLE MAX I HAVE A TOP SECRET THING TO TALK TO YOU ABOUT OK?

I handed the paper over to him and he glanced back at me, confused his eyebrows, then read it, and wrote back. He handed the sketchbook back over.

sure thing guy.

I FOUND SOMEONE'S JOURNAL IN THE WOODS.
IT'S A SERIOUS JOURNAL. I HAVE STARTED TO GO
AROUND INTERVIEWING THE GROANUPS ON MY
STREET. I NEED SOME HELP.

(Now when I look at the pages in my sketchbook where we
passed our notes, I can't believe I ever thought Max would be the
best person to ask for help, but like I said, I was in *way* over my
brain.) Uncle Max wrote:

sounds like an adventure. where do I sign up?

NOWHERE. I JUST NEED YOU TO LISTEN TO THE
TAPES I WILL RECORD. THEY WILL BE SENT TO
YOU IN THE MAIL. THEY WILL NOT BE THE SELF-
DESTRUCTING KIND. YOU CAN LISTEN TO THEM
AND SEND ME BACK A REPORT LIKE IF YOU THINK
THE PEOPLE ARE LYING OR JUST STUPID OR IF YOU
THINK THERE WAS A CLUE THAT I MISSED OR IF YOU
THINK I MIGHT BE ASKING DUMB QUESTIONS. OK?

roger that. rendez-vous at the checkpoint in 0400 hours.

WHAT THE HECK?

I mean I would love to help.

SHADOW

I spend more time looking in mirrors than I should, watching "ME" ME ME ME ME, but I'm not convinced I'm related to my reflection. I'm not sure whether it looks like me or not, but it's not the image that throws me off, it's the way it behaves. When I move my hand, so does my reflection. *Always.* I've always thought I had much more in common with my shadow.

I'd much rather watch my shadow move, as it walks home through the snowy park in the night. I like how—no, I guess I really *respect* how when my legs cross over each other back and forth, they don't do the same in the shadow's reality. The thin black rectangles bulge up to accommodate a passing bump, or spill downwards off the edge of the path, then they leap back up onto the snowbank. When I approach the next lamp post and the icy ground glistens pale yellow, my shadow quickly reels itself in and cringes beneath me, buried under my feet, then starts to grow back, stretching way out in front of me. I can try to describe its motion all I want, but the truth is I never know exactly where I'll find my shadow, and often it's off somewhere I couldn't have predicted—wildly projected up onto a wall I've never noticed, or cloaking some window I myself will never get to look through—and I just like that.

WAITING

This sure is one big clean room. A couple of makeshift hallways shaped by padded burlap-chic barrier things, comfortable carpet chairs with wooden arms and cushy seats, also burlap-chic. The tile floor pretends to be cleaner than it really is. The walls and wall things are covered in sun-washed posters from long lost eras of poster design, shouting the truth about chlamydia, smoking and depression in hyper-neon Technicolor. A wheelchair.

Everything seems wrapped in plastic, even though only half of it actually is. A suggestions box, a Tupperware crate of stuffed animals under a low table. The radio is playing the piece of music entitled "Eye of the Tiger." One of the wall's posters hangs from its feet, the top pieces of tape having finally given up, admirable, they've been holding fast since '83. Only the poster's pale back is showing. Everyone here looks annoyed and then bored and then annoyed at being bored. Does the flaccid poster secretly hold some key to it all? Why am I too well-behaved to go flip it and check? What could it possibly say? "LIFE IS JUST A BIG THING MADE OF SMALL THINGS"—"THE ONLY WRONG IS THE WORD 'WRONG'"—"THE REAL TRUTH ABOUT IT, THE WAY OUT OF THE

"HELPFUL"
CABINETIVE THERAPY

He didn't go in. They called his name and he said he had to go to the washroom sorry and he headed into the hallway, he was practically running to the elevator. Hours later now here he is having the worst coffee of his life. This is the only place that's open this late. This thing he is drinking has like two more names than he does.

Why didn't he go to his appointment?

It was like when he was sitting there he got thinking about it and couldn't figure out why he'd ever *started* going, or how he'd lasted so long. It's been like five months. E had suggested maybe he should think about it; he was already thinking about it. He needed something. He needed to take his mind off of her. No. He needed somewhere he could go and just talk about her for hours. Did it make him feel closer to her sometimes in some backwards way? Did it give him hope?

Did he do it for her?

No he *wanted* to go. And at first it was free through school. He had an initial half-hour consultation with one counsellor named Janet, in which he described the things that were going on in his head. He'd brought an epic web of a list that filled two whole pages of graph paper with black ink. He showed her the list, which contained every sorrow and habit and insurmountable obstacle—she glanced at it a moment and handed it back. How could she have overlooked it or consumed it so casually? It was the most enthralling list.

Janet left the room for a minute and then returned with a thin stack of paper, fresh with the smell of photocopying: fire and asphalt. When she handed him the pages they were still warm in his hands. He always loved the feeling of holding warm paper—it was one thing that felt precisely like hope. The smallest things could be comforts. The white sheets had tiny font typed in columns and bulleted lists, sprinkled with little clip-art illustrations of men with frowns, question marks shooting out of their heads. They outlined some "unhelpful" styles of thinking, and basic coping strategies. As he squinted at the papers Janet said he would be set up with a regular counsellor on a weekly appointment basis, to begin *cognitive therapy*. Cognitive therapy, she said, was a drug-free treatment, with emphasis on the conscious changing of thinking patterns, in the hope that negative feelings would change as a result. It would be a start. If he turned out to need drugs they'd address that later. It sounded pretty good.

Then the meetings were every Thursday with a psychologist named Ralph who had a short grey beard like a shag rug and a firm handshake. His office was a warehouse a few blocks off campus, fully stocked with table saws and belt sanders and nails and glue. The psychologist and the patient hung their jackets on pegs on the wall and washed their hands in the filthy square industrial sink and put on their safety goggles. Let's get to it, Ralph said at the first appointment, and started cutting two-foot squares out of a large sheet of plywood.

Together they began work on a complex filing cabinet system for the thoughts who came clawing their way into the patient's mind. They got three or four boxes built in the first couple of hour-long sessions. The patient was a slow carpenter, but Ralph said they were making great progress. Quicker than most patients, he said. When the patient returned the next week, even more cabinets had appeared: fifteen, sixteen of them stacked and waiting to be filled.

You worked on them without me? he asked.

I got to thinking, and figured we'd need a few more.

You didn't have to do that.

Sure I do. It's my job.

Soon the focus shifted and the patient did less of the building and began the filing. He sat in the orange upholstered chair in the centre of the huge floor and did his mindfulness exercise. He'd put the earmuffs on to save himself from the noise of Ralph's cutting and hammering and ladder extending. He made an effort to sit up straight and focus on his breathing. (When he got in the chair, Ralph would take notice, and, trying not to be obvious about it, he would make quicker cuts, wouldn't leave the saw running. He would hammer softer and walk on tiptoe. It broke parts of the patient's heart and made him want to try harder. He knew he could fix it.)

It always took a few false starts. His mind would be whirling, speeding in nine directions on nine layers at once. Something would surface—an image of E standing up from her bed naked in the morning with the new sun sparking a ring around her hair and showing off all her smoothest skin—then something long past—childhood, riding in the car through the poor part of town, June bugs on the porch floor in May and his bare foot crunching them into the rough wood—then an overbearing wonder about the future: what would he do when his lease was up, would he stay here again or finally scrap it all and be the vagabond he always pretended he might be, and then the gigan-ticness of having done it all *wrong*, of continuing to do it *wrong*, of everything right being embarrassing, everything wrong being worse, of being in all the wrong places at all the wrong times, having all the wrong heroes and wanting everything for all the wrong

Then he would catch himself, somehow, and be back again.

Start over.

Gather up the drawstrings from all corners of your mind and pull them a little tighter. Come back to your breathing, keep slowing it down. Close your eyes and let the thoughts come whipping by and try not to chase after them. Fold your hands together to stop them from grabbing. Instead of *being* the thoughts, just watch them run past.

Eventually the patient would recognize a thought and write its name on a sheet of paper.

~~It really did help you, you know. For a while. It did. It was embarrassing but not useless. You're just so fucking stubborn. You could still go back. Go back next week. It's collapsing, rebuild it. But why would you? You're already giving up or telling yourself you are, you don't know what you're doing, you can't keep going into something like that without being hopeful you are way past hopeful, you are desperate, hopeless. You have ALWAYS been desperate, you're never NOT desperate~~

Get up. Get up from the chair and drag yourself to the index catalogue you have written. It hangs from the wall on a bit of white string. When Ralph notices you do this, he will resist the temptation to grin. Don't let this make you feel like a guinea pig. Don't resent his goodness. Pick up the little book and browse through the categories:

OVERGENERALIZATIONS	O7
DOOMSDAYS	D4
BINARIES	B2–B8
SHOULDS	S10
MUSTS	M10
HABITS	H1–H25
GUILT	G4
EMOTIONAL MASOCHISM	(see "HABITS")
PERFECTIONISM	P7
REGRET	R10
RELIGIOUS SCRUPULOSITY	R5–R9
RELIGIOUS GUILT	(see "GUILT")
SECULAR GUILT	(see "GUILT")
ALL-OR-NOTHINGS	(see "BINARIES")
SIGNS AND PROPHECIES	S4–S8 (see also "DOOMSDAYS" subsection A)
SELF-HATRED	(see "HABITS")
NARCISSISM	(see "HABITS")
SOLIPSISM	(see "SECULAR GUILT," "HABITS")
BELIEF THAT SAD = TRUE	B9–B15 (see also "HABITS")

Find the section code you need and then consult the yellow numbers and letters stencilled on the polished concrete floor. Walk down the corresponding column until it intersects with the proper row and there you'll find the square on the floor marking where the correct cabinet will be: look up and find it suspended far above your head.

(The cabinet structure is growing enormous and sprawling in order to accommodate the exponentially increasing number of categories and subcategories. The wooden boxes, all connected at the sides, form a number of snakey armatures hung from the rafters with cables, filling the entire space just below the warehouse's ceiling. Like a maze of ventilation ducts, but wooden. And where air ducts would be dustily and unquestionably grey, Ralph has been painting areas of the filing labyrinth primary colours: lemon yellows, cobalt blues, cadmium reds, in accordance to some grouping method you don't understand, and which Ralph claims doesn't "really" matter. Sometimes you do like thinking of it as a Personal Ventilation System—admit this. And of letting your head breathe, and all the other pleasant and banal thoughts those of course lead to. Don't hate yourself for this. Breathe.)

Raise the ladder and climb to the proper cabinet and file all your bad thoughts away.

After a while you will get another separate assignment, concerning your journal. This is your *first* sad attempt at keeping a journal—remember how Ralph loved those two entries you came up with—but you were faking it. You were whining and bitching. Why me why me. You still had no idea what it felt like to be completely irreversibly abandoned. To have no way out. You were writing it for them and it didn't last. It was embarrassing. Not like you're doing better now—what are you doing now. You act like you're writing your fucking memoir, on your deathbed. The epic saga of Phil and his cabinets. Amazing. You're SITTING HERE. You did NOTHING today. You wandered around hating everything. It takes a lot of energy. Now you're here, you've spent two and a half hours in this place sipping the worst coldest coffee and savouring the most expensive brownie you can remember having. There is nothing to say here. Write your memoir.

Ralph said it would be a hugely useful practice for you to read over your entries a day or two later and eliminate all "unhelpful" words. To notice them. It would be a simple and effective way of controlling the influx into the DOOMSDAYS and

ALL-OR-NOTHINGS cabinets, and maybe even the GUILT. You were to first cross out the bad words, then cut them out of the pages with a utility knife and reveal all the holes in your worldview. So you do this, and you bring the stray words with you to the next session in an envelope. Then he shows you how to use the photocopier to enlarge the troublesome words. Blow them up to one thousand times their original size and print them on chalkboard-sized sheets of poster paper, one word each.

This is how big those little buggers *really* are, Ralph says, with your ~~EVERYTHING~~s and your ~~NOTHING~~s and your ~~ALL~~s and ~~ALWAYS~~s tacked up all over the warehouse. Roll them up. File them away.

And today you didn't go. They called your name and you ran away. It was supposed to be a way of ridding yourself of things, of storing the weight somewhere, and it worked up to a point, but now it ~~only~~ adds to ~~everything~~. The cabinets are ~~completely~~ stuffed and barely close, they keep moving on to newer and more convoluted structures: grouped now in secondary and tertiary colour schemes—~~complete~~ disorder. What was orange last week is now blue-green. Turquoise turned to violet then back to yellow. It's ~~total~~ mayhem. Obscene records line the walls—graphs and fucking pie charts outlining your progress to date, extrapolating your future improvements—it's ~~all~~ so calculated and hopeful, you ~~hate~~ it, it scares the shit out of you, you ~~hate~~ yourself for even going. As if you can find ~~yourself~~ by eliminating ~~yourself~~. ~~Everything~~ that has ~~always~~ been you. This is you, ~~Phil~~. It's not going to go away. It's not like the therapy doesn't work, it does make you feel better. A bit better. But the fact that you even NEED to go—you need to go, what are you thinking not going, who are you performing for? But then it's ~~always~~ when you're actually there that you feel your ~~worst~~. You're ~~always~~ embellishing and inventing things to discuss, to keep momentum. You turn ~~all~~ the small problems of the day-to-day into monstrous problems, cataclysmic, ~~only~~ to keep the system functioning and expanding—you take ~~all~~ your new terrifying ones—the ~~forever~~ ones the cages that ~~never~~ open—you turn them into small musings on the horizon of your meaningless life, you pretend and hope them ~~all~~ away, they don't go away, you are too good at lying. You ~~only~~ feel good talking to yourself and you will do it forever, write your life down, make it exist, catalogue it distance it, this is the ~~best~~ thing you have learned, most days you can't even manage *this,* tell your weak selfish little story to yourself don't fucking lie, maybe it will be enough help, the drugs will help the old ones were not the ~~right~~ ones. Relax and tell it and ~~never~~ stop writing, you can ~~always~~ go back you can but don't worry tell it be REAL—~~every~~ second hurts more than ~~anything~~, the reason you ~~ever~~ went in the first place was to STOP putting ~~everything~~ in boxes—it's FINE it's all fine just get it down now cross all the ~~bad~~ out and see what's left

BEACH

Remember? We're sitting on hot rocks on the beach—it's hot and humid—you share your water bottle—the walk here was a bit awkward—I was in an ecstatic high mood—so grateful to finally have this day together—you've been busy, with the summer class and with seeing summer friends, with summer, and work—you're working at the shop and the other shop when they need you—if I see you it's for a maximum of fifteen minutes per day—nowhere near enough of you.

So I've got this high to have this whole morning to walk with you—we slept together at your house, without blankets, it was the heat wave—we ran into each other in the park the evening before—it's such a small city—we got to your room and had the long talk about how It Can't Mean Anything—but how it seems bound to happen, unavoidable—we both want to so yeah sure—but how we understand that We're Not Seeing Each Other—neither are In Any State to be seeing anyone. But then breakfast is cheerful and exciting and decidedly Like Old Times—poached eggs on the grainiest bread, yogurt, coffee, and I convince you that today's the day for skinny-dipping—it's going to be another fireball of a day, a mushroom cloud, too hot already at 7:30—we got up early for you to get to work, we forgot it was a holiday. No work today. I convince you to come swimming.

I'm in a hyper mood, we're walking, you're sort of just neutral, laughing at me and rolling your eyes—I'm such a romantic—especially today—not fully letting yourself get sucked into the old dynamic, but you're warming up, I can tell. I'm thrilled—I can't be bothered with rules—you have a lot on your mind—You've told me at least three times now that we can't Be Together, if we hang out we have to find a way to Just Be Friends. I'm not paying attention—today it's all words.

We get to the beach. We're sitting there on rocks sharing an orange—two young deer with white spots all over come out from trees on the far side of the beach, walking in their alien way—tails swatting, new strange legs bumping—they stop dead when they see us, their knobby legs quivering—what do they think they see?—they disappear. As far as I can possibly tell you are thinking you do in fact want to go skinny-dipping—you're just taking your time—I keep going on about how it's the perfect day, the perfect place—and so on—I'm this giddy little kid.

I'm wholly focused on the water and getting you in it and the day—the water will feel so cold and good on our skin—just us and our skin—I'm imagining it even now—there's no one around—does anyone ever come here? Perfect. I grab the bottom of your t-shirt and start to slowly peel it up—you snap. You can take your own clothes off. Sorry. Silence. Then: We're not talking about this again.

(But I don't want to talk about it either and I just want to be in the water—I don't know what you mean or why it's coming up *now*) You growl. We're not—You stand up: I think I'm just going to go to school—I'm still sitting there—Here we go—You're impossible!

(I don't know what's going on, we've had the nicest morning, everything's fine.) Can't we just—

No. I'm going to go—DON'T go. Listen—What do you even want from me?—I just don't understand why we're fighting!—

This is what we DO. This is exactly why—No it's *different.* This is different, and you're just looking for it and so now it's happening. We're *friends.* We don't hate each other!

I'm going to school.

(You don't *have* to fight with me anymore. I can't believe it. I'm going crazy—Don't go, we don't have to swim—

Why do you even want me to stay? Is this actually fun, to you?

I don't say anything—I'm crushed into a ball, frustrated mindless—grinding my teeth—the distance between what I wanted and what the day is—I always had to imagine you—how could I become such an expert at fooling myself—a con artist out of work bored—I gave it endless chances—I am raving and pouncing at everything, I am nothing, I'm in a thousand places—

I want to die.

What the fuck—that's it—What?—You can't just SAY something like that!

What?

You're insane. I should have—I'm *going.* Don't come find me.

—

Goodbye Phil.

You pick up your bag and hurry so fast through the tall grass—I wonder if you're crying—do I want that?—you look back—I can't tell—you see me still here hunched over in a wretched pile of me—I knew this but never felt it so powerfully completely—I can't tell you anything about this even if I tried—it's coming back so sure and one directional, I am a mass of dark energy hunched with the surest goal—I am horrified—I can't remember if you really came or not or was it possible I even made it up—I wish I MADE YOU UP, I could forget, I have never been so completely nothing so alone, it never goes away, you went away.

ACCIDENTALLY TELEPORTED

THE DAY after Maple Day I was on my way to investigate the second house. When I was halfway there I saw Victoria Brown, the girl that lives up the street who Finch is always trying to french, walking on the other side.

"Hey Arthur!" She crossed the street.

"Yo."

"How are you today?"

"Good."

"Where are you going?"

"Secret. I'm investigating. Where are *you* going?"

"*I'm* going to play at Simon's."

"Finch's?"

"Yeah, Finch's."

"You're lying."

"I'm not lying!"

"You already passed his house. It's right over there."

"I wanted to see if you wanted to come too. I was going to *your* house."

"Oh. Well, I'm really busy."

"Maybe later?"

"Maybe. No."

She played with her white barrette, to make sure it was still holding her hair together. I was kicking rocks around. My thermos was already in my hand so I opened it and took a drink of cold milk and then shaved my moustache. I wanted to get going.

"That shirt is very *hand*some," she said.

"I always wear this."

"It's nice. I like the stripes." She straightened her dress a bit.

"Why are you going to Finch's?" I asked.

"'Cause he phoned me and said to come play."

"He just wants to try and *french* you."

Her face blushed and she tugged at the sides of her dress.

"Do you let him?"

"No!"

"Good."

"He doesn't even try."

"I *knew* it," I said. "He told me he asked you to be his *girl*friend, for crying outside."

"He did."

"What?"

"He *did*."

"What did you say?"

She was getting redder.

"You said no."

"No . . . maybe. What's in your knapsack?"

"Did you say *yes*?"

"Fine, *maybe* I did."

"You're weird."

She looked at me and smiled. Her eyes were brown but I imagined them as blue for fun, and then I thought I probably liked brown better anyway.

"Simon is a really nice boy," she said.

"Mmm-hmm." I rolled my eyes so far that they ached.

"You should come play."

"He's just so *annoying*. What am I supposed to do, come over and watch him try to make dominoes fall over? And listen to him tell me how he's the king of dominoes or whatever? I can't think of anyone who gets farther on top of my nerves. He's the *king* of my nerves."

"He's *nice*."

"Well anyway, I've got people to see." I took a step forward to leave. She laughed at me.

"Okay. Well you look *hand*some today."

"You already said that. Why do you keep saying it like that?"

She looked at her feet. They were zig-zagging as she kind of danced them around. I looked at my watch and just as I saw the 2:26, she attacked me. She kissed me, kind of like how Simon would on my cheek, but she was doing it on my mouth and she was sort of not stopping. Also, it's gross, but her lips were all wet and small. I think I stepped on her foot or something, and she hopped off of me. By that time it was probably 2:27.

Then it was stupid because we were both just standing there, and what are you supposed to say when someone just slobbers your face up? And it was even stupider because we both had to walk the same way up the street. But luckily she yelled "Bye Arthur!" and started running to Finch's, and I waited for her to disappear and then I walked and took my time. What the *heck*. Girls are the one thing I'll never understand.

At probably 2:28, Simon drove up in our little red car while I secretly wiped my lips off on the back of my hand. He pulled over and rolled the window down, which took a long time, because our car is awfully stupid and old and rusty.

"Hey chief. I'm just going to pick up a few things for bridge, you coming?"

"Nah, I don't really like playing bridge."

"No, are you coming to the *grocery store,* smart-guy."

"Nah," I said. I had forgot it was bridge night. Simon and Uncle Max had this bridge club that happened on Sunday nights, which was just a thing where Max and Simon and their guy friends would go to one of their houses and play a card game called bridge, which is a game that's not even worth talking about. Once one guy had to leave early so I tried to play for five minutes and then I woke up in bed the next morning. Simon said I fell asleep so hard there was drool on my cards, and I asked him if I at least had good cards and he said not really. That's bridge club. Anyway it was going to be at our house that night.

Simon asked me if I was sure I didn't want to come to the grocery store.

I said, "I'm really busy."

"Alright, just be home before dark, and be careful, alright?"

"Obviously."

"Actually, be home for supper, okay?"

"Ohh-kay."

"C'mere."

He messed up my hair a bunch and said "I love you."

I looked in the mirror on the side of the car and tried to straighten my hair a bit.

"Yep."

"See you at supper then. You still haven't changed those sheets."

"I will. See ya."

"See ya." He pushed up his glasses and drove away.

I stood and drank milk from my thermos and made sure to watch our car until it was all the way around the turn in the road and there was no way he could see me, then I started walking again. I unscrewed the lid of my thermos and looked under it, and carefully poked my messy haircut to check for tiny microphones and spy cameras you can barely see with a naked eye. I was clean.

The second house I had to investigate was the house right after Finch's house, on the same side of the street. It was technically Finch's next-door neighbour, but you could have fit four houses in the woods between them. From where I was standing at the end of the driveway, the whole place looked grey. It wasn't, of course: the house was pale blue with white shutters, the small car parked out front was something in between gold and green, and the grass and hedge and trees were green, obviously. But the day itself was another grey one, where the sky was bright but who knows where the sun was, and I didn't have a shadow, and it was making the whole house and yard and everything look grey.

I didn't even know who lived there. I guessed it was someone I'd never thought about in my life, and someone I'd never heard anyone talk about. I figured that this meant they must not be a dangerous person, or else they'd be famous like the hermit. I also figured this meant they must be a not-very-interesting person. Then I thought, maybe I was being too mean.

The mailbox right beside me actually *was* grey, and said "PETERSON." I thought, "Oh yeah, I guess I've seen that name before."

Just like when I went to the Beckhams' house, I got super nervous. Walking down the street to someone's house was simple. But going *inside* was completely another thing. I stood there literally shaking in my boots just like last time.

So I turned around, because if I hadn't even heard of whoever lived in the Peterson house, then they must not be very useful. They must not know anything. I was so shaky that that made a ton of sense. I started walking away, and my stomach felt relieved. I made it probably about two whole footsteps without thinking about Phil and then I thought about Phil.

"Ahhh fuck," I thought, but I didn't say it because I don't really swear. I stopped walking. My arms and legs and everything were shaking because I was being sawed in half again and needing to go to two places at once. I was going to go home and make a list of *All the Things in the Universe That Have Nothing to Do With a Person Dying Close to You* but whenever I took a step towards home I felt like I was being lazy and I took another step in the opposite direction. When I stepped towards the Peterson house I felt like I was being mentally insane but not lazy and that seemed better but it felt worse. There was something inside the Peterson house and even if it wasn't Phil maybe it was. My brain didn't even know what it was talking about. My feet were actually walking back and forth on the edge of the stupid driveway. At least there was no one around to see me acting so moronic.

Eventually I slowly walked towards the house. I thought, maybe whoever lives there is a very nice ten-year-old boy or girl, or a few of both, and I can ask them all simple questions and get simple answers and be on my way. My finger rang the doorbell. A tall grey-haired man with giant glasses answered the door in a few seconds and I thought, "Get *real*, Arthur."

"I beg your pardon," he said.

Then I thought I said my "Get real" out loud because of how I say things out loud by accident, and I said:

"Uhhhm, sorry?"

And he said, "Can I help you?"

And I said, "Hello."

"Hello," he said.

My knees felt almost as confused as my brain.

"My name is Arthur Williams. Are you ... Mr. Peterson?"

"Precisely."

"Can I come inside your house and ask you a question?"

He looked at his gold watch, as if he was asking it for permission.

"It's a bit of a bad time, I'm afraid."

"Why? What time is it?"

"No, I mean I'm right in the middle of something. Would you mind coming back another time? It's not terribly important, I hope? Boy Scouts or something like that?"

"No," I told him. I said "It's not important," but I was lying—it was only about the most important thing in the world. But I could tell the only thing he was "right in the middle of" was an excuse, and that meant that he was lying first, so that meant I had to lie too. That's how it works with grown-ups.

"Alright?" he asked.

"It's okay I guess. Thanks."

There I was, *thanking* him for making my life more terrible. I turned to leave, but he must have seen my gigantic frown and angry eyebrows before I was all the way turned around, because he said "Wait."

I stayed where I was, with my back facing him instead of my face.

"Well, I guess I've got time. Okay, come on in."

I wasn't expecting him to change his mind like that so I felt really shaky walking into his house but I did it anyway. I took off my boots in the hall and my feet smelled really sweaty, and a lot like extra-old cheddar cheese, and that didn't help.

"No socks?" said Mr. Peterson.

His house was small inside, smaller than the Beckhams', and much smaller than ours. The hall was barely a hall at all it was so short, and there weren't a lot of walls, and I felt like I could see everything in the entire house, with the kitchen on the left, a bedroom and a small bathroom on the right, and a living room up ahead. It seemed like everything important was on the bottom floor, and even though I saw stairs to the second floor, I couldn't figure out how anything else could really fit up there. Also, everything looked a lot newer than our house did. In the kitchen the counter was cold black marble and the chairs had no decorations and were really simple looking, like I could've built them myself with some broomsticks. The walls inside matched the walls outside: everything was light blue with white, except the kitchen.

Even though it was a new house Mr. Peterson had it smothered in old things, so it seemed fuzzy and dusty. The walls were covered all over the place with ancient maps of the world, maps of Canada, the U.S., Russia, Africa, and other places. There were black and white photos of boats hung up everywhere, too. Tall sailing ships, army boats, the *Titanic* I think, a couple tiny sailboats. The photos and maps and things had all turned different shades of yellow and brown from being so old, and the house kind of smelled like a basement full of rotting wood and human saliva.

"What's this?" I picked up a tiny rock off the shelf on my way into the house.

"Ohhh, that!" Mr. Peterson rushed over as if I was dropping it on the floor or something. He took it from my hand but held it for me to examine.

"*That,* is a fossil."

"Yeah, I know. But what's it of?"

"It's a trilobite. Well, it's just a portion, of course. You see the corner? I believe that's part of the cephalon, its head if you will, and then here there's a bit of thorax. Do you know what a trilobite looks like?"

"Obviously."

"Well there you go." He placed it back on the shelf exactly where it was when I picked it up, facing exactly the same way.

"How'd you get it? Because I thought they were really rare."

"A friend. Yes, they're very rare. Not unfindable, but rare. A friend, actually, a retired palaeontologist, gave it to me for my birthday one year."

"Amazing. When's your birthday?"

"May 17th."

"That's soon, kind of."

"True. I suppose."

"Mine's December 5th."

"Really."

Then me and Mr. Peterson stood in the hall for a little while not knowing what to say to each other. I glanced around the house more, and felt shy, and then felt shy about feeling shy, and I was trying to figure out whether it would be rude to say "uhmmm" or not but then he told me to "make myself at home" and he went in the kitchen.

I walked into the living room and circled it in detective mode, as Mr. Peterson started to boil some water.

"Something to drink?"

"No thanks."

"Are you hungry?"

"No. Thank you."

"Sure?"

"Yeah."

The thing about grown-ups is when you visit them at home, they always offer you something to eat and drink. And sometimes you just aren't hungry, is the thing. Still, if you say no thanks they make you feel like you're *insulting* them or something. Like you're calling them something awful, almost. It's like you're not letting them do their job, which is being a grown-up. Also, they always tell you to make yourself at home but they never stop offering you things, which makes no sense. When I'm at home making myself at home, no one's around, and I get things for myself and make cinnamon toast. You can't make yourself at home and also have a waiter at the same time. And they always expect you to sit down, it seems like. I was only on the second house but I was already getting used to the plan. Come in, get offered food, sit down, spill the beans.

After I was finished looking over everything in the living room—the model ships with flappy sails and tiny ropes, the photographs of the river and people I didn't know, papers in frames with little red stickers shaped like the sun, the collection of atlases on the small bookshelf, and the unbelievable old map of the world from way before they had discovered hundreds of countries we've found now—after I was finished looking it all over, I sat down in a very stiff armchair.

Mr. Peterson came out of the kitchen, and his navy blue slippers slippered across the wooden floor with a scorching cup of tea. The tea made sense: the place was tidy enough, but I'd found five empty mugs sitting around with tea bags still inside. He put down his tea on the coffee table—did that make it a tea table?—and sat in an armchair that looked even stiffer than the one I was in.

"So what's this about?" He got to the point, just like I predicted in my plan.

That was fine by me. I took out my tape recorder and put it on the tea table, and then I unzipped Phil out of my backpack and held it up like one of those special TV lawyers. It was fun to be creating a bit of a new routine.

"Exhibition A," I told Mr. Peterson, like the exhibitionists on TV.

"Exhibit," he corrected.

I kept my cool.

"Obviously."

"What is it, your journal?"

"Close, but no cigar. It's *somebody's* journal. I found it in the woods."

I realized I had forgotten to press RECORD on the tape player, so I did. I felt nonprofessional. But at least it didn't record me saying my wrong word.

Then Mr. Peterson didn't say anything for a little while, he just sipped his tea once and looked at me like he was trying to remember something, but the something didn't exist. He looked confused. I expected him to say "Can I please take a look at the journal?" I hoped he'd say "I know exactly where that came from." I *dreamed* he might say "Don't worry, because that guy is still alive," but he didn't say any of those things.

He said, "Well it's not mine, if that's what you mean."

(That's not what I meant.)

"No," I said, "I mean, do you have any idea where it could have come from?"

He looked like he was trying to remember what he was trying to remember.

"I'm not so sure about that."

"Well, do you know anyone named Phil?"

"Well, yes I suppose. I had a good friend Philip in school. In college. He . . . passed away this year, in fact."

My throat turned into a fist.

"I'm sorry to hear that," I squeaked.

"It's fine," he said. "It was a little while back."

"How did he die?"

"He got sick. Like most people, I suppose."

"Was he your best friend?"

"Oh . . . no." He scratched the back of one hand with the other one. "No. It was a while ago." He took a drink of his tea.

"Uhmmm," I said.

I looked around the room again and sat up straight to make the chair hurt less.

"So have you been running around interviewing the entire city then?" Mr. Peterson asked.

"Just the entire street so far."

"Looking for the author?"

"Looking for clues."

"But you hope to give it back to him? To this 'Phil,' is it?"

My throat had a crumpled up sponge stuck in it.

"Uhmmm," I said. "I don't think so."

"Oh?"

"I guess I was just wondering where it came from. How it got to our street. I mean it didn't just *appear*."

"Sure," he said.

He took another sip of tea and scratched the floppy part of his neck, below his Adam's apple. I didn't know what to do. I felt like it was useless for me to be there but I didn't want to just run away. I felt like I wasn't even there in the first place. Maybe there was a window I could climb out of, or a trap door. I wished I was a master escapist.

Mr. Peterson folded his arms on top of his blue sweatshirt. He gave me a really quick smile, and then scratched his neck.

"What is your job?" I asked.

"I'm retired."

" . . . Retired of what?" I said, because I was trying to be funny.

Mr. Peterson looked out the window. "A couple of things. I did some architecture, and some engineering later. I ended up doing a lot of both, really."

"What did you engineer?"

He looked at me. "Do you know the Vine Street Theatre, downtown?"

"Obviously." That theatre was actually one of my favourite buildings, if I had to like buildings. Sometimes Maxine would take me to a play there or to see a symphony, which was cool, but I never liked anything we went to see as much as I liked the gigantic chandelier that hung overtop of the audience there, which was like an upside-down wedding cake made of icicles.

"I helped build that, about thirty years ago," he said. "I don't know if there's anything else you might recognize."

"Amazing," I said.

I thought for a moment about that building, with all the gargoyles and things on the outside, and with the pretty chandelier, and how he had helped make it.

Then I said, "So if you're such a good architect, why did you make yourself such a regular house?"

Mr. Peterson frowned. He looked up at the light-blue ceiling. "I didn't design it, actually."

"Why not?"

Mr. Peterson looked back down at me again. Then he changed the subject.

"Later on I became the chief demolition engineer on some projects—"

"Demolishing engineer?"

"Precisely."

"So you built buildings..."

Mr. Peterson nodded.

"...and then you tore them down?"

He took a quick gulp of tea.

"I suppose so."

I was a little bit demolished. I took Phil from the table and held the corner of the pages and let them flip by really fast. I watched the page numbers flash by like an animated movie:

25, 27, 29 ... 35, 37 ... 41, 43

Just then, the tape recorder clicked off.

Mr. Peterson watched me as I popped it open, flipped the tape over and poked the door shut. I made a gigantic sigh, and hit RECORD again.

"What do you want to be when *you* grow up?" Mr. Peterson asked.

The thing about becoming a grown-up is that you forget how annoying it is to be asked by someone what you want to be when you grow up. When I was tinier I used to have answers for that stupid question. Silly answers. *A fireman. A garbage man. A dolphin jockey.* Pretty much anyone who got to ride on something. But it'd been a long time since I knew what I *really* wanted to be. Maybe forever. The most annoying thing about being asked what-you-want-to-be-when-you-grow-up is that you know the grown-up asking it thinks you *have* to grow up in order to be anything.

So I didn't know what to say. I stared at the tape recorder which was going to hear me say whatever silly thing I was going to say. I sat there for a while thinking about it and Mr. Peterson kept looking out the window, like he was just waiting for a deer to walk by. I tried to think of something not silly, something that made sense. Then I knew I was trying too hard, and I decided to say the next exact thing that came to my brain. It was pretty silly.

"Well one time I had a dream where I drew the Leaning Tower of Pisa really big, because I could cover the real thing with my drawing, because I made it not leaning anymore."

Mr. Peterson turned his head towards me again. His bushy eyebrows went up, and he had a small smile, like I made a joke that wasn't quite funny enough to laugh at.

"I guess maybe, I'd like to do that," I said. "I mean, I don't know."

I felt like a real live idiot.

"I see," Mr. Peterson said. "You know, that's got a lot to do with what I was doing, too."

"Not really."

"Sure it does."

The tape recorder recorded fifteen long seconds of silence. Then, the sound of Mr. Peterson yawning.

He pointed at a big photo of some war boat.

"Have you ever heard of the Philadelphia Experiment?"

"No. How come every time I say 'Phil,' everyone starts talking about *Phil*adelphia?" It was not fun to be creating a routine anymore.

Mr. Peterson laughed, which was weird, but then quickly became a corpse again.

"I hadn't thought of that. Anyhow, the Philadelphia Experiment is a strange story. A mystery. It's widely considered to be a hoax, but anyway there were miniscule pieces of evidence, suggesting that..."

(Meanwhile my *real* dad had discovered the last *living* trilobite known to man. He hiked through the woods to this cliff to search for trilobite fossils, but after he'd been digging for five minutes, a real live trilobite scurried between his legs. He was in shock at first. But he snapped out of it, and because he had such excellent animal communication skills, he followed it, and when it noticed him, he crouched down to show it that he was friendly, and he succeeded in petting it. Then my real dad took it in and cared for it as a pet. As even more than a pet—as a friend. After three months of study he became fluent in its language of high-pitched squeals, and learned that it was actually a she, and that she had spent millenniums searching for a mate.)

"... so not only did the electromagnetic field render the ship invisible to *radar,* it also bent light around it, so not even the human eye..."

(My real dad trained her to scurry faster than the fastest racing car, because he knew what they were up against. There was a group of scientists who were determined to hunt down the trilobite and perform all sorts of cruel tests on her to understand how she had survived the last extinction. My real dad wasn't going to let that happen. He built a wooden saddle chair for her back and he guided her from town to town, protecting her.)

"... the green fog returned, and instead of being visible again, apparently the ship was accidentally teleported. There was this flash of blue light and..."

(Every day was a tough day for my real dad and the trilobite. They rested in damp caves at night, one sleeping while the other kept watch. One night by the campfire, he asked the trilobite what he should name her. She asked what the point of having a name was, and he didn't know the answer.)

"... still the legend goes that people reported seeing the ship in both Norfolk, Virginia, and Philadelphia in the same day..."

(He never did find her another trilobite for company. In the end, he took a bullet for her when they were finally discovered. She escaped though, and they never caught her. As my dad sat against the cave wall, dying, he only had one regret. He had a wish.)

"... at almost the exact same time."

(He wished he could have met his son.)

I jumped when I realized Mr. Peterson was staring at me.

"Right?"

"W-what?"

"I mean, isn't that incredible?"

"Yeah. Amazing."

I felt like I got knocked out in a boxing match and woke up and a week had passed but I was still at Mr. Peterson's house. I thought maybe I'd look up whatever he was talking about on Wikipedia later, in case it really *was* amazing. But mostly, I felt confused and I really wanted to go home. I pressed the STOP button and started putting the tape recorder and Phil back into my backpack.

"Is the interview over?"

"Yeah. I got lots of stuff to work with—"

"So sudden?"

"I gotta get home for supper. I'm probably missing it already. Thanks for answering my questions."

"Oh, no trouble. Anytime."

I stood up and my back hurt from the stiff chair. I went straight to the door and put my boots on.

"See you later," I said, even though it was probably a lie.

"Goodbye."

WHEN I GOT home I checked Rosie's website for new updates but there weren't any so I just looked at all the photos of her in the most amazing places on Earth again and I read one more time about how you only get one life and I tried to grab things by the horns but instead I felt excruciatingly sad, for some reason. Then I didn't feel much better while we ate mini-pizzas for supper. And after that I went in the woods like always except everything looked different. I went between the first few trees on the edge of our lawn, down the reddish-brownish path into the thicker woods, over roots, past the treehouse, then I turned right and walked that way for a while. I jumped across the little ditch, heading towards the beach that's just a bit farther in, down at the bottom of the hill with the tallest trees that in the summer have dandelion-yellow leaves but had no leaves yet. The sky was so grey, and somehow it was like the trees were closer together than usual. They looked a bit taller, like they had all grown as tall as an extra person standing on top of them in the nighttime.

There was a lot going on in my brain. I kept thinking about the tree sap, for one thing, but for another I felt almost like there was someone else in the woods. I wasn't sure who, so I tried to make my imagination slow down, and I tapped each one of those empty dandelion trees with my branch as I slowly walked by. My brain was thinking amazingly hard because of how confused I was, and I was trying to picture who or what was or wasn't in the woods with me, but I couldn't.

I mean, obviously there was no one *there*. I looked around the whole place. I even sat down on the ground for a while, digging my branch into the earth, looking over my shoulder to see who was there, but it was no one.

It was really weird because I was always alone in the woods but I never really felt *alone* until right then. Not alone in a bad way. But also I felt like maybe I wasn't alone, so it was kind of scary. I usually never got scared in the woods. Then I realized that the feeling in my brain was exactly like one I got a long time ago when I first heard this one crazy question, and then of course the question came exploding back into my head until it was taking up most of my brain.

"If a tree falls down in a forest but there's no one around to hear it, does it still make a sound?" I still think about that question all the time even though it's years since I heard it, and maybe I'll think about it forever. Probably I will, because the thing about thinking about that question is that you can't, really. I mean think about it:

A tree falls down in the forest. (It doesn't matter how, because that's not part of the question, but anyway there's no person who knocks it down—sometimes trees just fall down by themselves, I guess, and even if they don't they do in this question because it's like in algebra when they only give you an x and you can't ask why.) So obviously when the trunk of this mystery tree cracks open and when its branches scrape the branches of the other trees around it, and when it lands with a big splash sound like a cymbal, obviously all of these things make a lot of noise, and in your brain you want to yell "TIIIMMBERRRR!"

But the thing is that no one is around to hear the noise or yell timber. Because everyone in the universe is so far away that they don't even know that the tree that just fell down even exists. So if the sounds of the tree falling never touch anyone's ears that means, "Are they really sounds at all?" And the *other* thing is that let's imagine that in our world any time a tree falls down and no one is around, the tree actually makes sure it *doesn't* make a sound. It is just completely silent. If this was true, we wouldn't even know about it, because we wouldn't be around to not hear the sneaky tree. So we can never prove whether it would make a sound or not.

So you can say yes and you can say no to this question but it doesn't matter because the point of this question is that both are wrong and you are left with no answer—just like when you try to ask where the big bang came from—and I guess that's why someone asks you the question in the first place, because they're trying to confuse you for the rest of your life.

The first time I thought about the tree question too much I kept going back and forth between answers and then I got more than confused, and I started to get scared, even though there was nothing real to be scared of. It was just an imaginary tree in an imaginary question, but that made it even worse. So it sounds stupid but I felt like I couldn't stop living inside that question so I tossed my branch and headed for the beach just to forget about trees.

I stepped off the path and my boots were on stones, these soft white pebbles that were in some places on the beach, and then the jagged grey gravel on other parts. I walked right up to the edge of the water and then kept walking, and I waded into the calm river just until it was halfway up my boots, so that there was a line on them where the red was suddenly dark red. I bent down and touched the top of the smooth water with my hand, and I held my hand there so the skin on the top of the water stuck to me like it does for the feet of those flies who are light enough to walk on water. The river was cold. It was really cold, of course, because winter was still trying to hang around, and it was before the water had even rose, but even still I took another couple steps out into it, because it seemed fun I guess, but then I was looking at my legs and didn't notice a little wave come out of nowhere and overflow my right boot, and I made a little noise because of how amazingly cold and soaking my foot was all of a sudden and I ran back towards the beach before the next wave came.

I limped back up the beach and sat on this big washed-up-log bench that was there. I yanked my boot off, and it made a *ploonk* kind of suctioning noise. I poured the cold water out onto the beach gravel. My foot was freezing. It felt blue. I put it back in my red boot. I was going to get pneumonia of the foot.

It was funny because the beach had been just down through the woods for the entire time our house had been there—obviously, beaches don't just sneak up on you or something—but I had never swam there, not even once. In the summer if I went swimming I always went to a bigger beach down the street, or to a sandy one on the ocean that was so far we had to take Maxine's car and make a family trip out of it. Anyway, I never really went to this beach even though it was so close to my house. I didn't even know whose beach it was.

Then I realized. I was where it happened. This was the beach—it had to be. The book was just up the hill a bit. It's stupid but I had been imagining some other beach far away. But then I somehow just got this feeling in my entire body like I knew. It was *this* beach, this exact beach that I never swam at ever, that I was sitting right on.

I started thinking more and tried to stop but couldn't and I just kept thinking more and more. I thought about where I was. I thought about Phil. The water was so cold. The gravel was so noisy to walk on, and the beach was so close. How come I didn't hear it? Where was I? Even if I wasn't around, how could I just not *hear* something like that? I wanted to punch things.

I pictured Phil alone with no one else there. No me, no anyone. I sat on the log picturing that for a long time until I couldn't anymore. I wanted to punch everything. I couldn't look at the water and hear the tiny waves make their horrible little crashing sounds on the shore. I couldn't hear the sharp gravel crunching or sit on the smooth wood anymore. Everything was punching me.

I kept picturing Phil and no one else. I kept picturing everyone else in the world so far away from the beach, talking and making jokes to each other and giving each other hugs and presents and going to each other's houses and visiting, without Phil. I couldn't stop picturing Phil alone on the beach exactly where I was.

So I ran home to get far away.

When I left the woods it was almost dark out and there were a million cars in our driveway and all over the stupid street, because Simon's bridge club was there, like I should have expected. I walked into the living room really fast and there were a bunch of adults sitting around at square tables. Uncle Max was there, and Simon's friend Matthew, and Max's friend Andy. But like I couldn't possibly have expected, there were girls there too. At one table Matthew and Andy were both sitting across from their wives, or girlfriends or whatever—one's name is Allie and the other one I don't know her name—and at the other table was Simon and Max and Maxine. The only person I didn't recognize was the lady sitting across from Simon. Simon was holding his cards and resting his hands on the corner of the table and talking loud and slow, like he had been going on and on about something, which was weird, and the lady was staring at him in the eyes with this big smile.

"Heyyy buddy!" Uncle Max called out when he noticed me standing there.

"Hey Arthur," said Aunt Maxine.

Everyone in the entire room turned and smiled at me and said "Hello" and waved and laughed. Then Simon said "Arthur, this is Maureen," and the lady said "Hi Arthur" in the way that grown-ups think you're supposed to talk to babies.

"Hi," I said. Then I asked Simon if I could speak to him for a moment in private, but I said it really loud by accident, like I was yelling.

Simon put down his cards. Everyone else went quiet.

"Sure, chief. Is something wrong?"

I didn't say anything except with my eyes that said, *"Obviously."*

Simon followed me into my room.

"Shut the door please," I said calmly.

He shut the door.

"What is going on!?"

"Please don't yell, Arthur. What do you—"

"You guys NEVER have girls over. It's a *men's* bridge club."

"It was Max's idea. We just thought we'd mix it up. It's not a big deal."

"It IS a big deal!"

"Arthur. *Please* don't yell. You'll notice I'm not yelling. What's really going on? Do you mind telling me where you've *been* this whole time?"

"So do you like her!?"

"Who?"

"Do. You. Like her!?"

"Maureen?"

"Do you?"

"I don't know, Arthur! What do you want me to say?"

"Typical."

"Arthur—"

"You're ruining my life!"

I sat on my bed and didn't look at Simon. I scrunched my fingers into balls and bit my teeth together and I didn't look at him at all except out of my peripheral vision but I couldn't help that.

"I'll talk to you in the morning. We'll discuss whatever it is when you've calmed down."

"Fine."

"I'm going back out there. Okay?"

I didn't look at him.

"Goodnight, Arthur."

I heard him close my door. I lay down on top of my bedsheets, with all their stars and galaxies, and I remembered that he wanted me to change them and put new sheets on. So I didn't.

He was probably back out in the living room playing bridge and having a great time. Bridge is the stupidest game *ever*. You need four people to play, but only three people ever do anything important. Because the rules are that one person always becomes the star of the show, and tries to win, and the other person on their team becomes the "dummy" and sits there being bored and boring and wasting space. Then the other two people team up to ruin everything for the star of the show. The stupidest thing was how the bridge-playing guys would always go on and on about how bridge is exactly like life. But who knows, maybe they were right. It's not like life was any better.

I went to my closet, opened it, and took out the clues. I looked them over. I took deep breaths and moved some pieces around and went over what happened that day. I thought about Mr. Peterson building a chandelier and then smashing a chandelier to smithereens. I got a new strip of paper and wrote on it:

-I have no idea what I want to be when I grow up.

But it was supposed to be things I knew, not things I didn't know. I crumpled it up and chucked it at my garbage can, because if I started collecting things I didn't know then I would have to collect everything and collect for a million lifetimes and I only had one. I thought about Simon and wrote something else.

-I will NEVER EVER GROW UP!

BUS

Some mornings like this morning I wake up already so down and so aimless and with my mind grinding and tearing to such degrees there's no chance and I wander the kitchen so sure it's a bear trap there's nothing I can do about it biting its way in and shrinking and burning until a miracle of courage and I kick my front door open and run from the flames as firefighters bravely run past me and I can't stop running inside me until I reach the bus and pay my $2.50 and get my transfer and my seat, then I close my eyes and pray my mind will just override itself turn off and kick into silent emergency mode I'm not in control but if I'm really really lucky the smell of the smoke fades and I inhale slowly and sit waiting for it to happen and it does—this drifting slow ecstasy finds me, and it's like I'm sitting beside myself in the rain.

And I am. It's raining inside the bus now as much as it's raining outside, and I can watch my chest filling and emptying and feel my heart's kicks get farther apart, the rain is warm but tastes like a glacier. I see Ecstatic Phil tilt his head back and open his mouth. Piano music softly plays and Phil looks up front and it's the driver, he's playing the three *Gymnopédies* waiting for the light to turn, the windshield wipers as metronome. And every atom of Phil wants nothing but to surrender to this rainy hope, this rapture of the crowded bus and of finally loving every person on it so completely... look at them all:

The pale guy with big neon headphones and soul patch can feel it. The old black woman with the tubes connecting her small waxy body to the oxygen tank, in her green and white striped shirt, in everything and despite everything she can feel it. And these are not strangers and these are nothing to hide from or to make the blood pump so fast and hot and these are the ones Phil has everything in common with and they must all be dampened by the same rain. They must all *feel* it no matter what, even as the bus grows more and more crowded it must be *increasing,* somehow, and Polite Phil stands to give his seat to a stressed red-haired woman. The rain still falls and now it's changing colours. Oh, look at it. Every drop is a different solid colour and to look through them all as they fall is to be simultaneously aware of every colour, all bound to land on the same floor, and man they're *heavy* these raindrops but they don't bruise.

And soon ~~Enlightened~~ Phil will have to get off this bus and he will but whatever breakfast diner soon holds him he'll make sure to bring the bus with him in his pocket. He will bring it in 1:1000 scale size and do laps of the placemat—WELCOME BIEN-VENUE—and sit and transfer the bus to his journal in whatever way he chooses and then walk to the library, and he will remember the great boundless joy of life and the communion of everyone so alone—the euphoria of a crowded bus taking you and *everyone* just where you need to go. And at night when he forgets it and sees himself sitting on top of his own head kicking spitting and howling HE WILL NOT FORGET and he will LIVE IN that joy and EVERYTHING WILL BE OK.

STACKS

I'm stuck here. We were here, we were *right there,* there we are, we were a couple of people studying in silence at that table, all wood and metal exactly like this table, a replica, but completely different. I can't get out. I woke from a dream of it yesterday and lived in remnants of the dream all day, now I'm here, this is not why I came here or is it, of course it is, to watch an empty table from across the room, to read invisible books, to no doubt soon walk home alone with nothing but demons, to never stop imagining, trying to squeeze every bit of pain I possibly can from this, WHAT is wrong with me, what else do people DO.

We were whoever I was a year ago and whoever you were, Phil and E, they got up, she held the door for him, they went downstairs and she returned a few books and they went outside. He grabbed her hand and held it, but the air was piercingly cold, just about to be December, and she soon unhooked her hand from his and put it in her pocket. It was decidedly hands-in-pockets weather. Was he disappointed that she'd withdrawn her hand then, in the cold?

They were keeping silent, just climbing up the icy steps, focused on not slipping and breaking necks. They walked along the sidewalk in the type of silence that only five hours of reading dusty books produces. Exhausted silence. But he was glad then, to be exhausted and silent.

It was *exactly* how I'd always wanted my life to be, it was how I saw it: me in an exhausted delighted mood and walking home slowly with *her,* it's just getting dark, there's such complete certainty about her, there is no one else, just us walking in silence or not and it not mattering which.

Then she said Isn't it strange how they call them "the stacks?" and he asked why, and she said Because they don't actually stack them. The books. They just stand them up next to each other, on shelves. They don't *stack* them, that would be insane.

She then proceeded to create a new library for him out of thin air. She said maybe it would have been built in a very small town, an isolated place, where they haven't been informed that the proper "stacking" arrangement is side by side, not literally on top of one another. And they certainly haven't been told about Dewey and his decimals. In this library, if you want to get a book out, you have to swiftly yank it out of the middle of the stack, as the iconic magician snatches a tablecloth out from under a feast. They would grease the covers of the books when they returned them to the shelves to make this possible, although still not safe, and people would be required to sign a lengthy waiver when applying for their library card. The librarians' poor little arms would end up in plaster casts, and they'd never get as much injury compensation as they needed, but no one would ever step in and show them a better system, because they simply wouldn't know one. So they would keep it up. After decades passed, and after enough book avalanches and broken bones, the librarians would get fed up, would let themselves get lazy, and they would start to reshelve the books via the tops of stacks, instead of trying to heave the pile up and slip them back into their correct spots in between. All the while, the soundtrack of the place would not be the usual passing whispers and shuffles of feet, but rather the irregular thundering, the CRASH CRASH *CRASH* of pillars of paper slamming down as the library patrons pull out their choices.

It wasn't so strange of you to be going on like you were, but you seemed to really be on a roll that night, so I didn't interrupt. I listened. I did my best to remember every detail so I could save them for you later—for *me* later, for future remembering. I did that with so much of you, too much, all of it, like grasping at one long dream image fading in the stubborn morning. Vanishing. Too much detail to possibly capture. Still I feel like I know it all, like I could recite everything, I can't let go, HOW DO PEOPLE LET GO. What does that even *MEAN?* Do some people actually get there? This is not why I'm here. I was looking up poetry and then didn't get any. I got distracted and ended up in places no one should ever be. They have a whole suicide section here, if you're into that, apparently. Lots of psych stuff but then weird stuff, too. I found practically like a how-to thing. I read way too much. I made myself reshelve it. So yes so then the worst part of all, you claimed, was that the most popular books, those borrowed most often, would always end up on the tops of stacks, tossed by the scowling librarians climbing their towering ladders, creaking around on their stilts. So the stacked books would then tragically go in approximate order of most popular to least popular from top to bottom, and some people tragically would even go as far as to assume that all the *best* books were therefore on the top, and the very *worst* at the bottom, and wouldn't bother with anything below heart-level. The whole scenario then became a survival-of-the-fittest deal, with the "best" books actually crushing and mashing the "worst" books into a pulp.

By this time you were walking at about half your normal pace, and poking one of your hands with the other with each new development. *Then,* you said, would come the minority fans, the lovers and rescuers of literary underdogs: snobbish, offended old men and women who'd make monthly pilgrimages to their favourite underrated and overlooked books and put them back up on the tops of the stacks, in the hopes they might be spared, or even read, and *then,*

Then you let out a sigh and resumed your normal walk. The library dissolved. I didn't know how to respond, I never did, so I just leaned my head in and kissed you on the neck. When I got home I meant to write it all down, but found myself just living inside it instead. I couldn't get over the way you'd constructed it, in such a cause-and-effect way. The books would be stacked, so then logically this would happen, so then logically this would happen… Everything was so easy for you, so fluid. I had ideas too, sometimes, but for you it was different. For you life *was* a long chain of good ideas, with no space in between. Hundred-watt bulbs popped into the air fully lit at all moments, hovering, falling to your heels and shattering. A trail of broken glass music followed you.

I needed to be around you forever, it was so clear to me. I had never wanted anything more. I used every idea of yours as fuel for my own dream of us, I told you I loved you. Kind of out of nowhere. How romantic. You didn't answer that first time until a few hours later in your room. I appreciated that. That you had thought it out. I was ecstatic pretending to be calm. Then I woke you up by accident, I thought you were still awake, you could be gone in an instant, I woke you asking if I could use your idea for a film. You were annoyed: What idea? The Stacks. Oh, you said, Yeah sure. Fine. You said you didn't own the idea, it was just an *idea,* and it just happened to have come out of *your* mind. You said you didn't *invent* your mind. That killed me. I couldn't sleep so I watched you do it instead.

STACKS

But I *was* this library, and you constructed me! I *was* a misinterpretation of a simple word. I was every librarian who obeyed the system with a faith that overcame paper cuts and broken bones. I was every stack of books, forever shifting and pounding and being pushed and rearranged but remaining essentially the same; I was every book in every stack. And I was a town of well-intentioned and good-natured citizens, all avid readers, not knowing any better system than the one they had learned. And I was every citizen who had left town on vacation and visited far-off libraries—quiet ones where things flowed smoothly and all was accounted for and on equal footing—but who felt uncomfortable, confused, even *wrong* to borrow a book there, without some massive effort required of them, without some permanent risk, and not even just in the finding, the ladder climbing, the heaving and pulling and crushing, but in making sure to put their whole soul and well-being on the line. I was everyone who knew an easy read was no read at all. And I was every resident of the surrounding townships as well, who'd heard of the painstaking library and visited it, and found it endearing and ridiculous. I was every reason for and against the stacking, and I was made out of the same metal as every shelf. But you were someone who saw the whole predicament from an even higher vantage point.

~~You were the cloud drifting over the entire province, blowing in and out of shapes and observing the towns and the situation below, and seeing through it all and finding it all so peculiar.~~

You're none of those things. You're not even the girl in these pages. She is nothing like you, and she knows nothing of you. I know this now. An eye-test chart isn't *you*—it makes me sick. You're not the details I tried to save—primary source documents written, drawn, even the ones I tried to keep safe and pure in my mind. "A trail of shattered light bulbs" isn't you. If you knew the things I compared you to you'd kill me. I could gut this library and build the stacks myself and work and live here until death and still I'd never happen upon you in any aisle. Everywhere, every book and every shelf would only be hideous monuments to me. Even if you actually came back I wouldn't recognize you. You'll never be *you* in my mind or these pages or my life and you never were. I couldn't let you. I know. No matter how hard I tried to understand and then how hard I tried to stop trying, only *you* were you.

~~And I know this now.~~

And I'm *sorry*.

BLAH BLAH BLAH

AFTER THE Mr. Peterson day, I took a couple of days off from interviewing. I tried to forget about how I hadn't even found one single clue, and how I knew basically nothing. The last house I'd have to check out would be the hermit's house, but I definitely wasn't about to just walk up there unprepared. I was going to need some time for doing research, and manufacturing bravery.

On my second afternoon off I went to Finch's house after finishing my school, because what else was I going to do. Victoria came over, too. We were all playing Scrabble, which was Victoria's idea, because she was bored after Finch made us play Frisbee on his lawn for all eternities. Victoria wasn't very good at throwing a Frisbee: it would always go way over my head or straight into Finch's ankles, or more often would just end up miles away some place, in some mucky ditch or sharp hedge, and then one of us would have to walk excruciatingly far to get it back. Victoria was a really good catch though. Better than both me and Finch. She was pretty fast at running, and she would almost always catch the thing, even if me or Finch had a bad throw. Of course Finch tried to do all these crazy throws: upside-down ones, sideways ones, behind-his-back ones, but they mostly were horrible, and would just launch the Frisbee in some moronic direction, and then Victoria would run really hard and usually catch them. It was pretty hilarious. "I used to be able to do it perfect yesterday," Finch kept saying, and Victoria said, "Can we please go inside now?"

So we played Scrabble on the dark green carpet in Finch's living room. I was winning, but Victoria was close.

"That's not a word," I said.

Finch looked at the letters he'd just put on the board, and then back at me.

"Yeah it is," he said, "triple word score."

"Trane isn't a word," I said.

"Are you retarded?"

"It's T-R-A-I-N," I said. "Take it off the board."

"No way. Pass the dictionary."

He never believed me until he looked in the dictionary. I sighed loud enough for him to hear so that he'd know how annoying he was being. He didn't seem to know. I looked over at Victoria. She gave me a kind of smile that made me feel weird, one like she was very happy to see me. It was a smile she'd been making a lot lately.

"If you don't believe me, then why don't you just ask your girlfriend?" I said.

Finch froze. After a second he looked over at Victoria, smiled quickly, then glared at me.

"I'm *looking* in the dictionary. That's how you do it."

"Arthur's right," Victoria said finally. "That's not a word."

"Fine," Finch said. He started flicking the trane letters off the board. Some of them ran into other letters in the words that were already there.

"Hey, you're messing the game up."

"Whatever."

"Don't be a sore loser," I said. "Just make a real word and keep playing."

"I don't even wanna play this retarded game anyway."

"Simon, come on," Victoria said, "don't be a baby."

"'Baseballing' isn't a real word either, for your information," Finch said, making mean eyebrows at Victoria. "You can't just add I-N-G onto anything like that, but we let you keep *that* one."

"At least it's spelled right," I said.

Finch got up and walked out of the room. On the way, he stepped right in the middle of the board, and all the letters fell out of their words and spelled a bunch of nonsense all over the place. I looked over at Victoria and she was trying hard not to laugh.

"What's so funny?" I asked.

"He's just so *serious*," she said. "He takes it so seriously."

Then I laughed for a little while, because I agreed with her and because it's really easy to laugh about Finch.

"Do you want to set it back up again?" I asked.

"It's probably because I dumped him," Victoria said.

"What? When'd you do that?"

"Yesterday."

"How long were you his girlfriend for?"

"Four days."

"That's weird. Why are you at his house?"

"You guys invited me over."

"Yeah but, why'd you say yes?"

"I don't know," she said. "What else was I going to do?"

I didn't say anything. I swept all the letters off the board and dropped handfuls of them into the slippery plastic bag they belonged in.

"Maybe I want you to be my boyfriend instead."

Victoria was looking down at the carpet and tracing circles in it with her finger. I didn't know what to say, so I still didn't say anything. I kept putting letters into the bag.

"Arthur?"

"Mmm-hmm?" I didn't look up at her.

"Maybe I want *you* to be my boyfriend, I said."

"I heard you."

"Well why aren't you saying anything?"

"I *am* saying things."

"You're being a jerk."

"I can't be your boyfriend."

"Why not?"

I stopped putting the letters in the bag. Victoria crossed her arms. I picked up the Scrabble board, folded it in half and put it back inside the box.

"I don't know, I'm busy. I just can't. You should just go out with Finch, he's not *that* bad."

"What are you talking about?"

"Nothing—I don't know. I just can't be your boyfriend."

"Do you hate me or something?"

"No way. Obviously I don't—"

"Well then why'd you kiss me yesterday?"

"You kissed *me!*"

"You hate me."

"I *don't.* Do you have any idea how old we are!?"

Victoria's mouth twisted into some new kind of smile that I had never seen anyone make before. It was kind of like a smile of someone who knows something you don't, who is keeping a secret, and also kind of like a sneaky bad guy's smile, except she wasn't a bad guy. It wasn't an *evil* smile, just a curious one. I didn't know why she made it. She always made the weirdest smiles.

"Fine," she said. "But some day you're going to be in love with me."

"I'm going home," I said, and then I went to the hall, put my boots on and left Finch's house. I had no idea where Finch disappeared to.

It was beautiful outside again, finally, and I walked home thinking about how silly girls can be. They were only boyfriend-girlfriend for four *days* and she broke up with him. And then suddenly he thinks it's fine to go around spelling fake words like "trane." How come every time people dump each other they go mentally insane? I mean, come on. They never even hugged or held hands or anything whenever I was around—he barely even talked to her. And she said he never even *tried* to french her. I didn't get it. Maybe she actually was in love with me instead. What a weirdo.

I was glad to have escaped. I was in a good mood, for some reason I was feeling like I was just one tiny kid in the whole universe, but I felt OK to be that. I could do whatever I wanted: if I felt like spending all day in the woods, I could. If I felt like never talking to anyone ever again, I could. I was ten years old. I didn't need Victoria to be my girlfriend, I mean look what it did to Finch. Besides, I saw her all the time anyway, whether I wanted to or not. I didn't need anyone. I ran for a little bit, because it was fun to go fast, and 'cause I was in control of the whole solar system. I ran until my lungs burned fiery from not breathing enough, then I slowed down. I had infinite energy. I spotted an especially pretty rock on the side of the road, one of those crazy quartz rocks that looks like kind of a lumpy diamond. It was a big one too, almost as big as a baseball. I kicked it up the hill a bit—it flew along the ground for a while and stopped, then slowly wiggled and rolled back down to me. I kicked it again farther up the hill, and in a while it rolled back down to my foot again. I carefully kicked that one single rock all the way home and left it in our driveway.

I couldn't wait to start preparing for the investigation of the hermit's house. I would be brave and go there and draw a map of his whole property first, sitting far enough away in the woods. And I'd write down investigation strategies on the side of the map. I already saw it in my head: a top view of the crazy cottage with all the measurements really precise and also showing how scary it looked, and with diagrams paying close attention to the scariest parts.

In order to safely go there and make the map I would need a way of being invisible, and hopefully silent. But I had ideas about that. The first thing I would do was I would get some old clothes, like a shirt I didn't wear anymore, or maybe one of Simon's dirty old sweaters he uses for gardening, and a pair of old jeans, and I would lie them down on the forest floor like a two-dimensional person lying on their back, and take my white glue and pour it all over the clothes and spread it around with the edge of a stick. Then I'd pick up handfuls of leaves and also green cedar branches and soil and dump them all on top of the gluey clothes. When it dried in fifteen minutes, I'd flip them over and do the other side too, and when the clothes were all done I'd put them on and no one would be able to see me sitting in the woods making my map because I would camouflage into the trees like lots of animals can do without having to wear anything, and like humans should do when we finally evolve smarter.

To be silent, I had an even easier idea. I would just find two clumps of green moss about the right size, and find some pieces of rope somewhere, and I would just take my boots off—which were red, so now that I think of it I'd probably need to paint them green first—and I would just tie the clumps of moss onto the bottom

of my boots with the mossy side down, so that when I walked I would make a sound so soft it wouldn't even really be a sound. And once I manufactured the camouflage suit and the silence boots, people wouldn't even know I was there, and I could sneak onto the hermit's property and do all my research. Plus Simon wouldn't be able to see me, or Maureen, or Finch or Victoria or anyone. Because it would look like I didn't even exist at all, like a zero-dimensional person, except secretly I did exist and I was getting stuff done, so really I would be a secret shaped like a boy.

I walked through the white door on the front of our house and took my boots off. I balanced against the wall with my right hand, wobbling but carefully taking my boots off one at a time, like a boot surgeon. Old crusty mud broke off of them even though I was being so careful, and it dissolved on the floor. I quickly swept the sand into the corner with my bare foot, plopped my empty thermos on the kitchen counter, and hopped into the living room.

I was about to attempt a cartwheel when I noticed Simon on the couch. He was sitting there like a statue, and he was camouflaged into the room. Simon *never* sits in the living room. He looked up from what he was reading, which was a black and white speckly covered notebook.

My cartwheel arms dropped and my heart felt like it was underneath hot water. But I tried to keep calm.

"Where'd that come from?" I asked, being sneaky.

"Why don't you tell *me* where it came from?" Simon said, being nosy and difficult.

"Well the big bang, technically," I said.

Simon said nothing.

"I mean, if you go *way* back in time, of course."

Simon still said nothing. What the heck was he doing reading Phil!?

"And before that who knows, but I guess it just—"

"Arthur. Where did this come from?" It wasn't that he didn't understand the quantumed physics of the big bang, it was that he was being really serious and worried. He wasn't smiling. Where had I left the book so that he found it? I usually kept it under my pillow. What a stupid place to keep something like that. Did he just go around looking underneath everybody's pillows for important things and then taking them away?

"Did you at least give Uncle Max the package like I told you?" I said, trying to change the subject and act like things weren't a big deal, so that maybe I could just get the book back and that would be it.

"Yes, he picked it up. They left something for you, too."

Then Simon sighed and got up from the couch and walked around the living room looking at stuff. He wasn't saying anything. I just stood there being nervous, and I didn't know what to do so I just started to explain.

"I found him in the woods. I mean, the book. I found it in the woods."

I waited a long time for Simon to say something.

"Did you read all of it?" he finally asked.

"Yeah. It's the first book I've ever finished," I said. That was actually a lie, but it sounded really good at the time. I don't know why I said it.

"I read it all, too," Simon said. "I came across it just after they left, and then I've spent all afternoon just sitting here, reading it."

"It's really good," I said. I was just about to remind Simon what the *New York Times* had said about it, but he turned around and looked at me, and he still wasn't smiling. I think he was smiling even less now, if possible.

I avoided his eyes by looking over to where Phil lay open on the coffee table. I recognized Page 43. The neat and tidy handwriting at the top, with the shaky writing at the bottom. The way everything was crossed out. The way it filled the whole page to overflowing. The butterflies in my stomach were crawling out of their cocoons and having a discussion. They were really worried and flapping around and not knowing what to do. They had smaller butterflies in their own stomachs. I pictured Phil sitting somewhere on the beach writing that page. I pictured what his insides felt like while he was writing it and my insides felt worse and worse. They were getting shook up like I was seasick. I pictured how bad my insides would have to feel for me to write something like that but I couldn't. I couldn't picture how inside someone's heart could feel that bad. I thought really hard about not throwing up.

I scrunched my damp toes under my bare feet and scratched my head. Simon walked over to me. He scooped me up and tossed me on top of his shoulder. The sharp corner of him stabbed at my stomach. I didn't throw up.

He tapped me twice on the back and said, "I hate to be the villain here chief, but I'm going to keep the book."

My entire body stiffened up and I almost got launched off his shoulder. I screamed into his back.

"What!?"

"I'm sorry, chief. You know I try to be fair, but—"

"Put me down!"

"I just can't see it being of any positive—"

"PUT ME DOWN!"

I kicked and flailed and roared until Simon had no choice but to drop me to my feet. I almost fell over.

"I can't believe you!"

"Arthur, don't take that tone, I know you must—"

"I only had one house left!"

Simon shoved his eyebrows downward.

"I only had *one* house left to check!"

"You've been trying to find this guy?"

"Well, yeah! I've been *trying* to find out where it came from."

"Ohh, Arthur," Simon said quietly. "That's going to have to stop, too. I'm so sorry."

"It's not going to! It's *not* going to stop!"

Simon rubbed his eyes underneath his glasses.

"How dare you!?" I yelled, "You're not even my—"

Simon looked at me.

"ARRR!" I roared and ran to my room.

I slammed my door and looked at my bed. My pillowcase and sheets had been changed without my permission, and now they had stupid superheroes all over them instead of outer space. Because I didn't change my own sheets even though I left Phil under my pillow, because I was such a gigantic moron and now everything was doomed.

I slumped into my desk chair and punched the switch on my lamp. I put my head down on my arms on top of my desk. I scrunched my forehead and my eyes against my arm and the skin on my arm got wet. I was shaking, and I stayed shaking for a long time.

CLUES:
- How it makes funny jokes not funny anymore.

After about a month of shaking, I noticed there was a light blue envelope beside me on my desk. It was all bulgy. I picked it up. Usually Maxine sent me really normal flat letters with nothing in them, but this one was heavy at one side, and the paper was tight and covering something square. The flaps on the back barely closed, and it had clear tape on the seams to keep them from bursting.

I wasn't exactly in the mood for Maxine trying to help snap me out of my problems, but I was in the mood for just about anything to distract me from Simon. So I tore open the envelope. And I made sure to rip it open viciously like a rabiesing animal.

Onto my desk thumped a cassette tape in a clear plastic case. That looked pretty curious, but there was a letter inside too, so I pulled it out and unfolded it, because that's what you're supposed to do when you get a present with a card, or a cassette tape with a letter: you do the reading part first.

April 16th

Dearest Arthur,

Dismal weather lately, but the snow's almost completely melted! I can feel summer coming on. You must be excited: school winding down, trees about to bloom, everything just waiting to get bright.

I hear you were a bit shook up about Maureen. I just wanted to say that I have some idea of how you must feel. It's mostly the lack of choice, right? Not having a choice can be tough. I don't want to go into it too far, I don't mean to upset you. Arthur. You have every right to all of your feelings. But I do know what some of them are, and I've had some of them myself. You know, I didn't get to choose your (step) grandfather. I was a bit older than your age then, but I can still remember the patterns of my thoughts. It was the silliest things, the smallest things. Like why couldn't he have had lighter-coloured hair? I couldn't stand to see my mom with a guy with such dark hair. And the way he walked, like he was a bouncing ball. And his dopey green car. Why couldn't he have had a blue car, a nice deep, royal blue? My friend Annie's father drove this dark blue Cadillac, and he looked great.

Arthur, I'm rambling as I always seem to do, but even worse this time, I'm afraid. The point is, Arthur, it took me a while, but I did get over these things. I didn't get to choose him, but I got a different choice, one that was hidden at first. It was a bit ridiculous. I mean, there was really nothing wrong with Frank. He really was a loving man. Si figured it out before I did, I think. I'm stubborn. But you know, we both did get a choice. We *had* to make a choice: we had to choose our attitude. If Mom wanted a green car, and black hair, and a quiet, thoughtful guy who bounced up and down when he walked, then she deserved that. And I could choose to see that or not.

And then one morning Frank was going out the door and I heard him say to her, "Wow. Nice shoes." (Mom always wore the prettiest, most unique shoes. She seemed to wear shoes at all times, even if she was just inside at home. Even if it was the winter, she would wear her nice shoes inside. She had this one pair of shiny red heels, I believe she was wearing those.) And I just remember thinking, you know what Frank, she does wear nice shoes, doesn't she? I almost cried, I swear. It sounds ridiculous, I know. But he noticed.

People are like puzzles, Arthur. In a couple of ways. Firstly, it takes a long time to figure them out and piece them together, and lots of times you never do. But those ones are the best people! I think that the pain of feeling like you've figured somebody out is actually much greater than the pain of never quite getting them. Wait, that's not what I was trying to say. Gosh!

Secondly, people have shapes. All we do and say and think and believe cuts outlines around us like a jigsaw. And sometimes, you run into a person who seems to fit right beside you in the picture. Someone who sticks out where you dent in and zigs where you zag. And there's a strange feeling when that happens, Arthur, and you feel like there isn't much you can do. And you feel so happy and you feel so awake. I'm just talking about friendship, Arthur. I'm just talking about fitting.

I'm sorry. I'm getting out of hand. All I'm trying to say is that Maureen seemed to like Simon quite a bit, but it's perfectly natural for you to feel confused about that. You can—it should go without saying—talk to me about it anytime. Write me!

(But she also said that she thought you were the cutest, and anyone who can see that can't be that bad, can they? Well actually, I guess any old fool would know that. But still.)

Blah blah blah. Here's your word. "Circumnavigate." Like many of our recent words, it's got two main definitions: 1. to travel around; make a circuit of, by navigation (to circumnavigate the Earth), or 2. to avoid, by manoeuvring around (to circumnavigate heavy traffic).

Enjoy the word! And the warm-ish weather!

Love as always,

Aunt Maxine

P.S.—Max says you're on some sort of secret investigation. Good luck with that!

I didn't really read the whole letter right then, because it was so long and looked boring, and I was so angry and how could she expect me to read all that? Also I saw the name "Maureen" somewhere in it and didn't really feel like reading anymore. I just skimmed through the rest, reading a couple of words here and there. OK sure, whatever you say Maxine, Maureen's great. She's practically Miss Universe. I wasn't convinced, but you can't have an argument with a letter very well because it's just paper, so I kept skipping ahead until I got to the vocabulary word. How'd she get a letter about Maureen to me so quick? News travelled way too fast in our weird little family.

P.S.—What on *Earth* did Max think he was doing telling Maxine about the investigation!? That was *top* secret. How much did he tell her? Why was everyone trying to sabotage me all over the place, and what the heck was on that cassette tape?

I opened the clear plastic case and slid the tape out into my hand. It was a ninety minute one (that's half an hour longer than the ones I used), and it was all multicoloured. It had blue and yellow labels on black plastic, and on one side Uncle Max had written with a black marker: *FOR ARTHUR'S EARS (AND DANCING FEET AND ARMS) ONLY!!!*

What the heck? I went and got my tape recorder. I popped Max's tape inside on Side A and hit PLAY. The speaker crackled and buzzed for about ten seconds and then it clicked and there was a steady, gusty noise. Then Uncle Max's silly, wobbly voice.

"Good day, Agent Arthur. I have reviewed the tapes which were forwarded to me from H.Q. Excellent work on all fronts. You have proven to be a proficient interrogator and are moving up in the ranks. The information you extracted was of limitless value. Arthur, this line is tapped so I don't have much time. What follows is . . . a celebratory address. Get ready. This tape may self-destruct if the listener fails to dance. Or the listener may self-destruct. The eagle is on the descent. Over and out . . ."

Four seconds of silence, and then some drumbeat started banging so loud that I had to turn the volume down to keep Simon from hearing all the way out in the living room.

boom, chatt,
boom boom, chatt chatt!

It was *so* loud. Then this screechy womping sound: Max's electric organ. The beat kept going and going and the organ kept buzzing and womping.

womp womp—womp!
womp womp—womp!

And then this voice. I couldn't recognize it at first, it was all sped up and chipmunked.

"Phil-Phil-Philadelphia!
Phi-Phi-Phi-Phi-Philadelphia!"
womp womp—womp!
womp womp—womp!

And then slowed down deep voices, too, like:

"Brrraaasss taaacksss,
Brrraaasss taaacksss."
wom-womp—weeem!
wom-womp—weeeooo!

"You'll, you'll never guess!
You'll . . . . never guess!"
weee-ooo, chatt chatt!
weee-ooo, chatt chatt!

wom, w-w-womwom, weee
wom, w-w-womwom, weee

Because Max took my Brenda Beckham interview and turned it into the most moronic thing my ears will ever hear.

"Spring feeeeeeverrr,
Spring—"

I smashed the STOP button. Who did Max think he *was*, sending me some kind of stupid dance mix tape like that? Did he have any idea how important everything was? I bet he played the tape for Maxine. I bet he made copies and gave them to all his friends with their tape-playing cars so they could all zoom around town and blast that idiotic remix of Phil's death and dance behind the steering wheel and almost get in accidents and make *other* people die. I bet he even told Simon about it, and that's why he went snooping for the book. Did Max even have a clue about what TOP SECRET means?

I rewound his tape all the way to the beginning to tape over it. I pressed RECORD.

"Dear Agent Uncle Max what the *hell* do you think you're doing making fun of everything like that, did you really think I was going to *dance?* And I bet you set Simon up with his date, too! You're about the most clueless, idiotic, scaredy-cat . . ."

. . . I said as many bad things as I possibly could and by the end I was probably yelling. Then I hit STOP. I took the tape out and put it in an envelope and I was about to write Max's stupid name on it, but then I didn't. I stared at the blank envelope for a couple of eternities. I knew I couldn't send it.

WE BOW

LOOK HOW the storm leaves us: our leafless branches sheathed in transparent clothing. We are pillars and ropes of glass. The ice slips into every crevice and our evergreens' tiny needles seal together, they are matted locks hanging heavy, glazed and sparkling. Many of our tallest and most slender actually bend to touch the ground. We are a gallery of crystal archways, a fractal pattern of white tunnels for squirrels and foxes to navigate. Draped and still in the windless morning, we grow silent.

The two walk near us. She in her goldenrod-yellow and he in black. He kisses her neck. They turn their heads toward an approaching rumbling in the distance that scrapes through the heavy air. A snow plow is making its way up the road. The man takes a disposable camera from the pocket of his parka while the two step up onto the snowbank that frames the street, their short boots pushing down through it in places, the snow frosting their woollen ankles. The man winds the film forward on his camera and waits for the plow. When it's about to pass, he raises the camera to his eye, waits, and triggers the shutter, the plastic flashbulb ignites for an instant and the plow is recorded onto the film. The man has been making bleak photographs of the solid white day with lone colourful things as their subject.

The plow is dazzling in its orange paint, the way its cubic forms dominate a blank crystalline landscape.

The two stumble through a buried ditch, the snow catching them waist-deep for a few steps, and they climb out and walk beneath us.

We are a world of prisms. See our bodies, sublimely coated, refracting and stretching the daylight to project full spectra; the world consists entirely of fractured rainbows, twirling and blinking on every surface. It is the most spectacular feast.

They walk together, making their way beneath our heavy branches, treading gently on the crust of ice above snow. He stops every few minutes and aims his camera off into the stringy glass world. They continue to wander. See the camera's tiny bulb sparking and its white light splintering into a thousand dashing fragments, layering atop those we already see, flaring through us, warping into vibrant colours. The brightest yellows waltz with brilliant oranges and pure blues against a boundless white backdrop. See the red, the violet. We are a collaged universe of mirrors caught in the midst of a silent fireworks display.

We love this, this assault of light. These silent visions are enough to keep us through the cold. And as the man showers us with his little light he takes our portrait, and we his.

But then he winds the film ahead quickly and points the camera at her. She is concentrating on her movement, focused only on lifting the heavy branch and ducking under, but when she turns to say something he clicks the camera and catches her. Her smile is gone. She looks him in the eyes, deeper than the eyes. Then she crawls out and moves back toward the street, quicker than before and less cautious, as if she now had a destination. He lets her go ahead. He puts the camera in his pocket and follows. He weighs more. His feet punch holes through the ice. He jumps over the ditch and once he's back on the road he runs to catch up to her. He rubs his hand against the back of her yellow coat and speaks but she doesn't reply. Now they walk in silence, and if they do talk their voices use deeper notes. They walk faster, as if the cold now irritates them. And they walk beside each other without walking beside each other. There are innumerable molecules between them.

And we know his error, and we know he begins to know. And though his photos of us can never be us, can only be souvenirs and sad captives, we will forgive his grasp. We will thank him for the light.

ICE

You hated having your picture taken, you said you always have. I told you when I got them developed I would tear this one up for you. And I haven't.

In total there were three photos I took of you. The first two from that first fall, we were down at the waterfront by the playground. I took two of you sitting on the pier, and then you said you actually kind of hated getting your picture taken. Those ones didn't turn out, you were lucky, I was too nervous and too in love to set the aperture, and you are a silhouette against fog. And so of course yes let's keep the romance going here let's pull out all the stops because this is THE ONLY photo of you that I HAVE:

- You are slipping under a heavy ice-covered branch, in your bright yellow coat, turning towards me. I'm on the other side of the branches—you are seen through them.
- We broke up the next day—this is our last official day. We did not break up because of this photo. But how could I ever get past how it tells the whole story. Maybe in thirty years I will be able to look at it and feel nothing—maybe.

- Your breath is a cloud. It hangs out in front of you dusting the air under the tree, one of your hands is raised to hold up the delicate branch and its smaller branches, you've taken your gloves off for some reason, your white fingers look frigid. All the smaller coated branches on the side make it look like you're stepping into a web of ice.
- You were talking about being present, about undivided mind, it all makes too much sense, you were explaining and making connections and laughing, I was useless, I couldn't stop trying to describe your laugh to myself. Was it like birdsong? Is birdsong so contagious? And I'm nodding and grinning and watching my feet move, taking photos. I ~~agreed with everything~~ wanted to agree with everything you ever said.
- It was February 20th. We had not done anything for the day that is known as Valentine's Day.
- I had wanted to.
- Because of the flash everything is all reflections and glitter, and you're stepping into a cage of light.
- How the things we did to each other could never not be signs.
- Not being able to stop ~~finding~~ looking for metaphor in *everything*.
- Your yellow is the only colour in the photo.
- Just before, when we stood on the snowbank and I kissed you just under your ear, on the spot where your jaw becomes your neck.
- The spot where your jaw becomes your neck.
- The way I could make you smile by kissing you, if I was lucky. Activate your cheeks and draw your lips up into a smile and light up your face.
- Your face is almost expressionless in the ice and calm in this

candid way, maybe vaguely mad, or do I just know too much, you're framed by a triangular hole in the ice matrix.

- I promise you I don't look at this photo every day.
- There are an infinite number of ways to describe it and absolutely no ways to describe what it makes me feel and how much.
- The same is true of you.
- I should give myself time, today might not be the day, there will be more days—will there be more days—some days are better some are impossible to ~~descri~~ survive I am trying I need you to somehow know that, today has been a nightmare I am *trying,* I am not giving up.
- I promise I will tear it up today.
- I took your picture, you hated that, I knew it, I did it anyway. We were less than a hundred feet from the beach where we would have the worst day. The things I said were automatic. How could I be expected to let go of something I never got to have, I need to tear it up and get rid of it and everything behind it and beyond it, what fucking drama, I thought it was the real thing, I thought it was it—I thought it was GOING to be the real thing—did you know you were only half in it the whole time—did you try—I wish you never had to try—we always had to *try*—think, figure it out, make a rule—I thought one day it would all become perfect, how do you convince someone. You don't. How can one person be so certain, I'm insane, I have made sure to fuck up every good thing I ever had, I can never just *be.* I can never stop caring. I was sure. I said we should skinny-dip there, if summer ever finally came. You said we would. I wish you would have told me I could let go and you wouldn't disappear. I wish I could have closed my eyes or let go—you are not a passing instant

to seal in ice—you are eternal, terrifying—I could never record even a moment of you so how could I be expected not to even try? I need to get rid of this, for you—I must have known the whole time—I will get rid of this for you I'm not lying I wish you could see, I had no idea how scared I was, I *made* it happen—I did it to myself.

IT GETS HEAVY SOMETIMES

I **OBVIOUSLY** wasn't speaking to Simon the next day. It was easiest at suppertime because Simon wasn't home anyway, so even if I wanted to I couldn't have said anything to him. I made myself macaroni and cheese, and I put the entire package of cheese in too.

After supper I was sitting in the kitchen drinking milk and thinking about how much my life was ruined and then Simon came through the front door amazingly fast.

"Let's go!"

He quickly tossed some plastic bags on the counter and threw some things in the fridge. He was doing a hundred things at once and I had no idea what he was talking about.

"Arthur?" he looked me in the face. "Let's go! I found her!"

"Found who?" I said, breaking the rule about not speaking to him.

When he said her name I couldn't believe I forgot. I was forgetting everything lately, even though I *wasn't* forgetful. I jumped off my chair and ran to the *National Geographic* calendar on the fridge. Sure enough, the day said:

"Rosie."

We drove a lot quicker than Simon usually drove, which still wasn't exactly quick. But he sped our rusty red car to the very end of our road, turned left and kept on going. He drove so fast I think he might have almost been going the speed limit. I kept my forehead pressed up against the cold fogged-up window and watched the night fly by because I had a lot to think about before we found her. It was starting to rain, and the rain tapped the car all over, making music kind of, and dripping patterns down in front of my face. I imagined Rosie running through the rain in the dark. Then, running through a different country full of snowy mountains and white cougars, then running through a thick rainforest, smelly sweat all over her, never stopping for a break. I imagined her doing the whole trip in one go, never even sleeping. I bet she could.

I saw her out there all alone, with only Icebird to protect her. I thought that Icebird was a really good name for a trailer, but maybe she named it that because she actually wanted to have a gigantic blue bird, like a phoenix but made of ice-feathers, that would fly above her as she ran and carry everything she needed in a chest tied to its back. Every night when she got tired it would let her sleep under its wing and it would sing gigantic sleepy

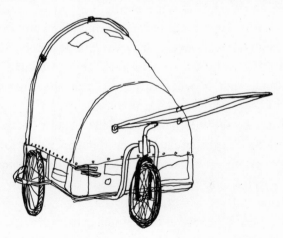

lullabies like a foghorn. I figured that must've been what she really wanted to bring on the journey with her, but she couldn't get quite enough sponsors for that so she just got a trailer instead.

I pictured her beginning in Wales and then also ending in Wales. Where her trip started and where it would finish were the exact same place, but that wasn't the important part. The parts in between were what I liked to imagine. When she got back to where she started, back to Wales, it's not like she had gone *nowhere.*

I saw her running and running still, maybe sometimes walking, maybe sometimes sleeping in a tent in a farmer's field. I saw her with enough energy to run around the whole world, even though she was old enough to be my grandmother. I wondered if it was possible she actually was my grandmother. It *was* possible. If she was, maybe that meant someday I could run around the world too, with my own grandchildren.

"When I spotted her it was right about," Simon paused, "...here."

We drove under an overpass near the highway, and the pitter-pattering of the rain shut up for a quick silence and then started again.

I looked very carefully out the window for her, but all I saw was the ditch filling with cloudy water, and power lines drooping up and down and up and down in front of the twilight sky and dark forests as we drove past them. I knew she wouldn't be that hard to spot because on her website she always had bright-coloured clothes and of course she was always pulling Icebird. We turned onto a ramp to get on the highway, because Simon said that if she was going around the world, then she'd have to head northeast out of the city. This was something that Simon didn't need to tell me, because I am not stupid.

Our car is stupid though, because it always does this stupid thing where one of the windshield wipers stops in the middle of the window and twitches like the kid on that commercial about seizures. When this happened, Simon always had to pull over and get out of the car and sort of punch the thing until it decided to snap out of it so that we could see again. This could sometimes take years to work. So he got out of the car, and as he was outside in the pouring rain doing the punching part, I thought about how it probably wouldn't work the same at all on that kid with the seizure.

Then I started to think different. Such as, what would happen when we finally found Rosie? I had been following her journey for months on her website, but she had probably never even *been* to my website. I didn't even know exactly why I wanted to see her, but I did. I had never really pictured what I would do if I saw her. I wanted to try and talk to her, obviously, because I wanted to tell her that I read her website every three days, on average, and that I thought she was really brave. And I wanted to get her autograph, so that I could hang it on my wall at home and show it to my grandchildren. I wondered if she'd be as nice as I thought she was.

Simon got back in the car and we started driving up the ramp in the dark. By then it was completely dark outside. We headed northeast on the highway for fifteen or twenty minutes without seeing anything except for a roadkill. Simon said it was a racoon but I wasn't so sure, I was pretty sure it was a mongoose or a Tasmanian devil. Maybe a zebra.

Then Simon pointed at some glowing orange dot way up ahead. When our car bounced, the orange dot strobe-lighted in the headlights, and soon it became a little orange square, then a bigger orange square with a yellow X, and then a person wearing a neon vest, and then Rosie.

She was running on the side of the road, and running slow, to be efficient. Icebird was attached to her waist with straps, and pulled behind her that way, instead of how I always thought it had handles on it, with her holding on to the front. She must have been so soaked. We pulled over onto the elbow of the highway and Simon stopped the car pretty far behind her, and she just kept running. It was weird. I felt like we were spying on her. Like we were being too sneaky; sneaky in a bad way. Our headlights were still reflecting on her back as she kept running and we spied on her. I was surprised she didn't check over her shoulder to see who was there. Lots of other cars and trucks were speeding by and they didn't know what they were missing.

"Wow," I said. I stared out the windshield watching her bright bouncy back get farther away and eventually slip back into the darkness. Half of me wanted to ask Simon to take me home. After a few minutes I looked over at him and he was already looking over at me. He asked if I wanted him to come with me. The brave half of me told him no. I took a breath that was very deep.

When I finally got out of the car, Rosie was an entire football field away from me, and the raindrops smashed my face. My hair was instantly wet and flopping in my eyes and I had to push it out of the way. I started jogging fast enough so I could catch up to her, but also slow enough so I could not catch up to her for a while. Why I was so hesitating, who knows? I practised things in my brain.

"Hi my name is Arthur Williams and you haven't met me yet but I go on your website every three days on average and I hope you enjoyed running through my town and you are really brave."

Too long. I kept jogging.

"Hi my name is Arthur Williams and I am ten years old and I am your biggest fan that I know of and I think it's amazing that you are going all the way around the whole world and you must be glad the world isn't flat anymore because what if you fell off the side and will you sign this hankie for my grandchildren?"

Even longer. And I wasn't saying what I really wanted to say. What *did* I want to say? I tried to calm down and make sense.

"Hi my name is Arthur Williams and sometimes I wish I was running around the world too and what was your favourite place so far and did you ever feel like it was too hard for you and maybe you should just quit and how much money have you raised so far and how many orphans does that save and don't your feet ever start to hurt and is it possible you might be my grandmother?"

I couldn't stop babbling even though my mouth wasn't open yet. Then I noticed how close I was getting, and even though I hadn't unboggled myself yet I was only a few more steps from Rosie, and I tried to slow down but it was too late and then she was right beside me.

Rosie looked down at me and her eyes widened and reflected Simon's lights down the road. Her sand-coloured hair was wet and bounced around. She looked surprised to see me at first, and then maybe happy. She smiled at me. It was more than a smile, it was one of the biggest smiles I'd ever seen. She had a huge grin on her face. For some reason, I had usually imagined her as sad. Brave, but sad.

"Well, hello!" she said, and slowed down until we stopped running.

A ball of words appeared in my brain and then somehow teleported to my throat. I wasn't sure what the words were, but Rosie was staring at me and the throat bubble just burst out of my mouth and unravelled itself out of my control.

"HimynameisArthurWilliamsandtenyearsoldyou'rereally brave!"

I am such a *moron* sometimes. Rosie laughed, probably because of how loud and squeaky I was. Then she just smiled again. She tapped me on the shoulder and said, "Come on."

We ran together. I stayed right beside her and kept the same speed, even though I could have run so much faster. We ran beside the highway, through puddles and mud and tried to avoid squishing the worms on the ground, and the cold rain soaked all the way through my sweater and my t-shirt to my skin. We ran past hundreds of trees and rocks and families of bugs and animals in the woods too dark to see. We ran below nighttime airplane flights and whole flocks of owls, and above whole cities of millions of tiny ants underground. The rain slid down our faces splashing on the ground. Her face was smiling, and after a while mine was too. Technically, we were heading for Wales. We ran on our one little planet that was called Earth, in the middle of an infinity of other galaxies. The line we were drawing made a squiggly circle around the whole globe.

After a while, I wished that Icebird had handles like I thought it would, because then maybe I could help her pull it for a while.

For some reason I thought that would be a very nice and brave thing to do. Another more scared part of me really wanted to just curl up inside Icebird and follow her for the rest of the trip. I just wanted to be more than a silly boy who ran beside her for two minutes. Maybe I could help her on the journey, and be her personal assistant or something. I sort of hooked my arm through the trailer's strap and tried to pull it that way. It was a stupid idea, really, because it would have actually just made it harder for her to pull. It was a weird angle. Or at least, it didn't seem like I was making much difference at all, and also I don't know if Rosie even noticed until Icebird bumped a little rock and jolted sideways all over the place.

She slowed down when she felt the trailer wobble. We stopped running.

"Whoo-oops," she said, with her quick voice and her accent, "you okay?"

"Yeah," I said. "Sorry."

She straightened her back out and raised her arms over her head, and leaned back to stretch. She took some really deep breaths. I didn't know what to do, so I copied her back stretch, and then I did some jumping jacks for some reason. I forgot that I'm not very good at jumping jacks. So I stopped.

There were so many questions I wasn't asking. There were so many things I wasn't telling her. I wanted to ask her for her autograph and I wanted to ask how much money we were raising. I took my handkerchief out of my pants pocket for the autograph but when she smiled at me, my heart felt weird and I wiped the rain off my face with it instead. I put it back in my pocket. I wanted to ask her if her feet were aching, and what size shoes she had. I wanted to ask about her husband. I wanted to ask if he was the true love of her life. Mostly, I needed to tell her all about Phil and how he was dead too and how awful that was. I had to tell her about my investigation and how I was only going around a whole street instead of a whole planet but it felt like the same thing. I had to tell her about how Simon had ruined it all. There was no way she wouldn't be able to help me out, I mean, she was running around the *entire* world.

I closed my eyes for a second and manufactured some courage. She had her back to me and was looking towards the woods. I tapped her on the arm. She turned around really quick and I panicked inside my brain.

"Your husband died of cancer," I almost screamed. I turned paralysed and swallowed so hard that it felt like it cut my throat. My feet scrunched up in my boots and my eyes shivered.

Rosie just looked at me. She was *still* smiling.

"Yes, he did." she said.

"And he was the true love of your life."

Rosie nodded. When she noticed that my eyes were starting to cry a little bit, she unhooked her waist straps and knelt down and gave me a hug. She was being very nice. She even said "Thanks for helping pull Icebird. It gets heavy sometimes."

The thing was that even though she was being so nice, I knew I was a complete *moron*. I hadn't helped her pull Icebird at all, really, and even if I did it was for about thirty seconds. I blew it, and she was just trying to make me feel better. I couldn't even ask her a *question*. She was hugging *me* because *her* husband died of cancer, and that didn't even make any sense. And she still knew nothing about Phil, and who *knows* if she was my grandmother. I still wanted to get her autograph, but I sure wasn't going to then, when she was hugging me like a baby.

I stopped hugging her and quickly got rid of my tears with my sleeve as best as I could. At least it was raining.

"You're a good kid. You're an absolute star," she said. "Everything's going to turn out fine."

"Thanks," I said, but I couldn't tell her about how nothing would ever turn out fine because Phil was dead and that was a real thing that happened and I couldn't make it not happen no matter how hard I tried, and I couldn't say that even if I was a star I was just one single tiny star in the middle of a whole universe of darkness, and that I thought maybe if I met her I would get bigger or brighter like her but of course I wouldn't. Because she was just one tiny person too and I couldn't believe I didn't know that until I saw her and she was real. Because she had to tie her shoes and wear her raincoat and get exhausted and cry like everybody else, and I was an idiot because I thought she was more special and brave than everyone but really I was just less.

I didn't tell her that we had something in common which was that someone we knew everything about died, and now we were going to places we'd never been before trying to find something that didn't exist. I didn't tell her that we had something not in common which was that *she* was actually good at it. I didn't ask her for help.

I just stopped hugging her and I said "Goodbye" and turned around towards the car. It was close to us which was weird because Simon must have been driving behind us really slowly the entire time so we could see better.

"Is that your dad in there?" Rosie asked.

I didn't tell her how my real dad is not my real dad.

"No," I said, and I ran back to the stupid car.

SMALL

When it happens it's like I all of a sudden get this feeling of deep
deep dread and I notice I've only been watching myself live. I
looked it up, it's a symptom of stuff—so much time passes me
unnoticed—hours or days or even whole months without having
one moment of full consciousness, I'm not in control, there is a
main character but it's not me, I'm not myself, I'm a list of every
characteristic of me and other sub-lists and histories of *Why I
Came to Be This Way* and *How I Try to Fix It*, and life is one long
detachment, a reading of the list, and my consciousness is just
like a tallying-up, an accounting-for of this precise meaningless
sum of myself.

Then I get this sudden jolt of a moment—some crisis or some
blessing rattles me all the way down into a new complete pres-
ence of my body, I realize and know my age with complete gripping terror, can remember each and every day and feel all their
moments and I'm under the precise weight of all that has passed,
the days are enormous, and in my gut are all the days still to
come. And I panic and my only panicked desire is to learn to
start existing IN THE DAYS and to never forget again—

And when it happens Phil zooms so far out and he shrinks
and now he's so so tiny, the top of his head is not five inches from
the grey carpet. He walks around his apartment and his little

life completely horrified in his new size, he already had enough and now this boundless detachment of mind and shrinking—what will crush him? It won't need to be much—an empty milk carton will easily topple and finish it all—a cereal bowl abandoned in the sink will be more than enough to drown inside, when he's this small death is SO CLOSE IT CROUCHES AND WAITS FOR HIM behind every chair leg it leaps down on him from every shelf he can't see it because it's EVERYWHERE. The gigantic world corners Phil out of nowhere until there's nowhere to hide but farther and farther inward and so he shrinks to cut the world off in its closing in—but now it's so enormous it's even more horrifying but there is space so much space if he could just get to it and someone once told him when an animal *thinks* it will die it panics but when it *knows*, when it is within inches bleeding to death and it *knows* and it is waiting, then it is so calm, it lies still, it can feel the space around it so vividly, it *knows*—it's almost high, euphoric—it's like *that*, and when E was his she responded immediately, she knelt down and opened her palm. She laid the back of her hand against the rough carpet and held it flat and Phil would step up onto one of her soft fingertips and walk towards her palm, stepping over the first then second pink creases on the belly of her thin finger then over the warm sterling silver bands on the borders between finger and hand. Her skin is so different from this viewpoint, so many more folds and lines moving in all directions making a stark texture under Phil's small shoes. In some ways it is like walking on the smallest desert planet but in so many ways it is *exactly* like being in the hand of the only person who took the time to really know him. Her magnified hand with its strange lines overwhelms him with its intricacy, a delicate perfection, he IS NOT ASHAMED to call it that. As he shrinks she only grows more perfect.

She lifts her hand from the floor and raises it slowly, carefully keeping her palm and her tiny lover upright, until the side of her pinky comes to rest against her collarbone, and Phil jumps up and grabs hold of her shoulder and pulls himself up. He sits there on her shoulder, on the soft furry terrain of that camel-brown sweater she wore so often, the one that matched her. He reaches and pulls some of her golden hair close to him and wraps himself inside its curl, and he sits and waits out the panic and the smallness. E puts on a movie and sits on the couch. She puts on something funny, or something beautiful or sad, and they watch. She says nothing about his shrunkenness, she doesn't make fun or ask why. They sit and watch and of course the movies are all about them and Phil casts them in the roles of the characters. When the movie gets too tedious—as movies do—they turn it off and brainstorm ending after ending and act them out, until they come up with an ending more fantastic and ridiculous and devastating and resonating than the dumb movie would have ever come up with. They make the very best endings—it's as if it's what they're really meant to do.

But now he shrinks and there's no hand to climb into and no warm shoulder—there's the cold white linoleum of the kitchen floor, endless violent things in all directions, him hugging his knees curled up against the baseboard foetal, tortured, still inventing ending after ending, and all of them dark and huge and close, him waiting. And my larger self somehow remains. My larger self walking around the kitchen hideous scrambling eggs and dropping knives in the sink, and Small Phil in this post-hysterical calm and mangled in the mousetrap and not yet killed but waiting and he is mystified by everything I do. Look at the way he walks, with his head hanging, does he actually pick his nose so often? Does he really not return June's call from last week, can he really not bear to even put the phone so close to his face, does he realize it's been five days since he said a word out loud?

And when I finally get to sleep Small Phil climbs to the top of my head and sits there looking off into the void and when watching himself among the hugeness grows too much to stand Small Phil crawls inside my ear and it's lightless and full of loud dull noise like a distended thud of a drum with no beginning no end—and he's in the stacks, he is passing through dark rows of bookcases yanking out the unfortunate books crushed and flattened at the bottoms of the stacks and dragging them back to the top. It's extremely difficult in his size and it takes hours, finding a heavy doorstop to wedge in the stack and wiggling and tugging and kicking a poor book until it budges and can finally be slid out. Then with all his strength he totters and heaves the broken book upward balancing it precariously onto a protruding edge of one higher, climbs up and moves it a bit farther by the same method, bit by bit, one gargantuan book and one miniscule inch at a time, until every underdog and loser and overlooked and underestimated book has its shot.

Then he gets on his stomach and slips under the library's back door and he's back in the blinding fluorescence of the warehouse, filing and refiling. He writes a new user's manual to the warehouse for me, mumbling and scratching at paper, he is outlining a simpler way, a hopeful way, a way that's realistic, possible. He repaints the filing cabinets and polishes them with a scrap of rag.

And when he's done he crawls back out and sits on top of my alarm clock and waits for me to wake up. He gets impatient and steps on the buttons setting the alarm an hour earlier. He drags my pills out into the middle of the hallway floor so I can't miss them. He goes through my mammoth notebook crossing out words.

And God smiles down on this tiny saintly Phil and Small Phil kneels, he has such warm faith and he is so certain in his blind calm, waiting for me to wake, he puts his small hands together and says a small prayer for huge me despite his knowledge and despite himself and despite the sureness and gentle crushing of everything he prays for me and for my mind and my heart and for the huge things I won't ever learn and can't be taught and all I haven't done, he prays for some end to everything. ~~He asks for my soul to be spared, he asks for it to return to my body, he asks it to exist~~

He sits talking with God and waiting and he says to himself He's going to be OK. I know it. Soon, he's going to be just fine.

And God says Of course. Of course.

~~GONE~~

Then she was leaving. She'd talked about leaving all summer, we both had, but then she was really doing it. In a few weeks she'd be gone and there would be no more needy half-reunions, no more vicious contests. There would be no more laughter, or moments of sudden understanding, nothing tender.

He kept his distance because he had to. She was so busy. There were worlds of things she had to do, and no more worlds for them to drift to, no more space. Time was the denominator of every situation they found themselves in, good or bad or anywhere in between: he pretended to hate her, how she could and would and wanted to disappear so easily, they smashed each other to pieces, or they came together and slid into a desperate tough spot where everything became so unclear and honest again and they loved each other so completely and cautiously, not because things now made sense, but because every day was the last day. ~~But it wasn't love, this last time. It was time.~~

Just fucking tell it like it IS. You went by her house tonight.

It's not even her house anymore, and you had to walk five blocks out of your way in one direction and then four in the other, and it was the coldest night yet but you went there anyway because that's just the type of thing you would do.

When you got close you pictured yourself just walking by like it was any other house on the street, and for about twenty seconds you'd actually convinced yourself that was something you were capable of.

Just don't make it up! It's pathetic but own it and say it anyway! It's all there is, you stopping and standing under her window and leaning on the tree. You thinking about how the light feels the same, the twilight, how twilight is right between day and night—how it's the start of an ending. You standing thinking about that for so much longer than you should have. Standing precisely in the last place you ever saw her. When she left so immediately. Unreasonably. Not even telling anyone exactly which day—and you climbed the stairs that night and knocked and she was just gone. Who does that? Who just disappears?

YOU DON'T EVEN KNOW HOW TO TALK TO YOURSELF ABOUT IT. You don't even know who you ARE. Stop hiding! Who is "Phil"? You don't know who you're talking to!—you haven't decided if you are listening!

And she was so much still there, beside the tree, the streetlight shining yellow through the leaves and her hair, she was so there that it showed you one more time how much she isn't. How the city is a parody of itself, a husk. How many times will you have to remember? It's WINTER now. IT'S NOT EVEN THE SAME SEASON NOW. Soon it won't be the same YEAR. It's not the same ANYTHING.

But you went anyway! You stopped on the sidewalk and looked up at her window and it was lit up and you pretended no one else lived there now because how could they?—how could anyone else live in the room you used to spend half your life

in—maybe more? The room where you were thrilled and com-
forted, blessed, where you were heard, where you finally felt
safe. The only room you belonged in. That warm room—how
could they have thrown out her plants, and why didn't you ever
remember what they were called, and how could they use the
same white curtain?

You walked home crying but that's normal for you, it's a
50/50 gamble these days whether you'll be in tears before you
make it to the door or after.

Then you checked her email. Because you still know her
password because she hasn't changed it. You read the message
from her brother, from her dad, from her best friend. Her ex-
boyfriend had not written. A new boyfriend had not written.
(This didn't make you feel better.) There was no mention of you
in any of the messages. You searched your name and a sentence
from an ancient message came up, with the word "*philo*sophy."
"*Phil*istine" came up. "Pedo*phile*." But not you. You marked the
messages as unread. You started to write her a message from
herself telling herself to please change her password, but you
didn't send it. You deleted it. (Emails are easy to delete. Other
things aren't.) (If only you could ask God to find every place
someone existed in your life and delete them all one by one. Or
every moment you existed in your own life—

GONE.

Like two weeks before you vanished I went to visit you at work—
you were filling in for a friend at the store—and I went to find
you on a slow Saturday. The place was deserted except for you.
When I came in the door you jumped up and ran out from the
desk and hugged me. We weren't together but we weren't not

together, and you weren't cold. You were warm. How could we ever hug in any acceptable way, in any civilized or neutral way? Our hugs even now—especially now—were too tight, too long and too close, and my chin always wanting to touch the soft skin open on your shoulder and it does—the hug that too many times and too easily turns into a hug full of sparks, and a gravity and a pulling close, and you putting your cheek against mine and the tiny blond hairs glowing all over our skin at the near-microscopic level brushing and our noses touching, us kissing, gently and slowly like we always tried, it was unspoken, giving, and our legs getting tired from standing for so long, then sitting on the edge of your bed when I only came over to ask you something, to just make something clear, but then look at us: lying there untogether, and holding unclearly for so long—

In the store we talked about our days like always, like we used to when we would every day, we became archives of each other's days, we had catalogues of each other's past year stored inside, and would remember every day of each other and share it all, and that was really one of the best parts—everyone knew that. But now day- and week-sized gaps were passing unaccounted for, so much time I couldn't picture you inside: what did you do yesterday, or the day before? What did I do? Anything?

We talked. About whatever. We talked about the music. We talked about the sun, other things. But we were pretending to stand so far from each other. I could feel myself growing stubborn, could feel myself splitting, slipping into a darkened mind, wanting—I could feel some place inside grow, and I didn't want to go there so I left. I said I should go and I went out the door. You were probably mad, but I had to go. Maybe I was even proud of myself for leaving. Seeing you now was watching a family carrying all their belongings out of the house and into the trunk of their station wagon. It was watching things get packed away in brown boxes, hearing a door close in some other room. It was a drive to an airport and it was waiting for a flight to take off. It was all of these things but it was *none* of them because it was something real and it was *really* happening to me, and it would make me cry walking down the street because this ending had no sense of public or private or tact and it found me everywhere. And maybe I can't believe I left you that day or that I'd ever leave you or refuse a minute with you, but it was impossible. It was impossible to pretend you'd still be in my life—impossible to keep pretending I was ever really in yours. You'd be gone.

WHY

WHAT BEING ALONE SOUNDS LIKE

CLUES:
- How you can't possibly think of anything else.
- How even when you think you're not thinking about it any-
  more you actually are.
- How it makes you really angry but you know angry is the
  wrong thing to be so you get even more angry.

When I got home from babbling to Rosie and making an idiotic moron of myself I went to my room and took off my soaking wet clothes. My wool sweater and t-shirt both already kind
of smelled like laundry that got forgotten in the washer too
long. They smelled like an old people's home, and they made a
flop sound when I tossed them in my hamper. I went to the bathroom and grabbed a towel and fluffed my hair with it all over. I
combed my hair, brushed my teeth, went back to my room and
locked the door.

I opened my closet, reached in and pulled all the clues off
of my bulletin board. I boggled them around on the floor to try
to put them in a better order. Then I took some new scraps of
paper and a marker from my desk and sat on the floor with my
legs crossed like a Native American and all the clues in my lap. I
made some new ones.

CLUES:

- How I will never be as brave as Rosie even though she is only a normal person.

Simon knocked on my door, *bang bang bang*.

"Yeah?" I got up quickly and tossed the clues back in my closet.

"Whatcha doin' in there?"

"Nothing!"

"What?"

I went over and unlocked the door and Simon was holding his glasses at his side with one hand and scrubbing his eyelids with the other. There was a book tucked under his arm. He snapped his eyes open wide and smiled at me.

"Whatcha doin', chief?"

"Getting ready for bed."

"Want a story?" The book he was holding was some red and blue covered thing I had never seen before.

"I'm really tired."

Simon frowned a little and put his big glasses back on his small face.

"Something wrong?"

"No. Something wrong with you?"

"Me? No, I don't think so," he said.

I turned around and sat down on my bed. I was obviously still kind of mad at him.

"Pretty big night tonight," he said.

"Yep."

I wasn't very interested in being read to by Simon. And like I already said, I wasn't exactly in an extraordinary mood, and besides, maybe Maureen wanted him to read *her* a story instead. On the phone, maybe. And then when the story was done she could ask him to marry her.

Simon put his hands in his pockets and walked over to one of my really old to-do lists that was still up on the wall. Lots of things were checked off but lots of things weren't. He looked at it for a while, but he seemed like he wasn't even reading it. I could tell because of how his lips slid sideways away from each other that he was thinking about something else. He took his hands out of his pockets, straightened the list and pushed the tack a bit deeper into the wall with his strong skinny thumb. Then he sat on my bed beside me.

"I'm sorry," he said.

"I'm still kind of mad."

"I know chief, I know. I'm sorry I didn't—"

"So you're going to give it back?"

"The book? No, I can't give it back. Not yet."

I knew he wouldn't anyway.

"Well then I'm still mad."

"I know. If I were you I'd be upset too. But I'm me, so for now I'm going to keep it, and I'm sorry."

I didn't even bother rolling my eyes.

"Listen, about Maureen, I—"

"You didn't call 9-1-1 did you?"

"About the book?"

"Obviously."

"No, I didn't do that. I'm still not sure what to do, to be honest."

He scratched his neck.

"Maureen's just—"

"I don't wanna talk about it."

Simon scratched his neck again.

"You don't *have* to be like this," I said.

"Like what?"

"Like a security guard or something."

"For now, I do."

"I didn't do anything wrong."

"No, you didn't. You're right."

"You don't make any sense."

Simon shook his head and looked at the carpet.

"The whole thing doesn't make much sense," he said.

"What does *that* mean?"

"I mean, how could somebody... I don't know. It seems so contrived almost, not contrived but—I don't know. You found it in the woods?"

"Yes."

"In our woods, right here?"

"Yeah, I already told you that."

"I know. It just doesn't make much sense."

"What are you talking about? I just found it in the woods lying there on the ground, I told you that a billion times."

Then he leaned down at me until I looked him in the eyes and he was making a completely serious look like he was a worried boulder. He said "Are you okay?" and I said "Yes." Then he said "Arthur, tell me the truth. Are you okay?" and I felt weird because he was being a little scary with how serious he was, and I said *"Yes."*

Simon didn't talk for a while, then he said "Alright. We'll discuss the book in a few days when I've... when I've given it more thought."

"Fine."

"So, no story?"

"No." I was about to tell him that there was actually one book he could read me a story from if he wanted, and that it had a black and white speckly cover and that it was probably hidden somewhere in the house, but I didn't.

"You brush your teeth?" Simon asked.

"Mmm-hmm."

"Okay. I love you."

"Sure."

Simon got up and stood with his hand on the light switch, waiting for me to get under the covers. I did, and he flicked the light off.

"Night, chief."

"Night."

My door closed and made complete blackness. That's maybe my favourite part of the day: when I can close my eyes and it looks the exact same as when I open my eyes. Not even Simon could wreck it. I stared up at the ceiling and saw nothing, and closed my eyes and saw nothing. Still nothing when I opened them again. Then my eyes woke up and started working overtime, and I saw the bright beginnings of some things. I became the pencil eraser guy on the black page of my room.

I saw a speck of yellowish white in the middle of the darkness and I rubbed at it with my eyes. Then at another and another one, and I could see the stars on my ceiling. I drew white lines to show some of the constellations. I erased white outlines for the pieces of paper on my walls, and then filled in the rectangles one by one. My glow-in-the-dark light switch, a few stray shirts, my half-finished igloo: brick by brick I erased all the bright things into my bedroom. It's silly, but I even scratched away with my mind and drew the Beckhams' white cat lemniscating at the foot of my bed, and Rosie's reflecting vest hanging on my coat hook. I could draw my own universe, if I wanted. I could make things exist that didn't, because in my room the big bang was *me*.

Finally when I closed my eyes there was nothing, but when I opened them: everything. I closed them again and let go of everything and drifted asleep.

MY EYES SLAMMED open and the rain wasn't falling inside my room and Rosie wasn't there. I was all confused in the brain. Did that stuff really happen? I was in my bed. There were my stars and my light switch. My igloo. It was a pile of white bricks on my floor, because it fell over again. That's probably why I was awake.

I lay there. It was one of those times when you think your dream life is real and your real life is fake. My brain started switching them back around. It must have been thinking about Rosie the instant I fell asleep and then turned it all into a dream.

In my dream Rosie said "What do you mean he's not your dad?" and I told her about how I didn't know who my real parents were and she asked me if I wanted to know very badly and I said yes and she asked why and I said I didn't know.

We were running on the side of the highway. The sky was pitch black. Instead of Icebird we were pulling a handle attached to our rusty car with Simon in the driver's seat reading a red and blue book. He never looked up, he just kept reading page after page really fast, and it was raining inside the car but there were windshield wipers attached to the top of his glasses and one of them was broken so he had to keep flicking it with his finger to make it go again.

I told Rosie that I was just about to crack the case of Phil when stupid Simon took him away. I told her there was no way that *no one* on the street had clues about Phil. I told her I only had one house left. We were getting soaked. I was really out of breath because we were sprinting full speed.

Then Rosie steered the trailer-car around a bend in the road and we went up a little gravel hill. She wasn't saying anything about all the stuff I was telling her, she was just silent and running.

Then we slowed down, and eventually stopped. I waited for her to say something but she didn't.

I looked around and realized where she'd brought me. The highway wasn't the highway anymore even though it had been the whole time: now it was my own curvy old street, and we were standing in the rain at the end of a gravel driveway and a hundred footsteps up ahead was the hermit's house.

There was one lonely orange window lit up.

I stared at the house. I was just about to ask Rosie what I should do and then I was awake.

I lay there wiping my forehead with my blanket, because it was wet for some reason. I couldn't tell if it was sweat water or rain water. The dream was so real, I could even remember what my hands felt like on the handle of the trailer-car. I could still feel the cold metal on my wet palm. I could still see the hermit's house. In the dream I was confused, but somehow I wasn't scared.

I sat up. My alarm clock said 1:43 and my body said "go back to sleep," but I was saying something different. I peeled my blanket off of me. I switched on my lamp and looked at all the superheroes all over my sheets, with all their flashy orange suits and huge round muscles and small pants. None of *them* looked like they'd needed to sleep a night in their lives. I tossed all the superheroes off of me and turned to the floor. I yawned my mouth so wide.

After I scrubbed everything out of my eyes, I stood up. There was a giant pile of clothes in front of my closet, because I was being so distracted and messy for the past couple weeks. I searched through the pile to find warm things. I picked out a dry black sweater and put it on top of my t-shirt. I put my black corduroys on below that. For some reason, even though I mostly hate them, I put socks on. I knew it was going to be cold. What I *wished* I could put on were my silence boots, but I didn't even have any.

I was the groggiest I'd ever been. There were the driest but stickiest snots ever in my nose, the kind that are no fun to pick because they itch. My whole scalp itched too and I felt sweaty all over. My mouth tasted like what I imagine coffee would taste like: disgusting.

Like a little field mouse I tiptoed out of my room, up the stairs, across the hall, to Simon's door. I looked at the doorknob, and wondered if it was going to squeak, and wondered if it was a friend or enemy. I couldn't believe I didn't even know whether Simon's doorknob was squeaky or not. What kind of investigation was I running anyway, without even having my own house on the back of my hand? I yawned, with no sound. I asked the doorknob, with my eyes, to help. Someone once told me that our bodies use a language that is a million times easier to understand than when we talk with words. I figured that it didn't work on doorknobs, but still. With my eyes I told it the whole story. It stared back at me, but not with eyes, obviously, because it was a doorknob. Still, in its metal way I thought I could hear it saying, well, I think it said, "Open sesame." So I turned it with the carefullest fingers I had, and I pushed on it. The door opened smoothly and completely silent.

"Thanks, doorknob," said my eyes.

"No problem, brother," whispered the doorknob.

I only opened the door Arthur-wide so that I'd fit through sideways, but not too much light would shine in from the hall. The hall was pretty dark anyway, but I couldn't be too careful. I slipped through, into the room. It was darker in there than the night itself was: there was a dim grey glow poking in from the window, in lines, creeping in between the blinds. The lines fell onto Simon's bed where he was sleeping on his back like a dead mummy. He was snoring, and I was glad. It was good to be able to know for sure that he was sleeping. I snuck over to the other corner of the room by the window, to his desk.

I opened the top left drawer with silence, which took about two ice ages. I looked inside. Paperclips and a pencil; that was it. I shut it just as slowly. Every movement I made so amazingly slow that they made no sounds. I inched the next drawer open. It was full of folders and paper, so much paper. I pulled on the bottom drawer and it squeaked. I turned into an ice sculpture of myself. The squeak was really loud, and on top of it I probably squeaked too. I waited. There was still snoring. I thawed myself out. There ended up being nothing at all in that drawer. Dust.

I left the squeaky drawer half open, because I didn't want to risk another sound. I must have been looking in those drawers for fifteen minutes, and nothing. Simon rolled over. I was starting to go a bit mental. I took a deep breath and sighed, a really slow sigh, to stay quiet and calm.

I took a good look at the top of the desk for the first time. Simon's laptop was there, and a mug full of pens and pencils. Beside that, there was a framed picture of me. Even though it was so dark I recognized the picture, it was this one where I'm in a yellow raincoat and I'm tiny, and I have my hammer and some blocks of wood on the ground in front of me. I'm in the woods near where the treehouse is and in the background you can see only half the treehouse because it's not all built yet. Simon isn't in the picture, because he took it, obviously. I look like I'm uselessly banging on the blocks of wood with my hammer for some reason, but also I look happy. The picture made me smell a smell in my brain that I hadn't smelled in forever, which smelled almost like the woods, and kind of like chocolate chip cookies baking, and then for a second I felt like I was way older than ten years old. Then I snapped out of looking at the picture and looked over on the far right side of the desk and I saw Phil.

"Right under your nose, man!" said the doorknob.

I couldn't believe Simon left it out in the open like that. Was he stupid? I felt weird picking it up. I held it tight in my hands, and I realized that maybe he didn't hide it really well because maybe he trusted me. All of the sudden I felt like a bank robber. The moon glow from the window blinds made stripes on my black sweater like it was a bank-robbing sweater on TV. I felt bad that he trusted me. I felt like a murderer. But I was trying to be the opposite.

I held onto the book anyway and tiptoed back to the door. I took another look at Simon. He was on his side now with his back towards me, and he was still snoring.

"Good luck, brother," said the doorknob, and I closed the door with him, giving him a quiet high-five.

Back in my room, I packed my backpack, putting in Phil last. I looked over the clues, and then I left my room. In the kitchen I pulled the biggest knife out of the wooden thing that holds our knives and I wrapped it in a dishcloth and quietly put it in my backpack too, which made me feel a little mental but also a little safer. When I got to the hallway I got a funny feeling. I went back to my room and picked up a bright green towel from my clothes pile, for some reason. I tied two corners of it around my neck like a cape.

Then I left. I was super quiet, and I snuck down the hall and past the kitchen and out the front door. It was definitely the first time I'd been outside by myself at two in the morning. It was just me and my breath. Every time I exhaled there was a puff of ice in front of me. I wanted to breathe on somebody and completely freeze them, not to be a jerk, but so that they could wake up in the future like I read about on Wikipedia before.

"Where am I?"

"I'm Doctor Arthur Williams, welcome to the year 3000."

"Where is my family?"

"There are some things we must sacrifice for the sake of science."

"You mean to tell me that I was just about to sit down to a lovely lasagna dinner, and now suddenly it's the year 3000 and you think that's just *grand?*"

"Isn't it fantastic?"

"Take me back."

But meanwhile back in the actual year, I was walking up the first small hill of our street, away from my house. I'd definitely walked up that street five thousand times in the past two weeks, but still it felt a little different every time.

This time the walk was longer and more freezing than ever. And darker. Gosh was it dark. I could kind of see my feet moving, and that was it. Our street had barely any streetlights, I guess 'cause of how far it was from downtown, and I could see absolutely nothing without my flashlight. I couldn't find the moon anywhere, even though I knew it was somewhere. I shone my flashlight to stay alive.

As usual when I walked, or as usual when I did anything at all, my brain became an infinite list of questions and memories. There was the hermit's *house,* first of all, and how terrible and destroyed it looked. There was the fact that I had only ever seen it from halfway up the driveway, and it still looked amazingly spooky. I knew it had a porch with a broken railing, and no railing at all in some spots. And the whole thing was damp and grey looking, and wood showed through the grey paint in really big patches on the front.

Then also Finch had told me that the hermit ate kids. While Finch was generally a person full of crap, it was still in my head. More realistic, I'd also heard he was a thief. And that no one ever actually *saw* the guy because he was such an anti-socialist. He stayed home, and then hunted his own meals in the woods after dark. To sum up everything I knew: he was a murderer, a cannibal, a crack dealer (whatever "crack" was), a robber, a vegetarian, an insane asylum patient, and he owned a bunch of guns. I wasn't stupid enough to believe that he was every one of those things, but even if he was only two or three of them I had a problem. Plus, I wasn't exactly as prepared as I wished I was. I didn't have my camouflage suit or my silence boots or anything. I figured maybe I'd just try to go right up and knock on the door first and try to just be normal, and then if anything especially evil happened, I'd have to improvise. When I imagined improvising my knees started to get shakier. I could feel the not-sharp side of the kitchen knife pushing against a bump on my spine.

My footsteps were getting closer and closer together. I was halfway there. My throat started to do funny things, like sometimes it would forget how to swallow, or try to swallow a big lump and get all shaky and tight. I stopped walking, and turned all around and pointed my flashlight quickly at everything. Nothing was around. I kept walking. There weren't really any sounds around either. Well, it just sounded like God was rubbing two pieces of paper together, forever. What I mean is, in that dark early morning on my street the wind wasn't quite silent, but it was close. It softly flicked millions of leaves in the woods all at the same time, so it made this *hiss, hiss* sound through the trees, and that's all I could hear. I figured it was what being alone sounds like.

When I was thirty steps from the hermit's driveway my legs started acting up. They sort of loosened up and shook around, as if my scared brains were in my kneecaps instead of my skull. My heart punched my stomach and the brains inside my kneecaps were asking "What the hell are we doing?" and I kept walking even though my whole body was thinking all over the place.

The driveway was about four times longer than all the other driveways on the street, and it went up a little hill at first with tall trees making dark walls on both sides, then it curved up to the left as the hill got steeper. I shone my flashlight up it for a while, but it wasn't much use. From the road, you couldn't really see where it went.

This was it. I was actually at the hermit's house and it was actually the middle of the most pitch black night. I was probably going to die. Here it was: the last day of my life. I was only ten years old. I hadn't even become anything yet. All suddenly I got this empty feeling inside of me, as if my whole body was a completely empty jar and time was on pause. I stood there on pause and even though it was springtime, the breeze was cold enough on the back of my neck that my bones shivered. And it was just so black. What the hell was I doing? The crazy hermit wasn't going to know anything about Phil; he didn't even leave the house. The trees hissed. It was the last house to check. I had to do it. I'd made a promise inside myself. I couldn't just give up. It's not like Rosie just *gives up* every time God decides it's going to get cold and dark.

I thought about Phil and Page 43 and maybe it was just because I was so groggy and my brain was mental but somehow I all of the sudden realized I didn't even care if I died. Or I cared, because it might hurt for a minute and Simon might be amazingly sad, but I also didn't care because if I actually did die it would be while I was trying to do the most important thing, so my life would have been a good life.

"Hello God," I said out loud. "Whatever you do, please don't let me get cannibalized."

I took one deep breath and then I was sprinting up the hill full speed, shining my flashlight on anything scary as I ran. I kept running like that, I just felt like it—like if I just kept going so *fast* and if I never lost my momentum then nothing could catch me and I couldn't chicken out. I ran up the curvy driveway, through all the mucky leaves covering the gravel and I didn't even think about the gravel on the beach because my brain was so empty and I went right up to the house without losing my momentum, splashing leaves everywhere the whole time.

I jumped up the four squeaky steps to the porch and rang the doorbell before Scared Arthur could tell me not to. Scared Arthur wasn't quite as fast as me. He was still running up the driveway and it was exactly when the doorbell ding-donged so loudly that he caught up and stood inside me so that we became the same Arthur and I realized. It was two in the morning. The porch light was on, but that didn't mean he was awake. I was so paranoid and I felt *so* annoying, and what happens if you annoy a cannibal?

I barely had the time to think about it before my knees started vibrating again. I crunched up my fists and made a squeak and stood there. I kept standing there. A sound came from inside the door and I was about to run but I closed my eyes. *Hello God, Hello God, Hello...*

I heard the door creak and I opened my eyes.

"Hello?" someone said.

It was an old man in a wheelchair.

"Hi," I tried to say but I didn't say anything.

The man smiled at me.

"Mr. Williams—what a delight—what the devil are you doing here, if you don't mind me asking? Shouldn't you be in bed?"

I couldn't say anything.

"Come in, first of all! Come-in-come-in-come-in!"

"How do you know who—"

"Come in!"

He was flapping his hand like a fish's tail.

I unlocked my knees. I looked backwards at the driveway and the yard, and I really hoped it wouldn't be the last time I ever saw the world. Then I slowly started to move inside the house, tiptoeing.

The man spun his wheelchair halfway around, in three tiny jerks, as if he'd been practising the move for years. He smoothly rolled through a doorway and into his living room, like how a swan swims. I mean like how a swan doesn't have to go really slow-motion to be smooth, and they can go pretty fast but still stay smooth. That's exactly how the man drove his wheelchair.

"Sit-down-sit-down-sit-down!"

I looked around the place and decided on the big red couch. It was red and black plaid, like a lumberjack couch. Somehow it was excruciatingly hard for me to do anything normal like sit down on a couch or breathe. But I eventually made it over to the red couch and it was so poofy that I sank really deep into the cushion. I put my backpack on the table right in front of me, which was so close to the couch that my legs almost didn't fit in between. I was still so shaky and my heart was still fast but I manufactured some more bravery and started the routine. I took out the tape recorder, set it down and popped it open. I slid a brand new blank tape into it and pressed RECORD. But I didn't want to give myself away completely, so I left Phil in my backpack for right then. The man just watched me start recording as if it wasn't weird at all, as if people came over to his cottage every day at two in the morning and recorded tapes of him.

"How are you *doing*, Arthur boy?"

Could he read my mind and see my name in there? I told him I was fine.

"You seem a bit... shaken up, I might notice." He had a way of saying half a sentence fast and half of it slow that somehow made it easy to listen to him. It made him sound kind of smooth or something, like how he wheeled his chair. It sounds stupid, but that's how it was.

"Maybe a bit," I said, and my voice shook when I said the word "bit" so that it sounded like two or three sounds instead of one. I laid my back against the back of the couch.

"Well I'm not going to *kill* you, for God sakes."

I blinked and looked at him. His face looked worried. He really wasn't going to kill me.

"Are you going to kill *me?*" he asked.

I looked at him for a second then shook my head.

"I don't think so."

"Good!"

He wheeled out into the kitchen, humming something I didn't recognize, from deep down in his throat. It sounded kind of wet and grumbly, but also triumphing, like some war-ending song or something. He was out of my sight soon, doing something inside the kitchen. I looked in and saw that his countertops were all half the height of ours at home, and there were no cupboards overtop, just photos and letters and things in frames. The walls were the same colour as robins' eggs, or maybe a little greener. I heard the sink running for a moment and then it stopped.

"You must drink coffee then," he yelled, "on the graveyard shift and all?"

"No thanks!"

"Water?"

"No thanks!"

"Milk?"

"Okay!"

"Chocolate?"

"Yes please!"

"'Yes please,' he says!"

I didn't think I was supposed to keep answering then, so I sat quietly and calmed down my shaking and kept checking out the place. The living room was a dark red colour, kinda like the colour of my room at home. It was either maroon or burgundy, whatever the difference is. As far as furniture, there was the lumberjack couch I was on, and the oval table at my shins, and a pale green comfy-looking chair with flowers on it, and a giant bookshelf full of billions of books, every size and colour. But the books were only on the bottom half of the shelves, with the top shelves empty, probably holding only dust. Ice ages worth of dust. There were three other square tables against some of the walls, and they had lamps and small stacks of papers and books, two cameras, big boxes of matches, and a pair of field glasses. The coolest thing was against the wall on the right side of the room, on top of a low dresser. It was a pretty big fish tank, and it was all lit up glowing green, with four little turtles swimming all around. They looked very young. I wanted to go over and put my forehead on the glass and say hello, hello, hello, hello to the four of them, but I was still nervous so I didn't.

His house was tidy. Everything was tucked away somewhere and there was nothing lying on the floor. The orange carpet spread to every room around except for the kitchen, and it was clean looking, but it had these pairs of skinny lines faded and dented into it, because they must have been the paths that the man's wheelchair took every day. There was a path from the door of the bedroom to the kitchen that was really faded orange, a path from the kitchen door to the dinner table in the corner which was almost as faded, and a path that went all the way from the kitchen to the woodstove on the back wall, and then continued over to the front of the turtles, which was lighter orange than I would have expected. I couldn't really find a path from anywhere to the front door.

There were also a whole bunch of old pictures on the wall of some beautiful woman. Sometimes she was alone and sometimes she was hugging some other guy. She looked really pretty, and I wondered who she was. She seemed to be in almost all the pictures on the wall. I took my field glasses out of my backpack and took the lens caps off and looked through them at the pictures of the lady. I looked at each one and held my field glasses steady and tried to find clues, because it seemed like the type of place to find them, but I couldn't get the focus right and the pictures looked blurry like I was waking up.

I heard the man's chair moving along the kitchen floor, and I looked over with my field glasses and saw a big blurry version of him rolling himself out of the kitchen slowly with one hand, pushing himself off the door frame and then steering towards me, while somehow holding a tray with a coffee and a chocolate milk in the other hand. I put my field glasses down and stood up, because I wanted to help him, obviously, but he yelled "Sit-sit-sit!" so I sat down again. It didn't make any sense how he rolled over so quick with one hand and put the tray on the table in front of me with the other, so I was kind of sitting there shocked. He drifted over to the woodstove, took a log from the box beside it, opened the hatch and tossed it in the fire, which had been crackling and rumbling the whole time. He was such an expert. He shut the hatch, zoomed over to the turtle tank, opened a container and shook some pellets of food in for the turtles. They flapped up to the surface and chewed at the food while I watched them. I finally got my field glasses focused, and the turtles all grew into full-grown adult sized turtles in my eyes. They kicked their webby green feet and floated at the surface and ate, and I watched them.

When the man rolled back over to the table he had his own pair of field glasses on his lap and he put them up to his eyes and sat there staring at me. I must have looked taller than the tallest tree in the world to him. He put his field glasses on the table and took a sip of his steaming coffee. Then I put my lens caps back on and took a drink of my chocolate milk, which was delicious, and shaved my chocolate moustache. Simon *never* buys chocolate milk.

"Thanks a lot," I said.

"Most welcome."

He rolled up the sleeves of his shirt, which almost matched the couch I was on, because it was kind of lumberjacked too except it was green instead of red. He scratched the front of his crazy grey hair.

"So what brings you here, Mr. Williams?"

"How do you know my name?"

"Oh, I'm sorry. I suppose that's right, isn't it? Francis, first of all."

He reached across the table and shook my hand and smiled. His hand felt like it weighed a ton, and he squeezed hard.

"Francis," I said for some reason.

"I know your father," Francis said.

"You do?"

"Of course of course. Simon Williams, what a man."

"He's not really my father."

"Oh yes," Francis said. One of his curly eyebrows went up and he looked at his knees. "Yes of course, my apology. But you know what I mean. He's a good man though, Simon. Talks about you all the time. You're a lucky little guy, you know. A *great* man... helps me a lot. Anyhow, don't suppose you came over here to chat about him now, am I right?"

"Right."

"Right."

Then I didn't remember how to explain exactly why I did come over and my head was a little boggled and I didn't understand how he knew Simon so without thinking about it enough I said:

"Are you a hermit?"

Francis started laughing really hard. "Sorry," he said in between bunches of laughs and then he kept on laughing even harder. His laugh was amazingly powerful. His eyes squinted and he sounded like some kind of jungle animal roaring or like a squawking bird mixed with a lion, with a big puffy chest and grey hair.

"Sorry," he said again. "Yes, I suppose you could call it that."

"What's so funny?" I said.

"No one's ever asked me that."

"Oh."

"I mean, they have. They've asked it a million ways, but never like that."

"I'm sorry," I said. I felt kind of rude.

"No no no no no. Don't think twice."

Then I tried to be more professional and get into detective mode better, so I asked "How long has this been your residence?"

Francis laughed again and then said, "Oh, must be fifteen, no... seventeen years. Yes, seventeen."

"That's longer than my whole life," I said.

"Wow, would you look at that," he said. "That's something."

"It's almost twice as long as my life."

Francis laughed but not as much and then said "Okay, okay" and I decided to try hard to stop being funny, even though I wasn't trying in the first place.

"So you've been living here all by yourself for seventeen years?"

"Mmm-hmm. That's right."

"Do you get lonely?"

Francis' big laugh started squawking all over again. "Arthur," he said, "you're going to be a damn comedian, you know that? Do you know that?"

"No," I said. I didn't get what was so funny.

"Lonely." He sighed. "Yes, sometimes. I suppose so. Don't you get lonely sometimes?"

I thought about it.

"Yeah," I said. "I guess so. But not excruciatingly."

"Well then me neither." He smiled and drank some of his coffee.

I was feeling kind of funny about how a hermit had just asked *me* if I was lonely. I decided to try and get back to sticking to the plan. I took Phil out of my backpack and put him on the table. "I found this in the woods by my house," I said. "Have you ever seen it before?"

Francis picked up Phil and looked him over, front cover and back cover, and his eyebrows slowly lifted. "You found a book!"

"Yeah."

"In the woods?"

"Yeah."

"I-see-I-see-I-see. Strange. And you want to know how it got there, eh?"

"Well at first I did, yeah. I wanted to know where it came from, and how it got there, but now... now I just want to know..."

I squinted and looked at the floor. My throat lumped a little, like brown sugar does when it won't come out of the bag into your porridge. I thought about Phil again and I couldn't swallow for a second. I pictured him alone and I didn't really know what I was trying to say and no one else did either. I looked at Francis and he was watching me and nodding and he looked really serious all of the sudden.

"Oh no," he said.

"What?"

Francis didn't answer me for a second. Then he said:

"Well I better read this, then." He looked at me. "Yes?"

"Sure," I said.

He held Phil and stared at his name on the cover for a while, and then he opened it and started reading the first page.

"An investigation," he said.

I nodded.

"Can't say I know who he *is* though."

"Nobody does. I asked the whole stupid neighbourhood."

He read all the way down to the bottom of Page 1 and turned it over. Then he kept reading Page 2. He read with the book on his lap and his body kind of leaned over it like the book tied ropes to him and was pulling him in. His eyes moved back and forth and every once in a while he scratched his hand through his grey jungle hair. When his head turned to the right a little and he was on Page 3, I realized he wasn't kidding around with me. He was going to read the whole thing. No one else had even looked inside it. Well, Simon did, but he wasn't supposed to. But Francis was the first person I interviewed who actually read any of Phil. I didn't even notice that was weird until then. But of course it was weird. How could anyone just not read something like that? I felt a little funny just watching him read. I decided I didn't really want to wait all week for him to finish reading, and I also didn't want to just sit there being useless, so I started explaining. Francis laid Phil down on the table so we could both have a look, and we went through the book together for a long, long time.

"Okay, you have to read *this* page," I would say.

Francis would read and bite one of his knuckles and say "Ohhh. Ohhh."

"This part's weird," I would say.

He would fold his arms together and hunch over and read for a while. "Hmm … Hmm!"

"And this is my favourite part. It's about creating the universe."

He bent forward even farther like he was looking through a special microscope that was built for looking at Phil.

We sat together like that, reading Phil. We read about when he made a masterpiece in the snow, and when the universe was nothing, and when he believed in God, and when it seemed like he sometimes didn't, and when he built filing cabinets in his brain, and when he became tiny, and when he was a library that didn't make sense, and when everything good that happened to him felt embarrassing, and when E was the love of his life but then she ran away, or their love did, and when his life was amazingly painful and things never got better and he was alone inside a cage, and when he never wanted to exist in the first place.

After we read for a long while I said, "So he just kind of wrote his life down, but he wrote it in all these weird ways. Sometimes it makes me laugh but sometimes it doesn't," I said. "And then he talks about himself like he's not himself, like he's not really there. Sometimes I wonder if he *wants* to be sad or something."

Francis nodded.

Then I turned to the next page which was Page 43. My throat lumped again.

"Then there's this page," I said.

I sat back a little deeper into the red couch. Francis read Page 43 in silence and I felt nervous for him and I listened to the gently roaring woodstove and I looked at all the paths in the carpet.

I looked at another photo with the beautiful lady in it where she was wearing a really pretty white dress and sitting under a tree on some grass in a park somewhere. She had the nicest smile, not just the regular kind that means you're happy, but the kind that makes other people happy too. I wondered what kind of smile I had, and if it was that kind or just a regular one. I wondered what kind Phil had. He must have had one. Was it a special kind that made other people sad?

Francis turned over Page 43 and saw that the next two pages were blank. He quickly flipped the rest of the pages which were also all blank. He said that's the last page and I nodded. He closed the book, sat quiet for a second with his eyes looking down, then wheeled himself very slowly to the turtle tank. He stared at the little turtles inside, swimming over and under each other and flapping their green flipper feet, climbing and sitting on the little island, then diving in again. He watched them for a long time. Then he came back to the table.

"So what are you going to do with it now? With the book?"

I shook my head slowly, to say that I had no idea. "I mean, what am I supposed to do? I can't do anything. There's nothing I could do."

Then Francis said, "Do you mind if I ask you a few questions?"

"Uhhh, sure," I said.

"Okay." He drank his coffee and rubbed his finger in the corner of his eye. "First of all, did you tell Simon about this?"

"About Phil?"

"Yes."

"No way. I didn't tell him anything, but he sneaked around my room and he found it anyway."

"Why didn't you tell him?"

I was starting to get a little bit unpatient with Francis because we were changing the subject and also because I felt like he was interviewing *me* instead of the other way around like it was supposed to be.

"What does that have to do with anything?" I said.

"Oh, nothing. Maybe nothing. I'm just doing my own investigation over here I guess. It's just that, the very first thing you said about Simon, if I remember correctly, was that he certainly wasn't your real father."

"Well he's not."

"Surely. Yes, I know. But the way you said it was as if—"

The tape recorder made a loud click noise because the tape ran out.

"Hold on," I said, and I popped it open and pulled the tape out, flipped it over and put it back in. I pressed RECORD. Then I picked up my field glasses and held them in my lap to have something to fidget with.

"Okay," I said.

"As I was saying, the thing about Simon is—"

"I just think Simon's so boring."

Francis looked at me for a second.

"Why?"

"What?"

"What's so boring about him?"

"He just, well . . . you don't really know him."

"I certainly do. Simon's over here quite often. He's a good man."

I made my face look so confused.

"Surely. When he first moved in, he came right up here to meet me. He sees me, in all my glory, exactly as you see me now, and can you guess what he says?"

"No."

"He says, 'If you ever need anything, you've got me.' And you know, I took him up on it too. There're plenty of times when I need something, even just some groceries, what have you, and Sarah's not in town, and sure enough your father, I mean, *your* Simon goes and brings me a roast or a bag of sugar, some small thing. Just last week, he wouldn't even let me *pay* him."

"He never told me that."

Francis shook his head and smiled. "He wouldn't. He's not the type of guy to give someone a hand and then go around talking about it. Boring? I can't think of anything farther from it."

I didn't say anything for a second.

"I know how they feel about me, Arthur. I'm surprised you even made it up my God-awful driveway, first of all."

"I heard you were insane, and you might be a thief, or a crack dealer, or a murderer, or a cannibal or a vegetarian or..."

Francis exploded with laughter.

"A vegetarian. That kills me—a vege*tarian*. Now, that one's new."

I thought about it and I laughed a little bit, too. I never realized how silly that one was.

"Arthur, what do *you* think of me?"

I thought for a minute.

"I guess you're probably just a really nice guy."

"Why thank you."

I thought some more.

"Okay, so if none of the bad rumours about you are true, why don't you just send around a letter to the neighbourhood that says 'Hello, I'm not a cannibal or anything, I'm actually just a really nice guy?' I could deliver it to everybody."

Francis chuckled again, I don't know why.

"I appreciate it, but that wasn't the point. If they want to, they can believe whatever they want. They *will* believe whatever they want."

"Who's Sarah?" I asked sneakily. I was getting curious.

"Hmm?"

"You talked about a Sarah. Is that her?" I asked, pointing to the smiling lady in the photo.

"That would be Sarah's mother," Francis said. "That's Olivia."

Francis smiled the type of smile that old people always do when they're remembering something amazing. The kind with the eyes that sparkle. Then he turned his head around and gave the same smile to the photo. I quickly pieced it together in my head: he seemed to think Olivia was amazing. Olivia was Sarah's mother, and I was about 90% sure that Sarah must be Francis's daughter. So Olivia must have been Francis's girlfriend or wife or something. Maybe he met her when they were really young. They met in school and they were best friends so they got married and now they were really old. But where was she now? Who knows. Maybe she divorced him and ran away? Was she in a wheelchair too? Francis turned back to me and I thought that his eyes looked just slightly more sparkly, like maybe they were a little damp. I couldn't tell if he was happy or sad; he looked both at the same time. I realized something. I suddenly knew that those were the kind of eyes you get when someone amazing isn't around anymore.

"Now Arthur," Francis said, "I doubt there's anyone in the world who can convince you of this, but I mean it, alright? Simon is not boring. He's certainly a heck of a lot less boring than everyone else."

"What do you mean?"

"I mean, seeing a kid like you, and to not snatch you up. To not see the absolute *bargain* they were getting. Now that's boring."

"But..."

"Hmm?"

"I just wish I could know who they actually were."

As soon as I said that I felt kind of funny. I was really letting my guts spill out to Francis. He had a way of giving me a serious look exactly when I needed him to give me a serious look, and giving me a smile exactly when I needed him to give me a smile. Things weren't just coming out of my mouth by accident and mixed up. It was like he had a way of making me say things on purpose that I never knew I wanted to say. It made my stomach feel funny. I wished people never had to bring knives with them anywhere.

"Simon must've told you that even he doesn't know."

"Yeah, I know. I just mean like, but why? I just want to know *why*."

"I hear that. Boy, do I hear that. We all want to know that, Arthur."

I didn't know what the heck he was talking about. Francis went quiet again and picked up Phil and held him in his hands.

"How does it make you feel?" Francis said.

"Simon?"

"*Phil*. How does he make you feel?"

My throat instantly got all lumpy but I tried to talk through it.

"I guess I just wish there was something I could do. I've been trying to figure it out but I've gotten nowhere. I obviously wish it didn't happen. I wish I never found the stupid book, because all I've been thinking about every day is Phil and it made me so angry because I couldn't even tell for sure if he's really gone. But now I just *know* he is, somehow, and also because why did everyone just leave him alone, or did he leave everyone else alone? Why was no one around? I can't stop thinking about him all alone and sad and what are you supposed to do about someone who was always sad and now they are forever?"

Francis didn't say anything. He breathed in a lot of air and filled his entire lungs and then let the air out slowly. He sat there shaking his head.

"I don't know what to tell you," he said. "I haven't got that answer. All I know is, some things, we could ask them our whole lives. Maybe we've gotta make sure we don't."

"What do you mean?"

Francis sat up straighter and looked me in the eyes. He looked curious. He reached and picked up his field glasses, put them to his eyes and looked at me. I must have been a huge giant Arthur to him, bigger than any Arthur ever was. He lowered his field glasses for a second and smiled. He held them tight in his hands and nodded at me and I knew he was telling me to use mine too. So I took the lens caps off my almost-great-grandfather's field glasses and held them up to my eyes and looked at Francis.

It was really dark and blurry, looking through them in Francis's house in the middle of the night. Once I got them focused I saw Francis's head, really huge. It filled my whole vision. All I could see was his scribbly grey hair and his puffy nose and the wrinkles beside his eyes. Then his eyes became shiny black circles because he was looking through his field glasses back at me.

"Pretend I am your problems," Francis said.

"What?"

"Pretend I am everything wrong. Look at me, I am every problem you'll ever have."

"Okay..." I said. We were still magnifying each other.

"So you look and you look and you look," he said. "Right?"

"Okay...?"

"You look at the problems very closely, and you wonder about them, and they just get bigger."

Francis became bigger because he was leaning a little closer to me.

"You look closer and you try to shrink them, you do all sorts of things but it's no use—the closer you look, the bigger they get."

"And blurrier."

"True. And so after a while, you can't even very well move, you see? Suddenly they're enormous. Bigger than planets."

"Okay?"

"So," Francis said. He took his field glasses away from his face and I just saw his gigantic watery eyes. I put my field glasses down too and looked through my regular eyes.

"So, what else can you do?" he asked.

"I don't know."

"Hmm," Francis said.

"Keep looking?"

Francis smiled and his eyebrows magnified a bit. "Is that all?"

"Uhhh," I said. "Maybe look at something else?"

"Aha," Francis said, "let's-see-let's-see."

He started moving his field glasses from one hand to the other and looking at the ceiling.

"So maybe you start asking yourself some other things. Something different. Maybe you start looking at other stuff besides just the things you can't answer. You don't ignore anything, of course. You *don't* start ignoring. But maybe you look at— well I don't know. Maybe you look at something you *can* answer. Or maybe just something nice. There's gotta be *some*thing nice around, right?"

"I guess."

"So maybe you ask yourself what you *do* have, for certain, and you look at that instead."

"Like a clue?"

"Like a fact. Yes, and you *really* look at it too, you spend a long time and don't give up. Okay, and then maybe eventually—so now what do you see?"

"I don't know?"

Francis took his field glasses and turned them around with his hands and then looked through the other side of them, the big side. I took mine and did the same thing.

"Everything is so small," I said.

"And beautiful!" said tiny little Francis. He was so far away he looked about the size of an atom. He was all the problems in the entire universe and he wasn't even as tall as an apple slice.

"Now I'm not saying there's no answers," Francis said. "The binocular thing's a bit silly. But I'm not saying there's no answers, it's just, sometimes you stop *looking*, and there they are."

My thoughts started bouncing all over the place in my brain and I couldn't really tell what was going on in there, and my eyes started watering.

"'Where did I come from?' is a pretty good question," Francis said, "but how about 'Where do I belong?'"

My throat was a complete lump and my eyes and nose got all prickly. The corners of my eyes felt heavy and got wet. I put my head down on my knees and I started shaking. I felt Francis's hand patting me on the shoulder, and I shook even harder. I cried for a long time, but I didn't even notice I was acting like a complete baby.

"Ohhh boy," Francis said quietly. "Ohhh boy."

After all that I sat up and wiped my face. I told Francis I should probably go home and sleep. He said it was after 3:00, and he should sleep too. I pushed STOP on the tape recorder, packed Phil back into my backpack and went to the door. Francis told me to come back and visit any time I wanted; I said that I would and I meant it.

As I walked out onto his porch, Francis started talking again.

"I guess it's really up to you what to do with it. The journal. I mean, *you* found it. As far as we know, it may well be his will and testament, first of all. I mean, it's up to you. Sorry I'm not more helpful."

"That's alright," I said. "I'm sorry I came over so late."

"Don't mention it!" Francis flapped his hand around.

"Goodbye," I said.

"Take care of yourself, alright? You're only what, eleven?"

"Ten."

"You're only *ten*, first of all."

"Okay."

Francis smiled and shook my hand, then watched me from the door as I walked down the porch steps into the night.

"And Arthur," he said.

I turned around.

"Nice cape."

I looked down at my bright green shoulder.

"Thanks."

THIS

You fell asleep with your hand resting on my back. We'd always try to stay tied together for as long as possible, but we could only ever fall asleep lying apart. (This is love: for both to give themselves over, wanting to fall into the same body together, some new body, some common home, but to be confronted always by one's aloneness. To find one's self ultimately only one's self.)

To bridge this endless gap, you just fell asleep with your hand resting on my back.

In that calm pulling space between world and sleep, as things started to slip and fall out of your universe, your hand tensed up and grabbed at nothing. Its small violent energy entered my back like a burst of miniature lightning, like a spark—like *you*, like this one searing instant of you—and I could feel the bolt move farther into your body—your elbow, your shoulder, your lower back, a kick of your leg. This was the most enchanting moment I'd known, this seeing you—this *feeling* you—so completely seized by the peacefulness you drifted towards. And I was the only witness to that little sensation leaping into you, so precisely shared through only your hand. My eyes were closed but I knew every one of your motions and in the dark I could see you. I saw you. And this was when I felt it. And this was what

I needed even though you didn't. And *this* was when I wasn't embarrassed to delight in something. And *this* was when I saw you and understood what they meant when they said: to love is to be entirely vulnerable at the height of your strength. That to love is to never know whether you are vulnerable or strong. And this was when I wasn't alone.

NaCN

Today Phil didn't crawl outside and over to the university and take a growling elevator three floors up to the chemistry department. He didn't meet a high school friend up there in the chalky concrete hall and he did not hold his breath and smile and nod through five interminable minutes of the most tedious small talk and he did not behave well and catch up on what was new in the old friend's life. He didn't invent things about his own life to sound busy—he did not say he was still animating and doing design on the side, he did not use finger-quotes to frame "on the side," eventually Phil didn't get down to business and ask if the old friend had found what Phil had not inquired about via email two days ago. The friend didn't accept the catching-up to be over like the kind self-assured angel Phil always knew him to be, and he didn't hand Phil a paper bag and ask what he wanted to use it for again, a flash of vague suspicion crossing his face, concern, Phil didn't smile to reassure and chuckle and tell the angel he needed to dissolve some gold. For animation. Phil wasn't lying. His hand was not palsied as he reached for what he could practically already feel inside him in the bag, the friend didn't laugh and take pleasure in this long lost gold-dissolving artist friend and let it make his day, didn't say it was "nice to see" Phil and then ask no further questions and tell him to be careful and Phil said no form of thank you and didn't say goodbye.

No because instead what he did was come home and have a steaming coffee on the front stoop with E and it wasn't freezing because it was almost summer again today not November and leaves were in bloom and the whole gang was there Phil and E and Small Phil on the bottom step and the real her the indescribable her the inevitable her and the vanished her and God was there too actually and they all just sat on the steps having a fucking great time and talking about how great of a time they were all having, and Phil talked to E and didn't even bring up the disappointment of the day at the beach in the summer when they walked all the way to that private beach in the funny little suburb in the forest to skinny-dip because they were together for once and they wanted to and that was reason enough and about how when they got there she didn't actually want to get in. And about how he had tried with every shred of self-control he had to just be patient with her and not get angry and panic and not try yet again to understand but it was impossible and the day became the day of the impossible and about the disappointment of everything, not just the skinny-dipping, but his entire tormented being and the shame inside everything whether it was for or against him and how he could destroy anything and she left him stranded on the beach, she had no patience, had already spent her patience on him a thousand times before and he couldn't make it back from the beach or into the woods and sat on the beach crying holding himself in a trembling ball like always—today Phil and E sat on the stoop and didn't make a list of everything they hadn't done together that they said they would and this list went on and on and it had no end and every day now is another addition and Phil just *let her be* did not argue or check her email or grasp at anything and he was doing a good job.

Then he walked her home like he does every day and he saw her for the last time again with tree and streetlight and her glowing hair against the dark spaces between leaves and the twilight and the beginning of the end and *I love you* and no answer. In the massive silence she disappeared again.

~~He thought maybe he finally should too~~

On the way home he thought about all the things he himself separate from her because she doesn't DEFINE him wanted to do but never did

He remembers everything he once naively thought he was and when there were things he could be and he starts making his own concise list and tomorrow at dawn he brings it with him and will cross EVERYTHING off ONE BY ONE SHEDDING EVERYTHING AND LET EVERY WORD WASH AWAY TO BLANK WHITE TO PURE NOTHING BECAUSE NOT LIVING IT WOULD BE TO LIVE THE MOST CONSTANT LIE AND TOMORROW IT ALL FINALLY BEGINS

WE ASK

THE MAN IS sitting on the rock. He wears white. Though it's late fall the morning is warm. He moves his dark hair out of his eyes. He stares.

We are here and watching. We are listening. See us standing over him and leaning close. Across the water more of us stand. In every direction more are watching.

He folds his right leg over his left. He opens his book. His pen writes quickly, then he studies the words. He strikes them out.

We are still here and have always been here. And this is what we've seen and will see, though we still look. He will stand, the book will be left behind—was it his intention?—he will disappear. Though we knew before he began to write, before he came to us, before. Though we always knew, we did not know.

Even as we lean and creak above him we do not know. We hear him, we see him but it is not enough. We will not feel him. We will listen and watch, and we will not stop. But we do not touch him. He tells us nothing and does not hear us.

In his last moment, just before the breathing swells we wait. He stares and is still. For now he is frozen inside this last breath, as are we, and we wait. Before he stands, before the book falls we are *here:*

There is no wind. The calm water makes no sound. And he stares and is still.

He is the size of a human. He is the shape of every one we have seen. He weighs as much as a human and moves as one does. This we know.

So we stand staring in this quiet breath and we wait, even though the next sounds have already echoed loud, as they will again, and now as they do.

~~NOTHING~~
~~FATE NOTHING~~
~~NOTHING ESCAPE END~~
~~WORLDS WHERE I COULD HAVE~~
<u>RIVER</u>

- ~~This has nothing to do with her (She knows this) This was before her~~
- ~~This was forever~~
- ~~(I'm SORRY) I'm sorry I didn't get around to it before I met you.~~
- ~~I CANT SEE MYSELF one day crawling out and being OK and I've known that forever.~~
- ~~I always had to keep looking for a reason to keep looking. You KNOW this.~~
- ~~And what kind of place is a place where you can't help imagining better~~
- ~~the beach is a good place~~   ~~The perfect place~~
- ~~the freezing water will take me so immediately and I'll be part of it and absorbed into nothing~~
     ~~I DID ALL I COULD TO MAKE NO ONE MISS ME~~
- ~~I can't remember the last time I didn't feel~~
- I ~~only~~ wanted ~~to give or know that something of me was worth giving.~~ I wanted ~~to be received.~~ I wanted ~~to not matter and for that to not matter.~~ I wanted ~~someone to know and not run away.~~ I wanted ~~some part of me to be worth sticking around for.~~ I wanted ~~to stick around.~~ I wanted

43

COMPLETELY IMPOSSIBLE

CLUES:

– Someone named Phil.

I started jogging down Francis's mucky driveway. My thoughts were moving around in a circle and putting themselves together like bricks in an igloo building itself inside my head. Some of them were things about Simon, and other ones were things about Phil. I still couldn't really tell what was going on inside my brain, but I knew something was.

I jogged as fast as I could without slipping and falling on all the leaves on his driveway. All the dead leaves from last fall that had landed on the ground and got covered in snow during the winter were exposed again. They squished under my wet boots, and my boots and the driveway were slowly composting them. It was weird to shine my flashlight on the old leaves and think about how they were still there, even in the spring, even after all the snow. I thought those leaves would have been history, since they were already getting replaced by new ones anyway. So there was something strange to me about the ghost leaves from last fall, basically, and if I owned money I would have used it to bet that Francis would have agreed with me.

I squish-squashed down until I reached the road, and the half-pavement half-gravel felt way less exciting on the feet. What I did though, was I stepped out of my boots and took off my socks and carried them. I don't know why. My heels got stabbed by sharp rocks every once in a while, but I didn't care. My brain was all screwed up sort of, because it was after three in the morning, and also I had never heard less noise. The parked cars in the driveways weren't making noise, the dark houses weren't making noise, the telephone poles weren't making noise. I thought that if someone was having a special late-night phone call on my street right then, maybe if it was kind of a sexy one, I would have been able to hear it come out of the wires. It was the quietest morning I had ever found.

Everything was asleep except me. The part of the street just before my house where the oaks make a ceiling sounded like it was snoring. That was the only sound: the trees all standing side by side, reaching as high as they could without having to stand on tiptoes, holding hands so they'd sleep safe without falling over, and the breezes making them snore and snore. They even smelled like what quiet smells like to me, like cinnamon, raisins, and something else. I was a little scared, to tell you the truth, but I kept my flashlight on the whole time and I walked all slow and silent in my bare feet.

(Meanwhile my real dad was the mayor of a quiet city where everyone had to wear silence boots all the time. He had made the law because the city was just getting *so* noisy, with everyone walking in so many directions at once and running into each other, and whenever anyone said anything no one could tell who was talking, if they could even hear them, and they definitely couldn't understand when anyone was telling the truth. So everyone learned how to not hear anything.

When my real dad got his brilliant idea and made the law about the boots, not everyone followed it at first, but some people did. They went downtown to city hall to pick up the two clumps of moss that my real dad's government gave them for free, and they tied them onto the bottoms of their boots. When they walked, they barely made a sound. The people who were still being loud felt stupid after a while so they got silence boots too and then everything was silent, and every day the people walked just as much as they always did, and got as much stuff done, except it was so quiet that it wasn't so annoying to do it anymore. Soon they realized that they were actually walking seven times farther and actually getting seven times as many things done as before. So the city became the best city in the world because it did everything a city had to do, except way better than other cities, plus with less noise.

It got voted the nicest city to live in, and everyone wanted to move there, so lots of people did. The moss on the silence boots would wear out every couple of weeks, but it was OK because they could always compost the worn-out moss and keep growing more on the moss farms, and decades later the council voted yes when my real dad proposed to pave the streets with moss instead of pavement, and replace the floors in buildings with moss. The glass skyscrapers, the parking lots, the fire station, the old theatre and the chandelier, the houses, the grocery stores, the pizzerias, the zoo: everything would be moss. It was an exciting and record-breaking day when the world's best city got mossed over, and all the streets and buildings shined when the sun hit them, like they were actually paved with emeralds. But when the news reporters whispered questions to my dad to ask him how he felt about it all, he didn't say anything. They showed him that night on the news, being quiet and smiling, and everyone realized that instead of talking my real dad was listening.

Eventually the entire planet decided to live in my real dad's mossy city, and the city got really big and expanded to all the continents but it didn't get any louder, it somehow got even more quiet the more people moved in, and the farther the moss creeped. And every day was so silent that people actually believed they could hear a microscopic noise which was the soft crackling of all the burning stars billions of light years away. Some people thought that was impossible, and the soft noise was just the quiet rubbing of all the boots on the moss. Other people thought that both were probably true. And *everyone* listened to each other instead of ever talking, and they understood each other perfectly even though nothing was said. They knew where everyone was going and didn't get in each other's way so much—and even when they did they just smiled about it—and they knew how everyone was feeling, which was usually quiet and happy—and even when they were sad it didn't last forever—and they heard the answers to all their questions rushing gently at them one at a time, like the noise of each star.)

When I finally nudged open the door and stepped inside, I was extraordinarily glad to be back in my house. I put my boots down silently and I tiptoed through the kitchen and put the silly knife back and then carried my socks with me back to my room. If I was in a movie or a musical or something, I would have knocked over a lantern or a box of nails, obviously, on my way through the living room. And Simon would have woken up and gotten mad at me and put me in a boarding school for running away like that in the middle of the night. But I'm not moronic, and I made it into my bed safely, without a sound.

I switched my lamp on and took out Phil again. Right then, I was mostly interested in one part specifically. I opened to Page 43. I closed my eyes and read it with them closed for a while at first, because I had it practically memorized. Then I got braver, and opened my eyes and slowly read Page 43. I read it again, and then one more time. I already said my brain was all screwy and I meant it. I thought about that page, and how it was the last one, and what it meant, and whether I was even right about what it meant. I went back and forth between believing it and not believing it and as usual I ended up on believing it, which made my stomach crunch up. To be honest I was going a little crazy. And then, I started wishing about things.

I yawned and lay back on my bed making wishes. Maybe Brenda Beckham could have listened to me when I said not to call her stupid son. Or maybe Mr. Peterson could have made sense. Maybe that white cat was with me, cleaning my feet. I wished that maybe Victoria would be Finch's girlfriend for real, and maybe they'd actually french, but that I wouldn't have to know about it. Maybe I could pretend to be a better friend. Maybe I could be stronger, and old and wise, and magical, and I could make all these things the way they were supposed to be.

Maybe everyone would get exactly what they wanted. Maybe I could have been less of a jerk to Simon lately. I'm telling you, my brain was malfunctioning.

As I was lying there with my eyes closed, my heart was shaking. No, it wasn't *shaking*, it was heavy. It weighed a thousand tons and it was choking me. Every time I made a wish I did it because I thought that maybe it would lighten up but instead it got heavier and choked me a bit more.

I wished that maybe I'd never gone into the woods and found Phil in the first place. Maybe I just wasn't there. But that wish was completely impossible. I *was* there.

Then I opened my eyes and grabbed a pen I had inside my pyjama shirt pocket. I knew what to do. It made just as much sense as how much sense it didn't make at all.

I flipped Page 43 over and stared at Page 44.

I told myself it was OK to do it. I took my pen and wrote some words at the top, but they were so stupid, and I crossed them out. What the hell was I doing? It wasn't going to make any difference. Still, it felt like what to do. But it was impossible. I didn't know what to write. I chewed on my pen, and I didn't start crying, and inside my head I said:

"Hello God, I hope you'll make me finish this."

Then I realized why it wasn't working. I wasn't in the right place.

It was almost four o'clock, and it was still dark and scary outside, but it made sense to go. I took Phil and my pen and my flashlight to the front hall, and got ready to go outside one more time. I almost put my jacket on upside-down, that's how tired I was. I put on my boots but didn't bother bringing my backpack. I crept out the door again into the darkness.

My treehouse was exactly like it always used to be, except it was dark. Dark, but not scary. I shone my flashlight beam into every corner and then climbed the slimy ladder up to the top floor. The floorboards and the wall were a little damp where I always used to sit but I sat there anyway.

I used to do the most important things in the treehouse there, on the top floor. Maps and lists and plans and things. Some of my very best drawings were drawn right there. But there was never anything at all like the thing I was doing that morning in the dark. Nothing *that* important. I shone the flashlight at the blank Page 44 in the notebook and thought hard. So hard. I saw the words I wrote in my room and they looked so horrible. They were like black rotten spots on a banana. I felt like I was at a funeral and I was laughing at the person who died and everyone there was embarrassed to know me. But I convinced myself that I wasn't doing that. I wasn't just trying to mess up the book. Every time I thought about adding something I thought about it too much until it became a bad idea, and I felt sick, and like I was doing something wrong. Like I was doing the avoiding kind of circumnavigating instead of the brave kind that draws a scribble around the entire world. Like maybe Phil would have been disappointed in me. It was like I was pretending, and I didn't want to pretend. What did I want?

I waited for the right idea, but ideas weren't coming. Usually I always had ideas in the treehouse. Sometimes I had so many of them that I couldn't even do them all. I never even thought about not having them. I waited. My page was still blank. There was no one around to give me anything to start from, it was only trees, but trees can't talk. I took off my boots and counted my toes for a while. I made a shadow puppet on the wall with my flashlight and my hand. I tried a lot of things to take my mind off of not having something to write. I was sitting there forever, trying everything. I even knocked on wood for good luck, on the soggy floor, but my page was still nothing.

Then, everything came. I made myself write one word and it made sense, so I wrote more words and I didn't stop. I don't know how, but suddenly inside my brain the only things were me and Phil and the page and my imagination, and my imagination was working so hard, and I concentrated so hard on what it was telling me that I didn't really have to concentrate anymore. I wasn't worried about pretending because I knew everything I was writing was the exact truth. And I wrote it all excruciatingly fast, without thinking about the last word I'd put down. I just wrote the next word I had to write, and then the next word and the next sentence and the next page. I even wrote more than one page. I was writing faster and faster and for so long that the sky started to get brighter than it was before.

When I finished writing it was almost 6:00 AM and I realized the sky was transforming into daytime. I climbed down the slippery wooden ladder and then down the stairs to the ground. It was bright enough that I didn't even need the flashlight anymore; I could see pretty much perfect. The sky was slowly turning orangey-blue instead of black and making the shapes of the treehouse and all the tree trunks into the hugest shadow puppets. I think that was the first sunrise I ever found. It felt weird.

I went to the sea turtle rock and walked down the hill a bit and leaned against the bent tree that Phil was near when I found him. I took five steps away from the river, and one sideways towards the house. I kneeled down and put Phil on the ground.

I took a last look at the cover of the notebook. I could see why Phil said he liked that pattern. It really was beautiful. It was just black and white, so it was simple, but at the same time it was extraordinarily complicated, and hard on the eyes. The black splotches jumped all over the white background. Or maybe the white patches were on top of the black background. It was both at the same time. It was like the splotches were fighting, or like they'd just stopped fighting and were becoming friends again and slow-dancing. If I stared long enough at it and covered some parts up by holding my hand out in front of my eyes, I could find pictures in there: maybe a little animal, or a face. The shape of a planet, or a whole solar system. Maybe if you zoomed way out in space, like maybe if you flipped your field glasses around and carefully looked through the big side, maybe that was what the whole universe looked like. Not just white dots on blackness, but maybe huge white patches and black patches the size of whole mysterious galaxies, reaching for each other, and it makes no sense and who knows what's on top of what, but anyway it's really pretty.

I started to dig a hole in the soil with my hands. But then I stopped. One, because I thought there might be a tiny chance I'd need to find him again someday, and two, because I thought maybe if someone a lot older and a lot smarter than me came along they could still notice it, and *actually* find out about him. But I was pretty sure both those things weren't going to happen and that I was saying goodbye to Phil.

And also I didn't bury him under the ground, because when I found him he was covered in leaves, not dirt. So I just took a handful of wet leaves and spread them overtop, and I kept adding leaves until I couldn't see the black and white speckly pattern anymore, and the pile was just a mix of a whole bunch of colours, all these reds and oranges and yellows, getting more orange and red and yellow every second from the sun rising.

I stared at the pile. I knew the truth about Phil; I wasn't stupid. Of *course* I wanted to save him. Obviously. And obviously I didn't. I couldn't. Because I was just a normal boy without real superpowers, or a real time machine, or God skills or anything. But I had to do *some*thing. And if you look up the definition for the word "save" in the dictionary, just like almost every word it means more than one thing at the same time. Besides to save someone's life, it also means to save them by keeping them somewhere, not like in your backpack or your thermos, but somewhere inside you, like your brain or your heart. So I guess I will probably save Phil at least once a day for the rest of my life. And obviously that's not good enough, but I had to do something anyway because I mean, I had to.

The weird part was, and I wouldn't make this part up, I started crying. Which I guess wasn't that weird, because it was like the third time I cried in the same week, but still, this time was different. I cried a bit after we met Rosie, and a bit more with Francis, but when I brought Phil back I really cried. I had to turn around and run out of the woods with blurry eyes so that I wouldn't dig him out again and ruin the whole thing. I had to run as fast as I possibly could, tripping over roots and boulders. Finally my shaking hand opened the door of our house one more time and I was back home.

WE SHAKE

THE BOOK returns to where it fell and the boy is running.

See him running as fast as he can.

See the windows of the house lighting orange squares in one sequence before dimming again.

And time accelerating for the book and the sun rising and streaking the blue sky quickly like a swinging light bulb, then setting in orange and rising again after the black. A rain, and a heat wave, and another rain. Winds stirring up leaves and tossing days and lifting the book's cover like a damp wing and holding it open. Pages whipping over and back like flags, wrinkling and weakening, they yellow and fray.

See the house barely trembling as life roars through it: the boy, the man, others big and small, questions and games, shouts and laughs and long days sped through. The white door fluttering closed and open.

See the tiniest creatures building a city and a world out of the book's pages, starting at the edges, then creeping in past the margins and overtaking the centre. Each page is as any other, and they do not sense an author, let alone two—the ink is only the raw texture of the land they've been given, and they feast. They flourish. See the treehouse with its borrowed parts, hear its boards creaking underfoot, feel the moss climbing the walls.

The hot sun rises and sets and rises and the summer sprawls out to become its next season, and the book is all but gone.

But it is not gone. We are reading and we are memorizing. We record the rippling sounds of the pages, the shape of each word they contain. We store these deep within us; we will not forget. The seasons shrink and blend and as the paper dissolves we absorb it; it becomes us. We have lent ourselves to its white fabric and now it returns. We draw it into our roots. We cannot forget.

Now time rushes faster and stretches out farther in all directions and is one. And inside this moment we hold everything, all vast and quiet and bright, and somewhere among it all, one tiny dot of this now is the boy, and it is his pages, and when we remember this part we shake. In this moment our limbs reach upward and we grow.

Actually Phil didn't really die at all because he actually

Meanwhile Phil was down on the beach walking to the water and Arthur caught up with him and Phil was naked. Arthur said WHAT ARE YOU DOING PHIL YOU SHOULD PUT YOUR CLOTHES BACK ON OR YOU MIGHT CATCH PNEUMONIA.

Phil said I'VE GOT SO MANY PROBLEMS I DON'T EVEN KNOW WHERE TO START. Arthur said ARE YOU GOING TO DROWN YOURSELF? and Phil said YES.

Phil told ~~me~~ Arthur that he was really really sad and angry. I KNOW Arthur said BECAUSE YOUR LOVE OF YOUR LIFE ABANDONED YOU AND ALSO YOU HAVE NOTHING TO GIVE TO THE WORLD.

BUT IT'S NOT EVEN THAT REALLY said Phil.

I KNOW Arthur said IT'S MORE BECAUSE YOU ARE ALWAYS SAD NO MATTER WHAT. IT'S BECAUSE YOU FELT SO ALONE EVERY SECOND OF EVERY DAY.

HOW DO YOU KNOW THIS STUFF? Phil said.

I FOUND YOUR NOTEBOOK IN THE WOODS BY MY HOUSE AND I'VE BEEN READING IT EVERY SINGLE DAY said Arthur.

Phil said NO ONE WAS SUPPOSED TO FIND THAT EVER.

WELL THEY DID Arthur said. Arthur started to cry like a silly baby and said PLEASE DON'T DO IT PHIL, IT'S A BAD IDEA.

BUT I HAVE TO Phil said. YOU CAN'T CONVINCE ME. WHAT IS YOUR NAME? Phil said.

ARTHUR said Arthur.

ARTHUR I'M SORRY MY BOOK MADE YOU CRY EVERY DAY OF YOUR LIFE said Phil. BUT I HAVE TO DO IT BECAUSE THE UNIVERSE DOESN'T WANT ME TO BE IN IT ANYMORE. IT ISN'T WHERE I BELONG said Phil. IT'S NOT A BIG DEAL. Arthur was crying this whole time but bravely made himself stop.

PHIL I DON'T THINK THE UNIVERSE WANTS YOU TO DIE EVEN THOUGH IT IS AMAZINGLY HUGE AND SCARY AND IT IS SWALLOWING UP EVERYTHING IT EVER GAVE YOU IN THE FIRST PLACE said Arthur. IT *IS* A BIG DEAL said Arthur.

ARE THOSE YOUR CLOTHES THAT ARE SITTING ON THE ROCK THERE said Arthur?

YES said Phil. Arthur brought Phil's shirt and pants over to Phil and gave them to Phil. Phil put them on after a while and sat down on a log washed up on the shore and Arthur sat beside him.

WHY IS EVERYTHING BEING SO MEAN TO ME THEN? said Phil. WHY IS MY BRAIN PUNCHING ME IN THE FACE AND WHY DOESN'T ANYTHING EVER MAKE SENSE?

I DON'T KNOW said Arthur. THERE ARE SOME QUESTIONS WE CAN ASK FOR OUR WHOLE LIFETIMES IF WE WANT.

LIKE WHAT KIND OF QUESTIONS? asked Phil.

LIKE IF A TREE FALLS IN A FOREST BUT NOBODY IS AROUND TO HEAR IT DOES IT STILL MAKE A NOISE? said Arthur.

Phil didn't say anything.

BUT ALSO OTHER ONES THAT ARE WAY HARDER said Arthur.

Phil picked up a really flat rock and skipped it across the water like 7 times. NICE SKIP said Arthur. THANKS said Phil. Then Phil put his head into his hands for a long long time.

I ALREADY ATE THE STUFF THAT MAKES ME DROWN said Phil. IT'S TOO LATE.

Arthur quickly reached into his backpack and took out the bottle of floatation pills he made and gave 3 to Phil. TAKE THEM WITH THIS Arthur said and gave Phil his thermos with milk in it. Phil looked at the pills for a bit and said WHAT DO THESE DO? and Arthur said I MADE THEM OUT OF THE STYROFOAM DUST FROM BUILDING THE IGLOO I WILL SOON COMPLETE INSIDE MY ROOM. THEY GO INTO YOUR BLOOD AND TURN HALF YOUR WHITE BLOOD CELLS INTO STYROFOAM CELLS SO THAT IF YOU GO IN DEEP WATER YOU WILL FLOAT INSTEAD OF SINKING. DOES IT HURT? said Phil and Arthur said ONLY FOR A MINUTE AND THEN NOT ANYMORE and Arthur took one of the pills himself to show Phil and then Phil put the pills in his mouth and drank the milk. YOU HAVE A MUSTASH said Arthur and Phil shaved it.

Then Arthur and Phil waded out into the river until it overflowed Arthur's boots and then they layed down on the water and they floated and didn't sink. Arthur layed on his back and so did Phil and they floated on top of the water which was very smoothe and warm and under the blue sky.

I'VE NEVER SWAM HERE BEFORE said Arthur. ME EITHER said Phil and they kept floating on their backs way out into the river looking up at the sky and using their feet like flippers and moving slow. They kept floating there and thinking until they decided to go back to the shore. They sat back down on the log and the sun tried to dry their clothes but Phil still had his head in his hands again.

PHIL I KNOW YOU THINK THAT DYING HAS TO BE BETTER THAN LIVING AND NO ONE IS AROUND TO CARE ABOUT YOU ANYWAY said Arthur BUT MAYBE IF YOU REALLY THINK ABOUT IT A LOT MAYBE WHAT YOU WANT IS TO STAY ALIVE FOR A LITTLE WHILE. I DON'T KNOW WHAT YOU WANT PHIL I DON'T KNOW. BUT I DON'T WANT YOU TO DIE. NOBODY WANTS YOU TO DIE. GOD OR THE UNIVERSE OR SOMETHING ELSE MADE YOU FOR SOME REASON AND I DON'T KNOW WHY AND YOU DON'T KNOW WHY EITHER BUT THAT'S THE WAY IT IS PHIL AND YOU BELONG ALIVE.

After such a long time of having his head in his hands Phil said MAYBE YOU'RE RIGHT and he started to cry excruciateingly hard which made Arthur cry a little more and put his arm on Phil's shoulder and say IT'S OK PHIL.

IT'S OK PHIL said Arthur IT'S OK IT'S OK IT'S OK.

I THOUGHT IF I WAS DEAD THEN I WOULDN'T HAVE TO NOT UNDERSTAND ANYMORE said Phil. I KNOW said Arthur. I KNOW. BUT PHIL YOU'RE NOT THE ONLY ONE WHO DOESN'T UNDERSTAND.

Then Phil kept crying for a long time.

Eventually Phil stopped crying and sat on the log for a while without talking and Arthur stayed sitting on the same log too.

Soon Phil and Arthur both stood up and walked up the beach and into the woods after Phil put his shoes back on. After an extraordinarily long time of walking quietly Phil and Arthur finally both started to smile again.

Phil had a nice smile that made Arthur smile too and he

said BY THE WAY WHAT REALLY HAPPENED TO YOUR REAL PARENTS?

Arthur pulled a green leaf off of a tree and twirled it around in his fingers while not saying anything at all for a minute to be mysterious. Arthur and Phil kept walking in the woods.

I DON'T KNOW said Arthur.

HE NEVER TOLD YOU? said Phil.

NO said Arthur. BECAUSE HE DOESN'T KNOW EITHER BECAUSE THEY WANTED TO KEEP IT A SECRET AND I WILL PROBABLY NEVER KNOW.

MAYBE THEY WEREN'T EXPECTING YOU said Phil.

MAYBE said Arthur. I WASN'T EXPECTING YOU EITHER PHIL.

I KNOW. BUT STILL WE ARE BOTH HERE said Phil.

Arthur stopped playing with the leaf and put it in his pocket.

SO WHAT DO WE DO ABOUT IT? said Phil.

Arthur shrugged his shoulders. OUR FAMILY HAS A BRIDGE CLUB ON SUNDAYS AND YOU CAN COME OVER SOMETIME IF YOU DON'T WANT TO BE LONELY said Arthur. SOMETIMES THERE ARE EVEN GIRLS THERE.

I DON'T KNOW HOW TO PLAY BRIDGE said Phil and Arthur said IT'S OK.